CURRENT Affairs

CURRENT Affairs

A NOVEL

BARBARA RASKIN

RANDOM HOUSE   NEW YORK

All rights reserved under International and
Pan-American Copyright Conventions. Published in
the United States by Random House, Inc.,
New York, and simultaneously in Canada
by Random House of Canada Limited,
Toronto.

Library of Congress Cataloging-in-Publication Data
Raskin, Barbara.
Current affairs/by Barbara Raskin.
p.   cm.
ISBN 0-394-57994-1
I. Title.
PS3568.A69C87   1990   89-43625
813'.54—dc20

Manufactured in the United States of America
Book design by Debbie Glasserman

BOMC offers recordings and compact discs, cassettes
and records. For information and catalog write to
BOMR, Camp Hill, PA 17012.

WITH LOVE,
TO MY PARENTS

ACKNOWLEDGMENTS

For their help and friendship, I would like to thank Charlotte Sheedy, Joni Evans, Julie Grau, Amy Edelman, Sarah Bloom, Julianne Fanning-Halberstein, Mina Mazaheri, Bethany Weidner and Helen Hopps.

CURRENT Affairs

#1 Down: "Flight-y free-lance foreign correspondent Stephanie Karavan" (*New York Times Magazine* puzzle, January 14, 1979).

S
H
A
Y

I t was never a piece of cake being the sister of Stephanie Karavan (a.k.a. Shay Karavan, a.k.a. Che Karavan), but things really got tough for me in 1975. That was the year she went to Ho Chi Minh City, the first American journalist to be invited there by the postwar Vietnamese government. During her twenty-day stay, Shay conducted thirty-two exclusive interviews with rehabilitated former Saigon prostitutes. On the return flight, she held on her lap a hand-carved ivory urn containing the ashes of an American pilot who had been MIA in Southeast Asia.

When Shay landed at Kennedy—wearing a *M*A*S*H*-green jumpsuit she'd repatriated in a clothes exchange with one of the former hookers—she posed for a swarm of TV cameramen, but refused to be interviewed. Then she hurried aboard Air Force One, which the White House had dispatched to fly her on to Paducah, Kentucky. Only a front-page mission like this one could drag Shay Karavan to Paducah, but once there, she quickly arranged an impromptu photo-op/ceremony during which she wept as she presented the ivory urn to the grieving parents.

Shay sold her article about the wartime lives of the Vietnamese prostitutes to *Newsweek,* becoming the first free-lance writer ever to score a cover story in that magazine. The details of how and why the Vietnamese government gave her the remains of an American soldier made the front pages of almost every newspaper in the world.

It was shortly afterward that I first came upon S-H-A-Y as an answer in a Sunday *New York Times* crossword puzzle. Later I encountered S-H-A-Y going in different directions in a lot of different newspapers:

#10 Across: "Nickname of radical feminist writer" (*Washington Post,* July 19, 1978);

#89 Down: "Female friend of Viet Cong?" (*Washington Times,* April 1, 1982);

#9 Down: "Popular lady Sandinista supporter?" (*USA Today,* February 12, 1985);

#43 Down: "Karavan to friends" (*Minneapolis Tribune,* August 8, 1986); and

#104 Across: "One Stephanie" (Northwest Airlines in-flight magazine, Summer, 1988).

Last March, *New York* magazine featured on its cover a hot-pink living room diagonally dissected by a satiny Miss America–type sash that read CHEZ SHAY. The accompanying article neglected to mention that Shay was only subletting the apartment from a plastic surgeon who'd gone off to meditate in a Tibetan monastery. Shay always had a terrible habit of redecorating other people's places if she stayed there long enough. Besides painting Dr. Rizer's walls hot pink without consulting him, she also had the carpeting pulled up because she thought it smelled like cat piss.

Her hairdo (really just a Jewish Afro grown shoulder-length and gone crazy) was known as the "Shaysie" in East Side salons as well as in Broadway no-appointment-needed-walk-right-in-unisex hair cutteries. There is even a sandwich called the "Shay Special" (corned beef, melted Brie and sauerkraut on a croissant) at Herb's, a Washington restaurant where writers and journalists hang out. Because a number of reporters in the national press corps still want to get in Shay's pants, they always pump me for poop about her. When she occasionally meets me at Herb's for a drink, all the guys go ape.

Actually, I was the one who gave Shay the nickname she made famous. Only about two in 1948, when Shay was born, I found "Stephanie" unpronounceable; "Shaysie" was the closest I could manage. When Marge (I never know whether to refer to Marge as *my* mother, *our* mother or just plain *Mother*—which is Shay's preferred affectation) also started to call her "Shay," the name stuck.

By the time she was twenty-five, Shay's nickname already embodied all the crossword-puzzle clues used to describe her. She was a radical, feminist, literally fly-by-night free-lance writer who ran around the world chasing hot news stories without any staff press credentials. Even worse, she had no responsible editor back home to curtail any of her literary or sexual excesses. Shay fooled around with lots of VIPs who played principal roles in major world events. She also carried on with lots of the journalists who had run away from home to join the international media circus.

Shay took her nickname for granted until 1964, when she had to write a paper on the Cuban revolution for her twelfth-grade civics class. Naturally enough, she fell in love with Che Guevara and eventually went to court and legally changed her name to "Che." Then she embarked upon a campaign to get all of us to say "Shay" with a hard C instead of a soft one. She would retell the story about Harold Geneen, then president of ITT, whose secretary instructed people to pronounce his name "not with a hard G as in God, just a soft one as in Jesus."

Whatever. No one in our family paid much attention since it was too late in the game for us to change what we called her.

venties and eighties, Shay's name became a concept,
did. "Shay" reflected a certain erratic, erotic,
proach to life that the public seemed to enjoy. Even her
...dships with revolutionary leaders from four far-flung conti-
nents were tolerated. America lets its celebrities get away with
murder so long as their antics don't scare any of the neighbors'
horses. Because people-watching is America's number one spectator sport, our country produces lots of characters but few leaders
who have any kind of character at all.

Anyway, I am Natalie Karavan Myers, Shay Karavan's older
sister. If I were placing a personal ad, I would describe myself as
a: WJMF DINK BBW/MSW ISO ☺ Translation: *White Jewish Married Female Double Income No Kids Baby Boomer with Master
of Social Work in Search of Happiness.* Although I fit the demo-
graphic profile, I am no yuppie. I suffer far too much to belong
to that euphoric elite. Also, I am a purely political animal, which
disqualifies me by definition.

If I ever become an answer in a crossword puzzle, the clues
would have to include:

- Former parlor SDS-er, now Working-Assets-credit-card-carry-
ing liberal
- Pro-choice owner of three stretched-out, faded I FORGOT TO
HAVE A BABY T-shirts
- Organizer and director of a Washington shelter for homeless
women that ran out of operating funds and was closed for the
summer of the Greenhouse Effect.

Sibling rivalry?
Shay and I made up the term. We make Joan and Jackie
Collins look like the Bobbsey Twins. We make the Ephrons look
like the Andrews Sisters. We make the Mitfords look like the
McGuires and the Gabors like the Lennons. Whenever I meet
someone new they always ask me, "Are you . . . ?" and I say, "Yes.
Yes, I am." Most everyone goes, "Gre-at," humming it like a

mantra. What they should say is "Tough break, Nat. That must be a rough row to hoe."

Growing up with Shay Karavan as my kid sister definitely qualified as a shitstorm of a learning experience. I am forever poking through the past to produce proof of certain preexisting conditions that help explain our present relationship. My index to the past is a large photo album filled with snapshots that I carefully culled from our family collection. I have studied these photos so intently that now the Kodak images—rather than the realities they recorded—trigger my emotions.

Here's the first picture in my album:

S N A P S H O T

That's me being held up high in my father's arms on the day after Shay was born. Daddy himself dressed me in my High Holidays peach-colored coat, bonnet and matching leggings before taking me to Swedish Hospital so I could peer through the newborns' nursery window at my only sibling. Daddy kept pointing toward a particular bassinet and I finally saw her. She was sleeping, swaddled like a Chinese doll. A speck of sand was lodged in the corner of one eye. I asked what it was and my father said the Sleep Fairy put it there. I believed him. "Peanut" is what my father used to call me. "Snookums" is what he called Shay when they brought her home to the square stucco house on the north side of Minneapolis that we shared with our father's parents, Bubbie and Zadie.

Things like Herb's oversized menu, the "Chez Shay" *New York* magazine cover, U.S. coverage of Shay's trip to Ho Chi Minh City (featuring articles with lengthy quotes from Shay explaining why the Vietnamese government viewed her as representative of the most enlightened and progressive elements in America) and all the newspaper crossword puzzles that used S-H-A-Y as an answer are taped inside a huge scrapbook our dad started keeping in 1967.

I inherited this reference work after Dad died because every family needs one sensible person who will save engagement, marriage and birth announcements, newspaper stories that mention relatives, graduation or recital programs, bylined articles, showbills, campaign literature and first editions of books published by, or about, any relatives.

Although Marge keeps these scrapbooks at home in the den closet, I am responsible for sending her all relevant materials. I became Shay's Boswell because, unlike my sister, I am systematic and organized enough to clip and paste, or at least *save* things. In other words, not only did I have to eat shit on a daily basis, I had to preserve it for posterity.

Am I bitter?

Is the Pope Catholic?

The melodramatic events that interrupted my life two years ago, during the Greenhouse Summer of 1988, finally dismantled the writer's block from which I've suffered ever since Shay took up journalism. I had always planned to be a writer, but the moment Shay matriculated at the University of Minnesota J-School, I switched my major from English to social work. Very few sisters have ever been successful in pursuing the same careers. Anne, Emily and Charlotte Brontë did it some hundred and fifty years ago. Now the Ephrons—Delia, Amy and Nora—as well as the Shanges—Ifa, Bisa and Ntozake—seem to be doing it also.

But they are the exceptions. Not long ago I heard that Joan Collins, who had studied acting since childhood, was outraged when her writer sister, Jackie, began turning up at London theatrical auditions to compete against her. Maybe that's why Joan wrote her own first novel recently. Catty sisters are always ready to invade a sibling's turf; they are instinctive crossover artists.

But who's counting?

Who's keeping score?

My sister began her serious invasion of my life on the Friday before the Democratic National Convention in Atlanta. Although my husband, Eli, and I ate breakfast together that morning, he was in a big hurry to get downtown to cover a Jesse Jackson press conference. Washington bureau chief for the *Minneapolis Tribune,* Eli doesn't really have to hustle all that much anymore. Lately, however, he seems to be in a big hurry to get somewhere else a lot of the time. A real big hurry.

After he left, I went outside to sit on the back porch while I drank another cup of coffee and did the crossword puzzle. Although I am a crossword junkie, the minute I saw 7 Down, "aridity," I let *The Washington Post* slip to the floor. Throughout June and July, crossword-puzzle writers, like everyone else in America, had become obsessed with heat and drought. Their puzzles were full of words like "siccative," "desiccate," "exsiccate," "evaporate," "dehydrate," "Gobi," "Sahara," "scorch" and "rivel." One week *The Washington Post* used "sere" five times.

So instead of doing the puzzle, I began to survey the devastation in our garden. My climbing rosebushes bore neither blooms nor buds. The hydrangeas had no flowers. Our huge mimosa tree no longer opened its buds in the morning or reclosed them at night. Instead, it was stuck at some half-mast position as if in perpetual mourning. Only a few of our old perennials sported any splashes of color. Indeed, the ground itself had begun to split and crack. It looked like land photographed from the air by *National Geographic* following an earthquake.

Washington had had no rain for thirty-four days. An open umbrella of haze shaded the city from morning to dark. The stench of dry rot pervaded everything, and government buildings had begun to reek from environmental as well as political pollution. I was thinking about rain, trying to remember where I'd been the last time it rained, when the telephone began to ring.

I recognize my sister's rushed breathing as soon as I lift the receiver.

"Nat?" she whispers hopefully.

"Oh, hi, Shay."

I emit an internal groan.

This I need.

"Natalie. I'm in some deep shit."

This I need like a hole in the head.

"What's the matter?"

"I can't really talk about it right now. Can you meet me at National this afternoon?"

Oh great. A little mystery to add to her mystique. A little London fog for atmosphere.

"Where are you, Shay?"

"Long Island."

Uh-huh. She's on one of her air-travel binges. My sister bops around the country collecting frequent-flier credits as if the airlines award Pulitzer Prizes for every fifty thousand miles.

"Who're you with, Shay?"

"I can't talk now, Nat. I've got to move fast to catch my flight. It's USAir eight forty-three and it gets into National at two-thirty. Can you meet me?"

"Jesus. I'm supposed to have lunch at one o'clock with Eli and some people we visited in Moscow. Why can't you just take a cab?"

"Well . . . actually . . . I *have* to talk to you right away," she says slowly, letting hurt hug each word before she releases it.

Translation: *How can you let your own sister take a taxi when she's in trouble? What would Mother say?*

Great. This is really great.

Just what I need right now is my kooky kid sister coming back to guest-star in my life for a while.

Last summer Washington was attacked by locusts, this year by drought, and now Shay's back in town.

I feel like the Passover pharaoh.

Personal plagues: My husband is unable to focus, not to mention anything more exotic, on me for more than five minutes at a time. This is a fact I can no longer ignore since it's been going on for several months now. Also, because my shelter has been shut down, all our local bag ladies are back on Columbia Road again, carrying their brown-paper weekenders packed for eternity. Down-and-out men hit the road; down-and-out women hit the street.

But despite my silent inventory of troubles, I capitulate to my sister, as usual.

"Okay, but I can't make it before three-thirty. The Nelsons were very nice to us when Eli and I were in Moscow. We stayed with them for almost a month."

"That's okay; three-thirty's great, Nat. Thanks a million. I owe you one."

You don't owe me one, I think, replacing the receiver.

You owe me a million and one.

A P W I R E S E R V I C E P H O T O

This is the best picture I have of Shay. It shows her on a cigarette speedboat knifing through the intercoastal waterway in Miami in pursuit of some Latin American cocaine king, possibly Carlos Lehder Rivas. Presumably she would have turned him over to DEA authorities (granted he was really in Miami) if he hadn't escaped under strange circumstances. Anyway, her pursuit of him—four years before his actual capture—became a national news story. In this shot, Shay's dark heavy hair is flattened back by the wind and that, plus the deep tan burnishing her skin, makes her remarkable blue eyes seem even lighter than usual. I always thought this shot shed a lot of light on the reason Shay can get away with everything she gets away with.

Over the years my sister has frequently been featured in the "Newsmakers" or "People" sections of the weekly news magazines because of her good looks. Everyone agrees that Shay's a stand-out beauty—even at crowded airports. But at three-thirty today, there is no sign of her outside USAir at what she regards as the low-rent end of National Airport. Shay thinks of the north terminal as a slum because all the shuttles leave from the main building.

As soon as I wiggle my way between two hotel minibuses toward the curb, an aggressive traffic cop begins signaling me to move on. I smile, wave and gun my engine. As soon as he turns away, I switch off the ignition and stay where I am. Circling National Airport at this hour, either in the air or on the ground, is suicide. Every minute I can stay stationary is priceless.

It's almost four when Shay comes running outside with her big red shoulder bag swinging back and forth like the Foucault pendulum at the Museum of American History. She is carrying an assortment of mismatched bags plus my pink umbrella, which she borrowed three years ago after promising to return it the very next day. Only Shay would carry an umbrella, *my* umbrella, during the worst drought America has suffered in fifty years.

Trotting along beside her is a man carrying several more of her bags. He is not a porter. He is just a man. Probably he was a passenger on her flight whom she vamped a little.

"You're late, Shay," I say as I swing open the passenger door.

"Ohhhh, have you been waiting out *here*? I was waiting inside."

"Inside? What'd you think I was going to do? Drive up to the ticket counter?"

"No." She is crestfallen. Crushed. Destroyed that she's done the wrong thing again. "I thought you'd park in that short-term lot."

"You mean the one that's always full?"

Nervously the man sets down Shay's laptop computer case and two leather tote bags. Shay gives him one of her sequin-bright smiles and then completely forgets his existence. He walks away, looking dismissed and disappointed. Since my sister frequently volunteers my chauffeuring services, I am surprised she didn't offer to drop him off at some hotel in congested Crystal City.

Standing there surrounded by her baggage, Shay looks like a

high-class, fast-track, sixties jet-setter. Ever since leaving her second husband eight months ago, she has been living out of suitcases, subletting apartments or staying with different friends and lovers in various cities, steaming out her clothes in other people's showers and using small hotel gift containers of shampoo, bath gel and body lotion on a daily basis.

Still, she's looking good. She's brown as a toasted muffin. Having always viewed tanning as a competitive sport, Shay takes a Caribbean cruise every Christmas to get a leg up on her competition before the official arrival of summer in North America. By July, she's cocoa-brown. This summer's ozone crisis has only enhanced the tone of her tan.

As usual, she's wearing a faded T-shirt tucked into her trademark white Calvin jeans and a pair of hot-pink thong sandals. Although her only makeup is lip gloss and black kohl eyeliner, Shay is a genuinely glamorous article, and the people making detours around her pile of baggage glance at her with small frowns as if she's someone famous whose name they've forgotten. That's okay for folks who don't do crossword puzzles, but it's a big risk for those who do.

"Well, get in, Shay. The cops are watching."

"God, you're such a doll to come get me," she says, ignoring my irritation and starting to toss bags into the backseat while broadcasting her gratitude toward me with a neon-white smile. "You look gre-at. That's a fabulous dress."

Uh-oh.

The last time Shay borrowed something from me—my much-beloved metallic raincoat—she gave it to a pregnant woman in the Miami airport who was on her way home to Chile. When I got angry, Shay was totally shocked. For some reason I keep forgetting her favorite leisure activity is taking *my* shirt off *her* back and giving it away to someone else. The name of that game is: "Oh, sorry about that. I didn't think you'd mind. I'll buy you a new one."

Uh-huh.

S N A P S H O T

There we are. Two dark-haired little Jewish sisters, four and two years old, sitting atop a ten-cent-a-ride spotted pony at the Farmer–Labor party's annual Fourth of July picnic celebration at North Commons. Surrounded by a crowd of little blond children, we are the only brunettes in this Scandinavian setting, where pale bland beauty is the standard and a shy quiet demeanor the norm. If you look carefully you can see that Shay is hanging on to (pulling?) one of my braids. By this time, our parents had long since abandoned *their* parents' socialism to become socialites. Avid assimilationists, they threw catered affairs in newly con-structed country clubs with open trenches still awaiting sewer and water lines. Although Shay and I were encouraged to assimilate and adapt to our surroundings, we somehow always seemed to stick out like sore thumbs. We certainly had more pony rides than the other children because Dad thought *more* was *better* in every situation.

"I'm so glad to see you," Shay continues fervently.

She's been gone maybe ten days. I wouldn't know for sure because she never tells me when she's leaving, where she's going, who she'll be traveling with or where she'll be staying. Anyway, I'm always so relieved when she's not around, it never seems to me she's gone for very long.

Shay checks the contents of a Bloomingdale's Big Brown Bag before setting it in the backseat and then, climbing in beside me, starts searching for her seat belt. Having finally admitted her mortality when she turned forty in February, Shay now wrestles furiously with all the different restraint systems she encounters, animistically assuming they are trying to confound her. Now she is fighting to get the cross strap locked into place.

"Do you put your seat belt over or under or between your tits?" she asks, scrunching down to find the lock mechanism.

Uncertain, I look down. My seat belt appears to be doing all three things at the same time, so I don't answer her question. Instead I ask:

"Where's Amelia?"

"At Christopher's house."

Amelia is Shay's three-year-old granddaughter, of whom she has temporary custody. Christopher is Shay's estranged second husband, whom she still uses as an administrative assistant and substitute baby-sitter whenever she has to go out of town. Christopher, once counsel to the Senate Foreign Relations Committee, is now a Woodrow Wilson Fellow who spends all his time translating Baudelaire and taking care of Amelia as a way of reingratiating himself with Shay. Considering he is only related to the little girl through his now-defunct marriage to her grandmother, Christopher has turned out to be an excellent primary caretaker.

What men will do for my sister still knocks me out.

When Shay is finally strapped in, I start the car and crawl along with the other traffic until we are past the north terminal, where everyone speeds up. That's when my sister lights one of her Merit cigarettes.

"Oh, Shay," I whine. "Do you really have to smoke when the air conditioner's on?"

"Smoking's a dirty job but someone's got to do it," she says, crossing her long legs and getting comfortable.

I can tell she is totally focused on telling me her story. Crosscurrents of excitement turn her into an emotional Jacuzzi. Although she can hardly contain herself (she's never been too big in the self-restraint department), Shay wants *me* to ask what's happening. That's why she's twitching with impatience. Any minute now she's going to raise her hand in good old kindergarten fashion and wave it in the air until I call on her.

"Okay," I finally relent in a slightly testy voice. "Let's have it. What's the story?"

"It's a real major story, Nat. I stole some government papers while I was out on Long Island."

"Oh, great. What kind of papers?"

"It's a copy of an interview the DEA—the Drug Enforcement Administration?—got from Fawn Hall." Shay's words come bubbling out like unchilled Perrier from a bottle. "It's so damaging they've kept it under wraps for a whole year already. Just suppressed it. But now I'm going to blow the whole story sky high. It's just what I needed to put me back on the map in a big way."

Shay's talking celestial navigational charts here.

"What'd she testify about?" I ask.

"Are you ready for this? She said she was a weekend cocaine user from 1985 to 1987. I bet she was doing coke in tony Georgetown clubs while she was working for Oliver North on the National Security Council. Doing coke while she was working at the White House! Isn't that wild?"

"Didn't she date some contra guy?" I ask, straining to remember a bit of gossip I'd read long ago. "A relative of a contra leader or something?"

"Yup. Arturo Cruz, Junior." Shay pronounces Latin names with an exaggerated Castilian accent she picked up back at North High School in Minneapolis. When she says "Nicaragua" it always sounds like she's gargling. "He's the son of Arturo Cruz, the contra general, or whatever he is. Fawn and Junior were a real hot item back there for a while."

"Jesus," I whisper, genuinely impressed.

Fawn Hall. The Republican Barbie doll. Captain of the White House cheerleading team. Oliver North's sycophantic secretary, who made Nancy-Reagan goo-goo eyes at her boss during photo opportunities and hid secret documents inside her bra to get them past White House security for him. Fawn Hall, seen driving a red Fiero with FAWN 3 license plates around D.C., was aide-de-camp to an inside traitor. Another pollutant to add to this summer's disgraces. Another hit on the list of scandals sprinkling down on us like acid rain.

Washington has become the crime-and-corruption capital of the world.

See Ronald Reagan pretend he can't hear reporters' questions.

See Nancy Reagan telling the have-nots to just say no.

See Fawn Hall, looking like a blond runaway from *Charlie's Angels,* say yes to drugs and contras while she fawns all over Ollie.

See Ollie twisting in the wind, still looking holier-than-thou.

Watch the Boy Scout leader and his secretary shred National Security Council documents.

See democracy go down the drain.

But—wait—maybe it's the bimbos who will finally bring down the government. Not the right, not the left. Not the skinheads, not the neo-cons. Not the Reagan royalists nor the distressed Democrats. Maybe it's the retired bunnies who will do the dirty work for us. Maybe it's the grown-up Barbie dolls who will finally destroy all the Kens who've diddled them for decades. Look how easily Donna Rice knocked off the Democratic front-runner.

Although no political challenger could unseat Wilbur Mills from his chairmanship of the House Ways and Means Committee, Fanne Foxe did it lying down. Foxe and Mills, Rice and Hart, Hahn and Bakker, Hall and North. Maybe Fawn and Ollie are making it. Maybe not. Anyway, it doesn't matter, because Americans believe it's worse for a man to screw his secretary than to screw his country.

So what's new?

But for Shay Karavan to break this latest Fawn Hall story is to let the fox do a feature on the chicken coop. Shay, too, is a member of the clubby coke generation. She understands all too well the health-club neurotic, macrobiotic, aerobic/phobic yuppified world of glitz, greed, drugs and personal defilement.

Shay's treatment of the Fawn Hall story won't throw any new light on Oliver North's Iran-contra caper. It won't discuss the illegal provision of ill-gotten drug dollars to the contras in defiance of Congress. No. It will only be a stylish profile of a drop-dead gorgeous spandex-sexy secretary and how she partied it up in Georgetown. And why does this bug me so bad? Because I'm getting the short end of the stick. I work in an area where there are few federal, state or private dollars to sustain serious social-welfare programs. I care about the needy; Shay's only interested in the greedy.

"You know, it's hard for people to remember what Contragate's about, Shay. If you could simplify things, it would really be helpful. People can't remember the sequence of events. Or the timing. Or even the players. Oliver North selling arms to Iran and then sending that money down to the contras to buy arms is just too complicated."

"Yeah," Shay says vaguely.

But now she is getting bored, fading out on me.

Real politics turn her off. That's why Shay should share this story with Eli. Let him do the political angle while she shines the glitz. Back in the early seventies, Eli did a lot of Watergate stories, sometimes even preempting the *Post*. But now no matter what stories break, what scandals surface, nothing can mar Reagan's image, so Eli has ended up feeling professionally defeated and personally cynical about both the presidency and the press.

It's one of the reasons he's so unhappy these days. Restive. Edgy.

"Anyway, Mickey Teardash and I are going down to Atlanta Sunday night to meet with some Dukakis people. They're deciding whether or not to co-release the story with us. You know who Mickey Teardash is, don't you? From the Georgia tobacco family? Last year he bought *U.S.A.* Actually he bought two newspapers and three magazines last year, plus that humongous public-relations firm—Images—in New York that's doing all the Dukakis television ads."

Shay cards her men. Each one must be famous for something.

At this moment I think I know how Sophia Loren felt when her sister married Mussolini's son. At this moment I think I know how Jessica Mitford felt when her sister Boud took up with Hitler, Himmler, Göring and Goebbels. Mickey Teardash is a walking symbol of Wall Street—the roaring eighties' national poster boy for terminal avarice. He is a junk-bond junkie, an LBO *luftmensch* and a corporate take-over kamikaze kook.

"I've read about him in the papers," I say carefully.

"Well, I told him we'd all meet him for a drink around eleven at Café au Lait. I *know* Eli knows him."

2

And this I have to live with.

I have tried to deal with it rationally.

I have tried to deal with it in the offices of high-priced shrinks.

Throughout our twenty-year marriage, Eli and I have tried to deal with it in positive ways. Eli's a great talker, and he's especially good on topics like family hang-ups. Because he'll stick to a subject until we run it into the ground, we have explored every facet of my overwrought relationship with Shay. These discussions are difficult and usually end with Eli saying the best thing about having a wild sister is that it strengthens a person's character.

Yeah, I always answer, so does a broken leg.

To my knowledge, nowhere is it written that sisterhood *has* to be difficult. There have been sisters who didn't insist on being diametrically and dialectically opposite types. There is no law that states sisters must use the Snow White/Rose Red fairy tale as their operative model.

Of course Eli knows him. Eli knows everyone. That's why Eli is so important to Shay. He's a valuable brother-in-law because he knows everyone and because everyone knows him and because he's an influential Washington journalist. Moreover, he is eternally and irresistibly interesting to Shay because he slept with her for several years before he married me.

That'll do it every time.

Frequently when Shay gets drunk, she brags that she's slept with Muammar Qaddafi, Fidel Castro, Michael Manley, one of *People*'s sexiest men alive (Sean Connery), one Nobel Prize winner, one MacArthur "Genius" Fellowship winner (that's her soon-to-be-ex-husband, Christopher) and two Pulitzer Prize winners, whom she never names, out of respect for me, since one of them is my husband.

"What this *really* means, Nat, is that the Democrats will have a better chance of winning the election in November. This could really help them. The Republicans will look awfully dirty after my story comes out."

This is a bit much for me to handle.

Once again my kid sister has found a piece of stage business for herself that is front-page news. As usual she is going to gild herself while she goes for the gold.

"Who'd you steal it from, Shay?"

"Actually, it's sort of a long story. See, I was out in the Hamptons working on an article for *Lear's* magazine. You know? The one for women who weren't born yesterday?"

I nod like older sisters are programmed to do.

"It's about September sex," she continues.

Another nod. Although I'm not sure what September sex is, with my luck I'm probably missing out on a good thing again.

"Anyway, before Mickey came out there to join me, I stayed with an old girlfriend of mine in Southampton. Remember Georgia Russo?"

"No."

Translation: *How the hell am I supposed to remember all the*

people in your life when you've got a goddam cast of thousands?
You still can't even remember the names of my two best friends—
or tell them apart.

"Well, one night, Jerry—that's Georgia's husband—got drunk
and started bragging about how he knows some of the lawyers
representing Fawn Hall and how sexy she is and all that kind of
shit. Actually Jerry's a real sleaze bag. He's got a practice full of
cocaine-dealing clients. Georgia's worried because it's illegal for
a lawyer to be kept on retainer by a criminal currently engaging
in criminal activity. That makes the lawyer an accomplice or
something. Anyway, Jerry dropped this bit about how the DEA
interviewed Fawn about doing drugs and that he managed to
pinch a copy of the DEA report."

Shay cracks her window and flicks her cigarette out into the
tinder-dry universe. Then she opens up her huge shoulder bag and
starts to rummage through its jumbled contents.

I have now reached the precarious point where 395 intersects
95 North. Like wild buffalo, cars are stampeding toward us, hurtling past the red nose of my little Ford Escort, which is poking
into their path. Since there is no one behind me, I decide to give
myself a break and wait for an easy opening. I'm in no big hurry.
When Shay's around I usually try to hang loose and take things
slow and easy. Actually, when Shay's around, I try to be a little
nicer to myself than I usually am.

"Anyway, the last night I was there, Georgia and Jerry went to
this party I didn't want to go to? And I was just sitting around
when all of a sudden I got this idea. So I went into Jerry's study
and looked in his filing cabinet. And there it was. Right on top
of some other papers in the top drawer. I almost freaked out when
I read it. So I just shoved it in my suitcase and took it with me
when I left there to move into Mickey's place over in East Hampton."

"This is really serious, Shay," I say, still watching the cars
rushing in from Virginia. "It's probably classified. You've probably broken some federal espionage act or something."

"Oh, I covered my tracks," she answers confid[...]
can prove I took the papers, and besides, Jerry [...]
notice they're gone until after the story breaks. In [...]
on what happens in Atlanta, Mickey and I migh[...]
the Dukakis people to release on their own so th[...]
credit for it."

Suddenly there's a break in the traffic.

I'm on.

Flooring the accelerator, I swing out across 95 [...]
around the circle leading to Memorial Bridge.

"So, as far as I'm concerned, it's a wrap," Shay p[...]

"Oh, absolutely," I say, not even attempting to c[...]
sarcasm. "It's in the bag, Shay."

"I can't wait to tell Eli."

Shay stares off into the middle distance while [...]
playing out her big scene. As an entertainer, Shay d[...]
waste herself on audiences of one. Especially if it's [...]
prefers performing for larger groups in SRO situat[...]

Shay's journalistic specialty is essay-style wrap-u[...]
tional trials, which she considers a form of American [...]
has written extensively about John Hinckley, Jr.,[...]
Bülow, the Walker family of spies, Roxanne Pulitze[...]
caro, Jr., Baby M, and most recently, Robert Ch[...]
Preppie Murderer.

"Eli is really going to freak out," she predicts hap[...]
just gonna *love* this story."

Look at lawyer-writer Flo Kennedy and her sisters, who call themselves the Other (read Black) Kennedy women. They get along. Look at Ursula and Gudrun of *Women in Love,* who linked arms and literarily walked through life together. Look at Beth and Jo and Meg and Amy in *Little Women.* Didn't they care *for* and *about* each other? Look how often the fierce feminist Gloria Steinem came to Washington to help her sister Suzanne take care of her six children when they were little. And didn't Erica Jong even write a poem to her younger sister full of love and warm advice?

Still, I guess I instinctively knew the truth long before I began my research:

(A)   It is impossible for sisters to be both different *and* equal.
(B)   Two or more sisters cannot occupy the same space.
(C)   One sister cannot be both a subject and an object.
(D)   Any action by one sister creates an equal and opposite reaction in the other.

It was Margaret Mead's sister, Elizabeth Mead Stieg, who announced that sisterhood was "probably the most competitive relationship within the family." *Let's hear it for Elizabeth!*

"Sisters are the crabgrass on the lawn of life," wrote Anon. *Allll riii-ight, Anon!*

Kate Millett's younger sister, Mallory, said that her relationship with Kate made her feel "like Milton Eisenhower to Kate's Ike." *Tell me about it, Mallory.*

Again and again over the years I have asked myself: Am I jealous of Shay?

And each time I have had to answer: Yes. Absolutely yes.

I am jealous of her looks, her career, her zingy clothes, her passionate pursuits, her notoriety. I am jealous of all the lovers she's had, who by now must number well into three digits. I am jealous because Shay knows all the glitzy glamorous celebrities in America, all the late-night talk-show charmers, the stand-up comics, giggly starlets, chic fashion designers, low-budget directors and far-out rock stars.

I am jealous because she knows all the movers and shakers who appear on morning network news shows—the media spin doctors, best-selling authors, policy-making politicos, Wall Street brokers, Olympic athletes, hostile-takeover honchos, Hollywood producers, foreign correspondents, Harvard pundits, diet doctors and French actresses.

I am jealous because she consorts with all the flamboyant hostesses and international CEOs and millionaire tennis stars and world-class yachtsmen and kooky artists—all the residual royalty in Europe, the smartest people in New York and the fastest ones in L.A. I almost lost it when I first saw whom she'd coded into her speed-dialing memory system. Her Rolodex reads like an index to a book by Stephen Birmingham or the key to a *roman à clef* by Dominick Dunne.

I freaked out when her name cropped up on the short list of Washington women mentioned as Gary Hart's *real* mistress—a woman known as a serious journalist, not just a bimbo. I couldn't handle it when a reporter from *The New York Times,* seated beside Eli at the annual Gridiron Dinner, asked if the rumor about Shay and Qaddafi was true. It blew me away when Ted Koppel asked Eli if there was anything to the story that linked Shay and former California governor Jerry Brown.

What I've learned from being Shay Karavan's sister is that a rumor is as good as the truth for boosting name recognition.

Over the years different shrinks have asked me, "Were you always jealous of your baby sister? When you were little, did you mind being older when she was so much bolder?"

Of course, I've always answered. Of course I did.

Did it bother you that she's had both a family and a career?

Of course, I answered. I minded that very much.

Did it bother you that Eli loved Shay first and only discovered you after she'd left him?

Are you kidding?

But when one shrink asked me if I'd exchange my life for Shay's, I said: *No, sir. No way, José.*

I haven't got Shay's temperament. We are drastically different. Even though I sometimes envy her life-style, I don't approve of her life.

Irreconcilable Difference #84: I happen to have inherited a particular synapse between purpose and caution that got left out of her genetic map.

Irreconcilable Difference #91: My conscience is integrated into my character so that I am a serious human being, while Shay is totally superficial. I am a person; she is a personality. I perform; she's a performer. I have character; she is one. I help; she hypes. She grandstands while I try to withstand the gross temptations of our society.

So how do I live with this sister of mine, who flits in and out of my life, using and abusing me, hogging the limelight, taking liberties and always just a bounce away from actually flirting with my husband?

Poorly.

"Ta *dum.*"

Shay has finally found the hairbrush she's been hunting. Lowering the sun visor, she adjusts the mirror so she can watch herself brush her thick, crinkly black hair. The dozen or so silver bracelets she always wears on her left wrist click like castanets each time she back-combs her curls.

"Any visitors in residence over at your place right now?" she asks me.

"No."

"So, then, would you mind if Mickey stays there with me over the weekend? He's coming in tonight and we'll be leaving for Atlanta Sunday. But, please, Nat, I want you to tell me the truth. If it's going to put you out in *any way*, we'll just forget about it and find a hotel."

I can't think of anything I would like less at the moment than having Shay and her new lover move into my home.

"You'll love Mickey, Nat. He's a real *mensch*. In fact, he might just be the right man for me. *Finally*. He's fabulously rich, you know, but he gives away pots of money to political organizations. And he's brilliant and funny and absolutely awesome in the sack. He's absolutely huge. Hu-ge. On top of that he's a good dancer and a *great* kisser. I mean *really* great. At least he doesn't drool spit into my mouth, which is a great improvement over Christopher, I can tell you that much. Anyway, I can't wait to get him to Atlanta so I can flash him around a little. Up till now we've been keeping a real low profile."

Eli is also going to Atlanta Sunday to cover the convention, but this year he didn't invite me to join him like he's always done before. We've attended every Democratic and Republican National Convention together since 1968. That's twenty years. So I have to admit not going this summer hurts a lot and forces me to admit to myself that Eli just isn't very interested in being with me anymore.

S N A P S H O T

This is Eli standing outside the National Press Building. He's definitely better-looking than Walter Matthau—but not much. He's a bespectacled, shaggy, baggy man—big, fleshy and comfortable. I guess he's sexy in the same way as a messed-up, much-used, slept-in bed. Being married to a Washington journalist is like being a doctor's wife—plenty of perks and vicarious status, but no personal satisfaction. Mates of Washington journalists are admitted into their members-only speakeasy by virtue of marriage—not merit. It is best they never believe they belong. Divorce brings death to the identity of the nonpractitioner. At best, the spouse of a journalist can hold conditional second-class citizenship in the elite world of the national press corps.

Eli didn't invite me to Atlanta this year because he's bored with me.

That's why I'd wanted a quiet weekend alone with him before he left. I have this fantasy of somehow making him remember how tight we used to be, how thick we were, before our cold war started this spring. Although I have been hurting over the state of my marriage for months, I don't say anything about that to my sister. Instead I say:

"Sure. It should be okay. Eli's just getting ready for Atlanta too, so he's feeling pretty mellow."

We are spinning across Memorial Bridge at 55 MPH. The city is baking, but there are still some joggers—federal office workers wearing satin running shorts—bobbing along the walkways. There are also two women guiding a string of youngsters across the bridge.

"Oh look, Nat. Look at all those darling little grandchildren," Shay coos.

I actually turn my head to see if she's flipped out.

Grandchildren?

"Imagine the teacher taking them for a field trip on such a hot day! But listen, Nat. And I want you to tell me the truth. Do you think Eli would mind if Amelia stayed over at your place with me too? If you think that'd create too much commotion for him, just say so and I'll forget about it. But really, she's begun sleeping through the night again, almost *every* night now."

I am squinting into the sun, scrunching up my face so my distress won't show.

"No, that should be okay," I say, concentrating on changing lanes. "I bought a new mattress for that little cot she sleeps on."

"Rea-lly? That's *so-ooo* nice. Well, would you mind stopping to pick her up right now on the way home?" Shay asks. "I get so lonesome for her I could die."

"Really, Shay. If I'd known you wanted to go to Georgetown, I would have taken Key Bridge," I respond tersely, letting ink-black irritation stain my words.

"Sorry about that. But can't you just take the Whitehurst Freeway back?"

"Jesus, Shay. Why didn't you tell me you wanted to go to Georgetown?"

"I didn't want to put you to any trouble," she says penitently.

"You always do the same thing, Shay. You make more trouble stalling around than if you just came right out with it. You knew you were going to ask me eventually."

But like a responsible older sister, I turn back to hang a right on the Whitehurst Freeway. As soon as I make the turn, Shay reaches over to clasp my shoulder.

"You're so terrific, Nat. I couldn't survive without you. Really," she says. "Thanks a million." Then she leans over into the backseat. "I bought you something in New York. I didn't even get a chance to wrap it, but I can't wait to show it to you."

The next thing I know she is dangling some lacy red thing in the air between us.

"Look," she says.

I take a lateral look.

"Good God, what is that?"

"A bra. And the cups unsnap."

"You mean a nursing bra, Shay?"

I'm a tad touchy on that subject.

"No," she squeals. "It's from Frederick's of Hollywood. It's to vamp Eli with. *You know.*"

"I can't look right now," I say, changing lanes again. My heart is pounding. It would take six of me to fill those two enormous cups. "Just drop it in my purse, Shay. I'll look at it later."

And shut-the-fuck-up, I think with hot resentment.

Just shut the fuck up.

Having brushed her hair until it is dancing with electricity, Shay now ties it back away from her face by twisting one long strand into a rope, wrapping it around the thick frizzy mass and knotting it near the nape of her neck.

"Aren't you afraid, Shay?" I ask her. "Aren't you scared?"

"No. Why should I be?"

There is no trace of anxiety on her face. Because I watched her grow up, I know Shay has no sense of personal danger, no internal alarm system. She operates on junkie logic, always did. From babyhood on, she acted as if she had blanket immunity from the consequences of her actions. She's perfect for these times.

S N A P S H O T

That's Shay, seated on her Schwinn two-wheeler. She is seven—
which is when she began riding in the street. Despite our parents' fierce prohibitions, Shay actually used her bike as a *mode of
transportation.* I obediently stayed on the sidewalk, which, of
course, led nowhere except around the block. I believe Shay acquired her sense of purpose from disregarding our parents' orders
and doing whatever she wanted to do whenever she wanted to
do it. This snapshot is like a movie still mounted in a glass show-
case beside a box office, freezing some climactic moment
plucked from a film. This snapshot blurts out the nature of my
childhood experience: Shay disregarding the rules and then
charging past me—atop her speedy Schwinn—to triumph despite her disobedience.

Of course she drove poor Marge crazy with her recklessness.
Actually, Shay and I have different mothers. At least we don't
seem to remember the same woman. Shay has her Marge and I
have mine. My Marge was always sweet and gentle. She wanted
me to be good, so that's what I was. Shay's Marge is a wicked old
witch who psychologically damaged Shay by claiming she was
difficult to raise.

"Listen, Nat," Shay says, lighting up another cigarette.
"There's something I've been wanting to ask you. Didn't you
have a doctor's excuse to get out of taking gym?"

"I don't know," I say. "Maybe. Maybe one year I did. I can't
remember."

The Whitehurst Freeway runs along the river, so I'm able to
steal a quick sideward glance down at the Potomac. It is a shocking sight. The water has receded, leaving the riverbanks bald and
exposing previously submerged rocks, tree stumps and boating
debris. The Potomac has shriveled up, evaporated. Another
Greenhouse Effect.

"I think you *did* get out of gym with a medical excuse," Shay
insists. "Anyway, do you remember Miss Tippy? In sixth grade?
She taught geography?"

"Sort of," I say, as the freeway bends away from the river.

Now we are on M Street, instantly and irrevocably stuck in rush-hour traffic.

Four-thirty on a Friday afternoon in July near the Key Bridge in Georgetown.

We are going belly-up on M Street, trapped in standstill traffic, while Shay tries to recollect our childhood.

"Well, do you remember that chart she used to pull down like a window shade over the blackboard? It had the five basic food groups on it? What we were supposed to eat every day? One was leafy green vegetables and one was cereal grains and one was dairy products. But I can't remember the others. Do you?"

"No." I shake my head. "I don't remember."

"God. I really wish I could think of it."

"What are you after, Shaysie?" I ask impatiently. "Why do you want to know all that stuff?"

"I just want to remember . . . correctly," she says, fiddling with one of the three emerald studs set punk-style in her left earlobe. "For some reason it feels important to me."

I sigh.

Here she sits, maybe making world history, and she's still worried about remembering the food groups from back in sixth grade when even the teachers were nutritional Neanderthals. I can't figure Shay out. I never could. She's totally inconsistent. Although she borrows things from me and never returns them, last year when she was in Chicago, she sent me a case of Nut Goodies—our favorite childhood candy bars—because they're only retailed in the Midwest. On the other hand, even though she's in Chicago frequently, she never has time to stop in Minneapolis to see Marge. She's been home only once since Dad died last summer.

A pale ribbon of sunlight is struggling to break through the haze hanging over Georgetown. Pulling down the sun visor, I suddenly see my reflection in the open mirror. In truth, I look a lot better at forty-two than I did back when I was twenty. Eli says I've started to resemble some Italian actress from a grainy Fellini-style black-and-white post–World War II film, pushing her own middle-aged envelope and looking raunchier and randier every day.

But what do I *really* look like?

A pale, blurred, tamped-down rendition of Shay, an under-developed Polaroid photo. I'm the faded sister, the vanilla sibling, the pale comparison. Unlike Shay's, my chest and ego are slightly underdeveloped—my skin and hair too thin, my temper too short and my memory too long.

S N A P S H O T

This is my favorite picture of myself and it was taken by the Motor Vehicle Department for my driver's license. Not quite an Avedon portrait, but what it shows is that I'm a Sigourney Weaver kind of woman. I belong to that class of brunettes—including Debra Winger, Ann Bancroft and Elizabeth Ashley—who light up from within, whose idealism illuminates their features and alchemizes relatively plain faces into beautiful ones as compelling as any gorgeous movie stars'. I think of myself and other brunettes of my ilk as the bushel-basket brigade, as in: "Don't hide all your charms under a bushel basket," which is what Marge used to say to me all the time.

Of course I automatically deflate my self-rating when Shay's around. She always puts a different spin on everything, especially how I feel about myself. Sitting beside Shay I invariably react like the little girl in the dirty joke who points at her diaperless baby brother and asks: "How come I'm so plain and he's so fancy?"

Shay whites me out like a typo.

All around us cars are shimmering like mirages in old MGM desert movies. Inside their air-conditioned incubators, the drivers look frazzled as they watch each other with drugged and distant eyes. Even their aggravated honkings, caused by some staccato stoppage, seem muted and remote.

Suburban Fairfax and Loudoun counties in northern Virginia have put water emergencies into effect. All nonessential usages—

the washing of cars, watering of lawns and filling of swimming pools—have been declared illegal. Courtyard fountains are forbidden to run. Commercial car washes have closed. There are periods of time in which no one can use any water at all: 1:00–4:00 A.M.; 3:00–5:00 P.M. Rain, which was ignored when it arrived at approximately appropriate times in proper amounts with foreseeable results, is now remembered, in its absence, as dear and beloved.

Everyone is waiting for rain.

"You know, the Gauguin retrospective is only at the East Wing until the thirty-first," Shay prattles. "Everyone says it's wonderful and there's only a few days left to see it. I think we should all go tomorrow."

"Oh, great," I groan. "I'll be sure to put that on my calendar."

It is almost five o'clock when we reach Christopher's.

Christopher lives on Thirty-sixth and Reservoir Road in a detached brick house that Shay convinced him to buy in 1980, right before they got married. Back then it had cost three quarters of a million dollars. Now it's worth two million, but that doesn't really matter much anymore because last year Christopher won the MacArthur Fellowship, which guaranteed him $300,000 a year for the next five years. In other words, he's now living on easy street right there on Reservoir Road.

Although Shay was thrilled about Christopher becoming a MacArthur fellow, she moved out of their house a few months later. She said it was boring to eat breakfast with him. She said she'd rather eat alone and read the *Post* editorial page, which she also hates, rather than listen to Christopher drone on and on about Baudelaire.

I should have known. I should have translated that message immediately:

I've met someone new who's much richer and flashier than Christopher Edmonds.

Pulling into the driveway, I deep-park Christopher's BMW, with its triangular yellow BABY ON BOARD sticker, and turn off my ignition.

"Listen, Nat," Shay whispers. "Don't say anything about the . . . Contra Papers to anyone yet, okay?"

The "Contra Papers." It's not an accurate title but it sure has the ring of history.

Sighing, I reach over to depress the lock on Shay's seat belt for her. In a flash she is out of the car, running toward Christopher's front door, all else forgotten. To be truthful, I have to admit Shay really does adore her little granddaughter. Not that that's hard to do. Amelia is the essence of lovable. Indeed, Amelia is almost edible. And that's good, because a lot of us have to pitch in to help with her maintenance.

In the lives of our family, little Amelia functions primarily as an indirect object.

Jealousy #786: Am I jealous that Shay has Amelia?

Absolutely. Positively.

For nearly twenty years I envied Shay for having her son, Steven, so why shouldn't I be envious now about her having a darling little granddaughter? The fact that I've been sterile ever since I had an abortion—which Shay arranged for me when we were students at the University of Minnesota—makes me jealous of any woman with children.

S N A P S H O T

This is the official hospital photograph of Amelia Amanda Yellen, taken at George Washington on the night of her birth, June 12, 1985. She looks like your basic exhausted newborn, sound asleep after a harrowing birth and still peacefully oblivious to the perils of babyhood in the age of the postnuclear family. Before Amelia turned one, her mother was committed to the Hazelden drug rehabilitation clinic outside Minneapolis in a last-ditch effort to save her life. Yvonne was already a junkie when Steven Yellen knocked her up during their junior year in high school. They were married in Shay and Christopher's garden on Reservoir Road. Yvonne wore a Mexican wedding dress that only half hid her protruding tummy. Steven wore a Greek wedding shirt and looked like he was in a state of shock. When Steven began his premed program at McGill University in September 1987, Amelia (then two) went to live with Shay.

I couldn't believe it when the court awarded my sister temporary custody of Amelia. Shay, who has no known address and one of the shortest attention spans in modern history, is as fickle a grandmother as she is a mother, mother-in-law, daughter, wife, ex-wife, girlfriend and—you guessed it—sister.

When Steven was born, Shay asked Eli and me to be his godparents. That had a sort of poetic justice because Shay and Eli had served as "godparents" at my abortion back in 1967, when they were engaged. Shay had found the two med students who agreed to do it and borrowed enough money to pay for it. Eli had driven us to St. Paul to get it done and let me use his apartment while I recuperated from the little illegal operation that left me with a perforated uterine wall. At least Eli understood the reason, some five years later, when a gynecologist told us we couldn't have a family.

That's how I learned that a bad abortion neuters a woman just like spaying does a dog. I always have to laugh when people say they're *fixing* their dog. *Breaking* is what they're really doing. I was *broken* and, like Humpty-Dumpty, nothing could put me back together again.

Anyway, I can't deny I'm jealous that Shay has a little granddaughter whom strangers assume is her own last-minute baby. Shay looks exactly like all the late-thirties first-time mothers pushing prams along Wisconsin Avenue. And, of course, she loves it when people assume Amelia is her daughter, because then she can shock them with the truth, which definitely dramatizes her youthfulness.

From the car I watch as Christopher opens his front door.

Christopher is ten years older than Shay and the WASPiest man I've ever known. He is very tall, very lean and still very blond, both inside and out. His personality is as blond as his hair. The exact antithesis of Shay, he is restrained, refined and reflective. He speaks slowly and takes action only after a great deal of forethought. He is low-key, low-profile and probably gets out of the shower to pee.

Obviously Christopher and Shay got together because opposites attract; they are apart now because opposites attract only briefly. The great pain of Christopher's life is his separation from Shay, whose comings and goings bedevil him.

Unable to contain his pleasure at seeing his estranged wife at the front door, Christopher bends down awkwardly to embrace her. But Shay, who is trying to see around him for a glimpse of the baby, doesn't even notice his effort to greet her. This realization splashes Christopher's face like a pitcher of cold water. It is followed by a chaser of plain old-fashioned pain and longing.

Now I can see Amelia edging around Christopher.

She is knee-high and wearing a yellow sunsuit. She has Shay's dark curly hair and her father's big brown eyes. Her little nose and mouth turn upward like a ☺ sticker.

Amelia sees Shay.

Shay sees Amelia and starts to dance a red-hot-mama number right there at the top of the stairs.

Amelia wiggles around Christopher to get through the doorway.

Now Shay starts doing the dirty boogie.

Amelia is clapping her hands and laughing. Now Christopher is laughing. Now Shay is laughing. They all talk excitedly for a moment before Shay comes running back to the car.

I roll down my window.

"Let's stay here and take a swim, Nat," she pleads. "Come on. It's so hot. A swim will feel great and I've got a bunch of suits inside. One of them will fit you. Just call Eli and tell him to come here after work instead of going home. Then Christopher can barbecue us something so we won't have to worry about dinner."

Shay uses Christopher's house as her cabana.

Although she won't sleep there anymore, she and her friends

use the pool, the patio, and the house (as an adjacent dressing room) any time of the day or night. Besides making frequent unannounced visits with small groups of uninvited guests, Shay also occasionally throws a big pool party there when she's in town. That's when she rounds up all the usual suspects so she can see the entire press pack at one time. Sadly enough, Christopher is pleased by this turn of events because it allows him to see Shay more often and stay in touch with her old crowd.

Jealousy #787: Shay's friends are legion and legendary; mine are anonymous and actually number only three, all of whom are away this summer. Shay's friends are Washington political hotshots who make things happen. Most of them are spin doctors, who appear on TV immediately following a news event to explain to the viewers what they just saw happen—oral instant-replay people. Shay likes these media *machers* because they blur the distinction between reporting and creating news. They act as both judge and jury.

Shay cannot remember the names of my girlfriends. She always calls Angie Annie and does not recognize Helen outside of my kitchen.

Since I've always found it easier to indulge Shay than resist her—especially on a hot day—I shrug and accept the invitation. So the next thing I know I am sitting beside the pool, still fully dressed, talking to Christopher, when Shay emerges through the back door wearing only the bottom half of a bikini. She is holding Amelia's hand and looking both innocent and happy.

Here's how Shay thinks:

I am her sister. I have seen her breasts.

Christopher is/was her husband. He has seen her breasts.

Amelia is her granddaughter and is absolutely *crazy* about breasts.

Since all of us have seen Shay's breasts, what could possibly be wrong with a collective screening?

What my sister consistently chooses to ignore is the metaphysics of human psychology. To Shay, her mind-set *is* reality; all the rest is sound and fury.

Totally unselfconscious, she approaches the pool.

Shay has Art Deco breasts, like the ones featured on the original paperback cover of *Darkness at Noon,* which Koestler described as fitting inside champagne glasses. It is obvious, however, that Shay has been swimming elsewhere, in less congenial pools, because both her breasts are quite white compared to the rest of her body.

Only the two toast-colored nipples match her tan.

Christopher looks at me and shrugs. I lift my eyebrows a little and sigh. Then we smile tolerantly at each other.

Once again we silently forgive Shay's transgressions because her sins are not venal.

She is out of control, but usually commits only victimless crimes.

Actually I am quite crazy about Christopher. In fact, I like Shay's first husband too. Barney Yellen has a storefront law office in Adams-Morgan, almost directly across the street from my shelter. Barney and I both belong to that group of advocates who continued working with anti-poverty programs long after the "Great Society" ended and they ceased being fashionable. Nowadays I see him more often than I see Christopher. Usually he's with his significant other, a good-looking blond reporter from the *Post* named Victoria.

Barney Yellen is an interesting man with a strong sex drive, a huge drinking problem, a lousy liver and a dirty mouth. Because his head is still stuck in the sixties, he continues fighting old fights and getting into trouble on Saturday nights. The day after Amelia was born, Barney gave Yvonne a copy of *Baby and Child Care* that Dr. Spock had autographed for Barney in a jail cell they shared in the Tombs in 1967.

"Aren't you coming in?" Shay calls out to us as she picks up Amelia and slides into the shallow end of the pool.

Amelia squeals with delight when the cool water licks her legs. Mischievously, she reaches out to clasp Shay's breasts as if they are water wings. Both of them are laughing as Shay begins a series of small knee bends to get Amelia accustomed to the water.

Then they play in the pool like two happy campers.

• • •

After a while, Christopher goes off to telephone Eli, and I move my director's chair, shaded by the thick wall of bamboo trees that encircles Christopher's property, into the sun. Living in the inner city as I do, where the homicide rate rises with the humidity, where water pressure is low and blood pressure high, I tend to forget about such amenities as pools and shaded gardens.

When Christopher returns, he sits down again and reports that Eli will arrive shortly. Then he begins chatting amiably, in his dry monotonous voice, about the mail and telephone messages awaiting Shay inside the house. I only half listen while I watch Shay and Amelia playing in the bright chlorine-tinted water. Within the wasted Washington landscape, only Georgetown remains green and fertile. Here, despite the drought, gardeners somehow keep the trees, grass and shrubs growing and the jewel-clear swimming pools cool and deep.

Never before have pools felt as counterfeit as they do this summer. Yet here I sit, in a cool corner of a well-kempt Georgetown garden, surrounded by all the embellishments of affluence that make people forget about political commitments and turn ideals into intermittent and conditional things. Now I have let my sister, the political lightweight, the loose cannon in my life, entice me into this garden, where my brand of personally painful, unrecognized and unappreciated hands-on politics is easily dismissed.

After spending most of June in my non–air-conditioned Home Away from Home storefront shelter for homeless women on Eighteenth Street, I felt my physical discomfort start turning me against my clients. Being hot all the time made me cranky and impatient with the pale, morose, overweight women who arrived dressed for a snowstorm in the Arctic. Suddenly the odors that rose from beneath their layers of clothing began to nauseate me. All the aversions I had finally overcome, with great effort, began to reemerge in the horrendous heat. I was almost glad when we had to close the place down.

But I have tried to do my part. For almost twenty years I have held down tedious, underpaid social-work positions that always made me feel whatever I accomplished was too little and too late for too few. Of course there were never enough public funds to support and sustain important projects that could have alleviated some of the suffering. One federal administration after another misdirected money into military budgets rather than toward welfare programs. Since Eli and I moved to D.C., I have worked for three different city agencies—housing, welfare and adoption. Two years ago I put together a coalition of local church groups to co-finance with the D.C. government my shelter for homeless women.

S N A P S H O T

This is eight-year-old Tyrone, who was my favorite client for three years and the reason why I left the adoption agency. I had finally placed him in a foster home with a woman who actually *liked* children. This was an exceptional placement, and it thrilled me— until my first home visit a week later. That was when Tyrone's foster mother announced she couldn't keep him because he upset her two foster daughters. "What's the matter?" I asked. So she beckoned me to the living room, where Tyrone was watching TV and milking his penis, which he had pulled out through the open fly of his blue jeans. "He does that all the time," his foster mother whispered. "He won't stop. That's why I can't keep him. He doesn't think there's anything wrong about doing it in front of people. He keeps doing it till he's done. Nobody ever told him he shouldn't do that, so he doesn't believe me when I say it's nasty. That's why I can't keep him. Sorry."

Being a social worker often makes me feel like an anachronism. Everything I care about has become passé. In this time and place, compassion for the wretched of the earth has gone out of style in a big way. Greed is in: Excess is our order of the day, outrageous excess in everything but human empathy. Sometimes I feel as if I'm the only one left in America who gives a damn. Beneath my breasts (with their inverted nipples) fierce political feelings flourish.

I am a secret subversive.

S N A P S H O T

That's me standing between my grandparents, my Bubbie and Zadie, revolutionaries who escaped from Leningrad in 1915. I'm maybe ten years old in this snapshot, so it must have been 1956. Every night Bubbie told us bedtime stories. Her favorite one was about a terrible midnight pogrom when the cossacks attacked the farm where she lived with her parents and thirteen brothers and sisters. According to plan, they all ran out to the barn to hide in the hayloft. Everyone climbed up the rope ladder and through the secret trap door in the ceiling. But their father, who climbed up last, couldn't fit through. His stomach had become too big to slide through the narrow opening. Bubbie's mother kept pulling him up by his arms, trying to unjam him, but when the cossacks rode into the barn they cut him in half at his waist, which released his head and upper chest into the arms of his family. It was that story which made me a political person. It wasn't by choice. I used to cry and beg Bubbie not to tell that story anymore and she'd lay off for a while, but eventually she'd put it back in her repertoire.

I am a political person. I have a politics, which is something Shay no longer has.

Having a politics is like a strong aftertaste in my mouth, a constant reminder that flavors everything else.

Having a politics is like trying to remember the lyrics of some old tune that keeps running through my head, driving me crazy.

Having a politics is like wearing bifocals that force me to see causes and their effects wherever I look.

Having a politics is something that I can neither avoid nor control. It runs unfettered through my system.

Actually, I don't have a politics. It has me.

3

Around seven o'clock my husband appears on the path that winds around the side of Christopher's house. Eli is a favorite male type among discriminating women. From the teddy-bear genus, he is of the cozy, cuddle-up-by-a-fire species. As children know, there's lots to be said for teddy bears. They remain the world's *número uno* choice of sleeping partners for good reason. Up until recently, Eli was as cozy and comforting as a stuffed animal in *or* out of bed.

He is wearing the khaki cotton suit I like best of all his summer clothes. By the end of the day, it is as wrinkled as his forehead. This suit makes Eli look like a foreign correspondent who's just landed in a new country with jet lag, a deadline and lots of currency from the last place he visited. Although Eli's probably annoyed about being summoned to one of Shay's command performances, he's wearing a noncombatant expression, which means he'll eat the inconvenience for the sake of some peace and quiet.

There is both good news and bad news about Eli Myers.

The good news is that Eli's a fabulous person. He is one of the most popular men in Washington. Unlike most other journalists, Eli is a fairly noncompetitive reporter—cooperative, supportive and accommodating. He is widely adored by the men in the national press corps for his high spirits and keen political insight. Women are nuts about him because he's smart, funny, sweet and sexy.

Very sexy.

Although after twenty years I have memorized most of Eli's sexual moves, he is so smooth and steady in the sack that I remain horny for him all the time.

That's the good news.

The bad news is that my husband has grown tired of me.

It's not something he wanted to have happen. It just has. His passion simply stopped, like a smoke detector that silently gives up the ghost without anyone noticing. These things happen. And, after so many years, why not? Maybe he's gotten tired of me—the way I look, the things I cook, the words I use, the movies I choose, the sweaters I wear or the shirts I buy him.

I don't know. In April we took a monthlong trip to Moscow, and Eli hasn't been the same since. He hates the smooth tyranny of our matinee-idol president and this now rigid, Republican city, which once offered him such great journalistic opportunities. His lack of interest in me started shortly after our return, and now it just hangs there between us all the time. I know my husband still *loves* me, that weary aphorism of late-night collegiate bull sessions; he's just not *in* love with me anymore. That's a big difference and, of course, it makes me crazy.

Eli crosses the brick terrace and comes over to me so he can thumb up my chin, look into my eyes and see how I'm doing. Eli doesn't like me to get upset. Since he knows how Shay affects me, he's worried I might be in a bad mood. But because Eli likes me to be a good sport and not make any trouble, I smile back reassuringly to show him everything's okay. That pleases him a lot.

Relieved, he is now free to say a few casual words to Christopher before turning toward the pool.

And that's when he sees Shay.

He takes a good long look. She is standing in waist-high water showing Amelia the Australian crawl stroke. This activity causes her breasts to sway slowly from side to side.

"Wow," Eli says to me in a minivoice. "How 'bout *them* apples?"

Narrowing his eyes against the sun, he continues to observe the swimming lesson.

"Isn't it about time for a drink?" Christopher asks, eager to interrupt our hushed remarks, which he knows are about Shay.

"White wine?" Eli asks me.

I nod and he relays my request along with his own to Christopher, who walks off toward the house as if leaving a battlefield.

"She's still got quite a pair there," Eli says dryly.

"Had you forgotten?" I ask him gently.

This is just a friendly reminder that he's crossing a field we both know is mined. That he loved Shay before he loved me contributes to the slow burn from which I've suffered for decades. It is the deepest, darkest secret of my life, next to the abortion. Those two facts comprise the dirty linen of my life.

From the moment Shay enrolled at the University of Minnesota (at the age of sixteen and a half) she created a new persona for herself. First she told everyone she was an "accepting" Quaker. A short while later she told certain people she was a "confirmed" Marxist. Then she started sleeping around with any movement heavy who caught her fancy and wasn't frightened away by her aggressiveness. In her sophomore year she joined the *Minnesota Daily,* where she learned how to write. Shay put a lot of herself into her stories, which probably helped make her a big name on campus. It's also the basis for her totally outrageous claim that *she* started the New Journalism.

S N A P S H O T

That's Shay and Eli at some Aquatennial hootenanny or something. They've just become engaged and he's got his arm around
her shoulders. I've always thought he was feeling her up because
of the way his fingers are dangling over her right breast. They met
when she was a junior and Eli came over to the *Daily* office to get
permission to reprint one of her stories. Of course he fell in love
with her. They went steady until she graduated and accepted a job
with a Headstart program in Jackson, Mississippi. The night
before she left, Shay returned Eli's one-carat emerald-cut diamond
engagement ring, even though she'd lost one of the two baguettes
flanking the stone. She claimed it had fallen out of its setting,
dropped into some rainwater and been carried away into a sewer
in front of our house. Shay took this as a sign she shouldn't marry
Eli. Eli took this as hard as a man possibly could.

As soon as Shay left town, I began to fall in love with Eli. Newly
equipped with a degree in social work, I spent that summer
looking for a job—which I never found—and comforting Eli
about Shay's heartless dismissal of him and her preemptive departure to Jackson.

After a lot of talking, Eli and I became good friends. We
remained just friends until one night when we drank too much
and made out together on the living-room sofa. In the early hours
of the morning, we drove to Green Bay, Wisconsin, and got
married. Maybe Eli thought he owed that much to the Karavan
family after sleeping with both their daughters.

Anyway, his parents and my parents were all shocked. Lots of
people were shocked. Even me. Although it bothered me that Eli
was a hand-me-down (hand-me-up?) from my younger sister, I
wanted him so badly I didn't care. Shay, of course, was thrilled:

"I'm so happy for you, Nat," she trilled over the telephone
from Mississippi. "I really missed Eli after we broke up and now
we can all be together forever."

Bingo.

S N A P S H O T

That's Eli and me sprawled atop a blanket beside the lake in Loring Park. He's much thinner and lankier than he is now, hungrier-looking and also happier. We have just rented our first apartment, in a rambling old mansion facing the park and the Minneapolis Walker Art Center. It is 1968 and we are very happy. We have begun meeting some interesting people, mostly a small crowd of liberals from the *Tribune* and from the Humanities Department at the U. of M. We visit our respective parents on alternate Friday nights for *Shabbes* dinners, but on Saturdays we make spaghetti-and-Chianti suppers for our new friends. On Sunday mornings we read the newspapers near Lake of the Isles, feeling lazy and relaxed as we tan in the sun. I have never been this happy ever before in my life. I am dangerously in love with Eli and thoroughly delighted that Shay no longer lives in the Twin Cities. Eli is a *very* imaginative lover, a long-distance runner of a lover, and our rich sex life keeps me crazy in love.

Christopher returns with our drinks, and shortly afterward Shay wraps Amelia in a large beach towel and carries her over to where we're sitting.

"This little girl is tired and hungry," she announces happily, rubbing her cheek against Amelia's cap of wet curls. "Hi, Eli."

"Hi, Shay."

For a brief moment it appears that Eli might reach out to caress Amelia, but then he cautiously recalls his outstretched hand. That's when Christopher stands up, takes off his shirt and tosses it toward Shay. She catches it easily with her free hand, but then looks puzzled, as if uncertain what to do with it.

"Put it *on*, Shay," Christopher says. "Cover *up*."

"Oh."

Shay sets Amelia down and absently pulls on the shirt, which envelops her like a hug, trailing down her slim body to a point below her knees.

Eli studies the bamboo trees.

I take advantage of Shay's momentary distraction to pick up Amelia and finish toweling her dry. Combining a little tickling with my rubbing, I make Amelia laugh until she begs me to stop. When Shay isn't around, I am Amelia's favorite mother substitute. This has caused me to fall completely in love with her even though the thought of myself as a doting great-aunt alarms me. I must actively dispatch images of old maids who wear tattered cardigan sweaters, drink herbal tea and make fruit cakes from scratch for the entire family every Christmas.

"Let's go inside," Shay suggests demurely. "I have to give Amelia her supper."

"Barney's picking Amelia up at seven-thirty," Christopher announces. "She's sleeping at his house tonight."

Shay's sun-flushed face constricts with disappointment.

"I don't believe it," she moans, stung by the irony of being separated from Amelia at such a convenient time for being together.

"It's *his* night, Shay," Christopher says flatly. "She's also supposed to stay with them all day tomorrow."

"Grandpa's coming," Amelia agrees, squirming off my lap.

Amelia has four sets of grandparents, a cast of eight individuals, half of whom keep changing. Amelia's maternal grandparents are divorced and living with fresh mates in neighboring New Hampshire towns, where Amelia visits them at Christmastime. Although she has never known anything but reformatted families, Amelia has clearly begun to view her ever-changing pool of custodians with some alarm now that both her parents have disappeared.

Because she doesn't like cast changes, Amelia focuses on trouble spots that threaten her precarious stability. Lately she's begun questioning Shay about her quarrels with Christopher, her arguments with Barney, her refusal to attend Victoria's birthday party and the whereabouts of several of Shay's lovers whom Amelia liked enough to call "Unkie" but have since dropped off the radar screen.

"I'm going to go get dressed and find Amelia some clothes," Shay says. "The air-conditioning in the house is too cold for her."

Then she walks off toward the kitchen. Amelia turns to watch her grandmother's departure until Shay has disappeared through the back doorway.

After a while, we all go inside.

The air-conditioning is indeed quite cold. As with other innovations in Christopher's home, there is a basic incompatibility between the original structure and its modern improvements. Most Georgetown houses feel the same—as if the parts are out of sync with the whole.

Actually, Christopher has left the place relatively intact, since it had already been renovated when he bought it. While the exterior looks like the Federal period in which it was built, the interior has been opened up in a manner favored by fashionable Georgetown architects. The kitchen flows into the dining room, which flows into the living room, which flows into a library, which opens onto a deck leading to the swimming pool. The only change Shay demanded was the installation of bidets in all the second-floor bathrooms.

Bidets, for some reason, are very important to my sister.

When (my? our? just plain?) Mother saw the house right after Shay and Christopher's wedding, she took me aside and asked, "Why couldn't he buy her a *new* place?"

So much for style.

S N A P S H O T

This is my favorite picture of Marge, *my* mother. I wasn't even born when it was taken, but it's what I envision whenever I summon up her image—a Marge I never knew. She is maybe twenty years old here, which means it's around 1937. Because she couldn't afford to go to college, she was working as a secretary for a St. Paul law firm. Someone had suggested she enter a typing contest at the Minnesota State Fair that summer, and she'd won the first prize of twenty-five dollars by typing 101 WPM. Dad took this snapshot of her fanning out the prize money like a hand of cards. She is smiling her usual shy, introverted smile. Her dark hair is bobbed and lacquered close to her head. She is wearing a middy blouse with a sailor scarf around the drooping neckline, a long straight skirt and sensible shoes. She looks happy. I guess she's happy because she has a boyfriend and can type so fast.

Christopher decides to whip us up some daiquiris.

After rummaging around for a while, he starts tossing strawberries into the blender from the center of the room, going through the motions of taking midcourt hook shots. This makes Amelia laugh hysterically. But when Christopher turns on the blender, the cover isn't securely fastened and the scream of the machine frightens Amelia and makes her cry. It also makes a big mess on the counter that will stay right where it is until the housekeeper returns in the morning and cleans it up.

"Let's watch the news in the library," Christopher says when Shay returns dressed in her shirt and jeans. "Meese made some new statement about his resignation today and I want to hear what he said."

So we all go into the den and watch Peter Jennings and Tom Brokaw back-to-back.

S N A P S H O T

Christopher and Shay's 1978 antique silver–framed wedding pictures march across the fireplace mantel. They were married in the church at St. Alban's School, where Steven, who was Christopher's best man, attended fourth grade. Christopher bought Shay a designer wedding gown that made her look exquisite. Besides the formal shots, there's a group portrait of the entire wedding party, taken the next morning at dawn down at the Tidal Basin. Christopher had rented the entire fleet of tourist paddleboats so we could sail around the basin beneath the cherry blossoms, which had exploded in time for their wedding. Eli and I are in the group photo along with Shay, Christopher, Steven, Hamilton Jordan, Peter Bourne, Pat Caddell, Jerry Rafshoon and Chip Carter. I was Shay's matron of honor, so it's just us two women with that gang of guys. Shay has always felt more comfortable with men than with women, but since I was her matron of honor, she had to count me in.

By the time the news is over, Amelia has fallen asleep tummy-down on the sofa; Shay and I are working on our third daiquiris. The men go outside onto the deck to start a fire in the hibachi. I watch them through the French doors.

Christopher spends a long time trying to coax the charcoal into action with his barbecue fork. Eventually Eli, now sucking a beer bottle, has to move in and do his usual mysterious thing that I can never quite see. Then both men back away from the grill, apparently pleased with the results. Soon I smell the fire and see Christopher appear with a large platter of chicken and a big bottle of Smokey Pit barbecue sauce.

When the doorbell rings, Shay leaps up off the sofa.

"Oh, Nat, please can you get it?" she begs. "*Please?* It must be Barney and I really don't want to talk to him right now. I've got to start the salad."

Without waiting for an answer, she rushes into the hallway.

Barney Yellen looks like some tough from a paperback detective novel. He has a crunched-up acne-scarred face, a drawstring forehead and a once-busted nose that spread out as it healed. His eyes are dark and speedy, his mouth a narrow slash above a square jaw. He has slick dark hair turning gray. He's runner-thin, almost scrawny, but compact. Built close to the ground. An infighter. You can't read Barney Yellen easily. He plays his life close to his chest.

"Hello, Barney."

"Hello, Natalie. Nice to see you. I've come to pick up Amelia."

"I know. Come on in. She fell asleep in the library. She spent a lot of time in the pool with Shay today."

"Shay's here?"

"Yes. She got in this afternoon."

Barney is wearing jeans, a graying white shirt with the sleeves rolled—not folded—up and worn-out running shoes.

He's his own man and his own best friend. Unthinkingly, Shay set him up for a great single life by letting out the word in left-wing circles that he was an extraordinary cocksman. This was the equivalent of paying him sexual alimony for life. Although they've been divorced for fifteen years, Barney is still stuck on Shay, linked to her by a passion that lingers between them like a naughty child holding each of them by the hand.

In the library he walks over to Amelia and stands there watching her sleep.

Shay and Barney met in Mississippi. He was an SDS officer sent down to serve as liaison with the SNCC leadership in the Delta. Shay went for Barney in a big way. Although she, too, eventually became an SDS organizer, Shay double-dipped. Not only did she have various political experiences, she wrote about them and then peddled her articles to various alternative and mainstream publications. It was during this Mississippi period that she began to develop a fairly large and faithful following of readers around the country.

Shay was three months pregnant when she and Barney finally got married and went off to join an overcrowded, overwrought commune in Kearneysville, West Virginia. Living among poor white trash, the communards all pledged to produce lots of "liberated" offspring to offset regressive tendencies in the Blue Ridge Mountain area. Steven was born the day after Shay's twenty-first birthday in the kitchen of the communal farmhouse—on a former butchering table—with nine people in attendance.

S N A P S H O T

This one I call "Our Lady of the West Virginia Commune." Shay went back to the earth in a big way. She definitely played hardball with Mother Nature throughout her pregnancy and early motherhood. This is a great shot of the young family: Barney in denim

hour before I summoned the elevator and he rushed into my arms, crying hysterically.

As soon as Barney accepts Christopher's invitation to dinner, Shay becomes totally disorganized. She decides we must eat by candlelight and scours the house for candles, carrying all kinds, including some red Christmas jobbies, out to the deck. There she sets them around the glass-topped patio table and, even though it isn't yet dark, lights them.

Finally we set out the dishes. When Shay discovers Christopher has let the chicken burn, she laughs like some southern belle, calls it "Cajun-blackened," and arranges the burnt pieces on a big platter, which she proudly sets in the center of the table. Everyone is fairly drunk by the time we collect the deck chairs and sit down to eat. Shay opens the door to the library so she can hear if Amelia wakes up.

Now all I can think about is the centrally cooled air leaking out into the dehydrated universe. Shay is cooling down Georgetown. Shay is combating the steamy heat of the Greenhouse Summer with Christopher's air-conditioning. She is subsidizing Pepco in her usual extravagant and urgent way.

While we eat, everyone talks about Jesse Jackson. We cannot get enough of talking about Jesse Jackson. Even while it was happening, we had to keep telling ourselves that we were actually seeing what we were seeing, that in our lifetimes we were watching an unabashed progressive black man make a move on the presidency. And even now, with the primaries over, we still share an excited disbelief in the history that we'd watched happen.

Drinking white wine and eating much too much, much too fast, we speculate about what will happen when Jesse arrives in Atlanta and how Dukakis will handle him. Christopher, now aware that Shay is going to the convention, begins to wonder aloud if it's too late to get a plane reservation and find a hotel room there. Shay, of course, ignores his logistical worries and forcibly changes the subject.

"I was out in L.A. a few weeks ago and the town is absolutely dead. The Guild's been out so long everybody's hurting for money. Real bad."

"At least they're killing off all those old shitcoms," Barney observes gratefully.

For Barney happiness is a strike in progress.

"Hasn't the Guild been great?" Shay asks him with warm confidence.

Translation: *Hey! Weren't we a team? Remember, Barney? Remember how tough we were when we were together? Weren't we something special?*

The divorced couple exchange a long look followed by a moment of silence, as if commemorating the death of a dear colleague.

Quietly the night has begun rinsing the last violet light out of the sky. It is almost totally dark by the time we finish our food and the last of our three bottles of wine.

I've got to hand it to Shay.

Here she is, talking to a group of four people, three of them men she's slept with, and the common denominator doesn't dawn on her. Shay's promiscuity is like the secret word that would release the little duck during Groucho Marx's quiz shows back in the fifties. If no one said the correct word the duck never descended. It's the same with Shay's sexual past. If no one says the P-word, the duck doesn't drop down and Shay doesn't have to deal with it.

"I stayed at the Beverly Hills," she continues blithely. "Really—that hotel makes you feel famous just standing in the lobby. I'd never stayed there before—"

"Yes you did," says Barney.

"I did?" Shay turns to look at her first husband. "When was I there?"

"You don't mean *when*, you mean with whom," Barney corrects her.

"Okay, so who was I there with?"

"Whom," Christopher edits her.

Since Christopher didn't know Shay during the period under discussion, he is immune to the jealousy that is clearly provoking his predecessor.

"Dennis Stein," Barney says definitively. "You spent a weekend there with Dennis Stein when you were covering Jerry Brown."

"Oh," Shay says vaguely, beginning to back-comb her hair with tense fingertips. "You mean after the Medfly fuckup? The night Gore Vidal called Jerry Brown 'Lord of the Flies'?"

"No," says Barney. "About eight years earlier, when we were still married."

Suddenly Shay remembers the right rendezvous and momentarily loses her composure.

Although she probably couldn't identify 50 percent of her lovers in a lineup, every once in a while she recalls some distant detail of sexual infidelity that upsets her equilibrium.

Now Shay's sexual history rises up like a sudden squall to disturb the surface calm of our gathering.

Both Shay's husbands look away, embarrassed by her confusion.

A small silence drifts down upon us.

I stare off fixedly into the hot darkness.

It seems to me I have spent a good part of my life being embarrassed by my sister.

It was only during the years when Shay was married to Barney and living far away in Mississippi, West Virginia or California that she was off my back. Indeed, those were the happiest years of my life. Between 1968 and 1975, Eli and I learned to know and enjoy and love each other. Life was nearly perfect when I didn't have to sit around, hot-faced with shame, waiting for some discomfort over Shay to subside.

Finally our embarrassment starts to dissipate and we begin to regroup like residents of some Texas trailer camp after a tornado. People who don't want to be where they are in the first place have nothing but fortitude to see them through those disasters that rain down upon church-chartered buses and mobile-home parks with unfair frequency. We who have long been tested by Shay's riotous past now take for granted chance encounters with some of her strange bedfellows, who appear like blips on the screens of our lives.

SNAPSHOT

Here's a shot of Shay clipped from the back section of *Vogue*. She really looks good here. It was probably taken in the mid-seventies, before she married Christopher. I do know that Studio 54 was still in business, because she went there every night. She was powerless to stop flirting, powerless to stay out of discos, powerless to stop drinking and dancing until dawn each day. Shay loved the death-wish crowd, the carousers who lived really close to the edge. She spent a lot of time with Margaret Trudeau during Margaret's love fest with the Stones in New York. Shay also spent one weekend on a yacht with Princess Grace. I know she once fainted at Régine's in Paris and had to be taken to the American Hospital to dry out. Shay followed the flight of European capital, running wherever royalty still reigned and partied. She skied with the Agnellis and was a spotter (identifying people) for CBS at some big party in Gstaad. During all this, Shay solemnly maintained that she was a member of the working press corps.

"Well," Shay says, after drawing a heavy breath to indicate her impatience with being misunderstood by both her former husbands, her former lover and her elder sister, "I'm going to find some clean clothes and freshen up a little."

She rises rather regally and walks into the house.

There is a fresh daiquiri in my hand. I take a deep swallow and relax for a few minutes before Shay reappears in the doorway. I can tell something terrible has happened as soon as I see her face.

"Natalie," she says to me. "Your car is gone. Someone stole your car."

For a moment no one moves. Then all three men rise in unison, as if choreographed, to hurry through the house.

I sit still, wrapped in a shroud of shock.

"Did you leave your keys in the ignition?" Shay asks.

"I don't know," I say, feeling panic pounding inside my chest. "Maybe I did."

I try to remember getting out of the car after Shay insisted I stay for dinner. I try to recall what moves I'd made, but everything is blurred and indistinct. When Shay's around, I feel like I'm the roadie with a rock-and-roll band, responsible for all the equipment, baggage, engagements, transportation and dope connections.

"I'll go look in my purse," I say. "It's in the kitchen."

I stand up and then look at Shay again.

"Do you mean you left your bags outside in the car with all those papers in them?"

My sister and I stare at each other.

This is unbelievable.

This is clearly a brand-new single on the LP album of our lives. As usual, Ancient Animosity, our rhythm-and-blues backup, strums the history of our endless discontent with each other. I go to the front door and gaze out at the empty space where I had parked my car. The men are standing on the lawn near the driveway, talking excitedly to each other. I don't go into the kitchen. I head for a bathroom, where I try to collect myself. For once I've *done* my sister, instead of vice versa. For once I've sabotaged her. Instead of Shay putting me down, so she'll shine all the brighter, I've messed her up.

It's not unusual for one sister to diminish the other so as to appear more dazzling, as all those savage sibling-sagas published by Danielle Steel and Judith Krantz amply display. I have always kept tabs on Princess Margaret and *her* sister, Elizabeth, the queen of England. I am always subliminally aware of Ann Landers and Abby Van Buren (twins who once didn't speak for seven years), the Gabor girls, Mariel and Margaux Hemingway, Marisa and Berry Berenson, Jackie Onassis and Princess Lee Radziwill.

My interest in bad blood between sisters borders on obsession.

The minute I return to the deck, my sister and I get into it in a big way.

SHAY: You dumb fuck, Natalie. You make a big production out of everything you do, but you never do anything right.

ME: Screw you, Shay. How could you leave important papers in a car full of suitcases people could see right through the windows? That's why someone stole my car. To get your damn luggage. Your laptop computer!

SHAY: For someone who's so hung up on doing the right thing all the time, why don't you lock your car? Nobody leaves their car unlocked with the keys in the ignition in nineteen-fucking-eighty-eight. What are you—crazy or something?

ME: Oh, no. I'm not going to get stuck holding the bag on this one. You're full of shit. You know damn well you were just using me. If you use people, Shay, you should at least tell them. Otherwise you have to take responsibility for what happens. So it's *my* car that gets stolen. Great! That's what I get for picking you up at the airport.

SHAY: But you *saw* me leaving my stuff in the backseat.

ME: Jesus, this is Georgetown. It's supposed to be safe here. Besides, nobody ever steals a Ford Escort. It's the least-stolen car in the whole United States. They can't even get one stolen for publicity purposes. You're such a bimbo, Shay.

SHAY: I can't believe you said that.

There is a long, agonized silence.

"So. Who do you think stole it?" she asks in a quiet, conciliatory way.

"How should I know?"

"I bet it was the CIA," she says.

Oh, sure. Shay always goes right to the top.

"Or maybe the FBI," she continues. "Or maybe they just sent the police to pick it up. They must have come here to arrest me, but when they saw my luggage in the car and the keys in the ignition, they just took the whole damn Ford."

Eli comes back out onto the deck. "Well, it's gone," he says, shrugging. "I guess we should call the police."

"God, no!" Shay wails.

"Why not?"

"Oh, Eli." For once Shay seems genuinely shaken. "I was so stupid. I stole some government documents out on Long Island but I left them in the car."

Eli leans against the deck railing as he processes this new information. Shay's confession, back-to-back with the theft of my car, is a bit much for Eli after a long day's work and so many drinks. When Christopher and Barney return we all sit down around the table again and listen to Shay's story about how she found Fawn Hall's testimony. When she's finished, she's rewarded with the perfect tribute of total silence.

Finally Christopher slams a fist down on the glass tabletop so that all the dishes and wineglasses jump in alarm.

"Well," he says, "this beats anything I've ever heard before."

"Shay, what have you done?" Eli moans, rubbing slow lazy fingers across his face, as if trying to erase his own identity.

"You mean Fawn Hall was doing coke in Georgetown while she worked for Colonel North?" Barney asks with a stutter of excitement.

Barney has always had a seductive hunt-and-peck way of speaking. The pauses between his words work like vacuums to suck in his listeners. Now he is looking at Shay with enormous pride.

"What a ball buster," he continues. "It'd be wild to release something like that and really nail those bastards."

"Well, you've sure done it this time, Shay," Christopher says grimly. "Someone's going to find those papers and turn them over to the authorities. They're going to throw you in jail and throw away the key."

"Oh, gimme a break, Christopher," Shay protests in a raggedy whine. "I'm a journalist. I have a right to release that kind of stuff."

"What you are, Shay," Eli says wearily, "is in a world of trouble."

Shay looks scornfully at both of them.

"First of all," she says with exaggerated patience, "if it was the FBI that took the car, they just might want to keep quiet about everything. Return the damn interview to the DEA and let me eat my story. I can't prove that I even *saw* the interview. I can't even prove it *exists*."

"What do you want to do about reporting the car stolen, Shay?" Eli asks in a flat, quiet voice.

"I don't know. I've got to think. What time is it?"

"Hopefully the questions won't get any harder." Eli smiles, looking at his watch. He is trying to be friendly. Supportive. Collegial. "It's ten o'clock."

"Can we drive over to Café au Lait?"

"Sure."

"But first I've got to find something to wear. Lemme just look through the junk I left here."

I see Christopher flinch as Shay's words strike him.

"Just give me ten minutes and then we can go."

"She's crazy," Christopher announces bitterly as soon as Shay disappears. "She's out of control. She's out of her head."

"This *is* a bit much," Eli agrees morosely.

We sit in somber silence, sipping our drinks, while the enormity of the situation envelops us.

"Why does she want to go to Café au Lait?" Eli finally asks me in a whisper.

"She's supposed to meet Mickey Teardash there."

"How does *he* fit into all this?"

"She's sleeping with him," I whisper back so Christopher won't hear. "I guess his firm's been doing some PR work for Dukakis or maybe he's made some big contribution or something."

Christopher is slouched down in his chair, clearly feeling imperiled. All he had wanted was a reconciliation, a resumption of his marriage to Shay, and now she's done something that effectively destroys his dream. He is staring off into the darkness with a mixture of hurt and resignation on his face.

Barney has begun pacing back and forth across the deck.

"Look. Even if the actual document is gone, we can still hold a press conference and announce its existence. Or we can leak it to Jeffrey Altney at the *Times* and let him investigate it."

"Hang on," Eli says. "We've got to see what Shay wants to do since it's her head that's on the line."

But it's *my* car, I think. Her head and my car. How come I haven't got the right to report it stolen? Where are *my* rights?

When Shay returns she is wearing a tight blue cotton dress that has clearly shrunk at least one size in some overheated dryer. The dress pulls across her breasts and stomach, barely reaching to the middle of her thighs. She is carrying an overnight suitcase and another Big Brown Bag. My sister, the queen of the bag ladies. My sister and her matching luggage from Bloomingdale's.

Eli jerks his head in my direction to suggest I stand up.

"It's good Barney's taking care of Amelia tomorrow," Shay murmurs as we pass through the library, where the little girl is still sleeping. "It's going to be crazy tomorrow."

We walk back into the kitchen. Shay reclaims her red suede shoulder bag off the counter and I retrieve my purse from beneath the table. My keys, of course, are missing. I have to admit that all of this is my fault and that I have really fucked up royally this time. Then I start trying to remember what was in the trunk of my car. I feel bad about the I AM A FONZ (Friend of the National Zoo) bumper sticker, which I know is no longer being manufactured. My favorite tapes, including Carly Simon's *Coming Around Again,* were in the glove compartment and my most comfortable shoes under the driver's seat.

Shi-it.

The men are clustered near the driveway when we get outside.

Shay and I stand side by side, looking at Christopher's BMW and the space behind it where I'd parked my Escort. At the curb is Eli's Honda and a pickup truck I've never seen before. Of course, I think. Barney must have traded in his Jeep for a raggedy redneck pickup now that all the yuppies are into Jeeps. He's still got to do his own thing. Fleetingly I wonder if he's got a baby seat in the truck and whether Christopher will remember to remind him to feed Amelia when he takes her home.

"Thanks for everything," Shay says, walking over to plant a polite kiss on Christopher's cheek. Then she turns to Barney. "I'll come by for Amelia around five, but I'll call you before then."

Assuming an almost militant posture, she walks purposefully down the stairs to the street.

We drive in Eli's Honda to Adams-Morgan, which is the Upper West Side of D.C. Although it is located in the predominantly white northwest quadrant of our still color-coded city, in the mid-sixties it became a truly "tan" community. Residents who stuck out several racially tense eras eventually found themselves living in a politically, culturally and artistically integrated area. On alternately quiet and raucous streets, haves and have-nots live next door to each other, constantly surprised by their coexistence.

Real District residents (not transients, like elected officials, who use the city as a temporary playground or a pit stop for getting their cleaning done between junkets) call their hometown D.C. They know a totally different place than the Washington recognized as the nation's capital. Real residents view the Federal Triangle—with its famous government buildings—as something, like the Colosseum in Rome, that has to be gone around on the way to the airport.

In the twelve years since Eli and I bought a house here in

Adams-Morgan, real estate values have tripled and political ones changed. A tidal wave of Hispanics arrived to adjust the color-contrast button on our neighborhood and tone down some of the edgier differences. Now yuppies kill to live here and affluent shrinks from Chevy Chase bring their wives and teenaged kids to Eighteenth Street to sop up atmosphere and eat Ethiopian.

Eli parks and we walk past a crazy cantata of commercial storefronts to reach Café au Lait, the sexiest bar in Adams-Morgan, maybe in all of D.C. The semioutdoor café is the hangout for Washington's stylish Eurotrash, the handsome progeny of sixties jet-setters and Beautiful People. The major assets of this new generation are long legs, lean behinds, cinnamon complexions, corrupt eyes and a working knowledge of French, German and Farsi. When they get cold sweats during the middle of the night, they get up and go to a disco.

Café au Lait makes people feel like they're somewhere else. Maybe down in the Big Easy. Maybe down in the islands. Maybe Down Under, having a few drinks. The place produces a laid-back attitude, as if life is easy come, easy go, easy does it. Every few months the management changes the decor and its pricey menu to imitate another exotic place . . . Rio, Istanbul, Khartoum. . . . Tonight, a huge papier-mâché dragon coiled above the stone raw bar announces Bangkok. Both inside and out, the place gives off heat. It's a moist, warm environment in which germs of intrigue can hatch and grow.

Wearily we hoist ourselves up on wrought-iron stools set around a small but tall marble-topped table situated half inside and half outside the building. With its wall of warehouse windows and protective grating retracted up against the ceiling, Café au Lait has only its potted palms to indicate where the city sidewalk shifts into private property.

"Should we stick with wine or switch to something else?" Eli asks, looking at Shay.

I'm used to that.

Jealousy #823: Shay's always the one who sets the tone and

picks the poison for our evenings together. She's the first to be consulted because she's in the know; she senses what's in and what's out. *The Washington Post*'s New Year's Day "In" and "Out" lists always feature some stylish item from my sister's repertoire that is about to become either a trend or a has-been.

"Let's drink wine until Mickey gets here," Shay decides.

Her face is glistening with perspiration and, even though her hair is still lassoed at the nape of her neck, some short curls have escaped their binding. Frizzed up by the humidity, they create a halo effect that offers Shay yet another dimension. Suddenly she begins a semihysterical inventory of her situation.

"Well, I've lost everything. *Everything.* I had four articles and a bunch of research in my laptop. My September-sex article was half finished, but I hadn't made a hard copy of it yet. And it was damn good because I wrote it on the plane."

Shay likes to believe she does her best writing aboard airplanes or in the coffee shops of hotel lobbies. Once she flew from New York to Acapulco just to break a writer's block. Another time, when she was staying with us, she drove out to Dulles and rode the bus that ferries passengers between terminals in an effort to trick herself into thinking she was catching a flight. She said it was like taking a placebo except that it worked because her creative juices began flowing again.

Although Shay insists she is inspired by travel and travelers, I happen to know what really turns her on is the male attention she attracts in highly charged environments. Ever since she left Christopher, she's been racing around and making all the scenes so as to maintain her fighting weight. Shay doesn't have to diet or exercise if she goes where the action is and runs with a fast crowd.

"I'll never be able to rewrite it the same way," she complains. "And all the clothes I liked best were in those bags. My jewelry. The B-fifty-two-bomber-tire bracelet I got in Ho Chi Minh. My favorite shirts. Everything. I can't believe it. I was really organized for a change so I could travel light. Mickey's finally convinced me traveling light's important. I'd even bought two great new dresses for the convention."

Shay doesn't mention my car. Eli bought it for me last year on our nineteenth anniversary.

Inside Café au Lait, all the pipes, electrical boxes and other infrastructural elements on the walls and ceiling are painted black and left exposed. The compact Salvadoran shucking oysters at the raw bar is wearing a black T-shirt and tight jeans like the rest of the male staff. Waitresses appear in black miniskirts, black spandex tops, spiked heels and spiked hair.

A Home Away from Home is only half a block away. But tonight the door is locked, with a chain that winds through the security gate, even though there is nothing inside to steal except a pile of thin old mattresses and some ratty pillows and blankets. In the small annex behind the main room are several coat racks hung with rummage-sale clothes that our homeless women study for hours before making a selection. But tonight my clients are sleeping elsewhere—in the park or on the street.

Again Shay starts up.

"But it's that damn interview of Fawn Hall's that's the real tragedy. Really. It could have been as important as the Pentagon Papers. It might have finished Reagan off. The Democrats could have won hands down in November."

She shrugs, stands up and trots off toward the back of the building without excusing herself.

I lean against the table and look at my husband.

My husband looks away.

I have lost Eli.

Or maybe I've only lost touch with him. I can see he is feeling logy from drinking too much, that he's tired and ready for bed. Instead, thanks to me, he's sitting here on the edge of an emotional abyss, on the brink of chaos, in the middle of Eighteenth Street, which at the moment offers him all the amenities of Cuba and all the charm of Panama.

Eli is sitting in a steaming open-air bar on a feverish night in a sweltering city trying to deal with my kooky sister. Chasing some classified document, floating around loose somewhere within the greater metropolitan area, which is still melting in a merciless three-digit heat that made the top of the evening news on all three networks last night, is not Eli's idea of a terrific way to spend an evening.

I have plugged my husband into this insanity and he is not happy. All Eli wanted was a little peace and quiet after a long day's work. Actually, Eli wants to be alone. Without Shay. Without Mickey Teardash. Without me, no offense intended. Eli just wants to go home. Our house is only a five-minute walk from here but, given our current situation, it might as well be in Baltimore. And I haven't even told him yet that Shay and Teardash are coming for the weekend.

Shay returns. Her face, lit like the flame atop a candle, announces she did a little coke while in the powder room. Shay loves all controlled substances and the sneaky thrill of getting an illegal high in a public place.

The waitress delivers three big balloons of white wine. Shay lifts her glass, drains it like ice water and then stares morosely out at the parade of people walking past. Eli and I watch Shay watching the street scene.

Jealousy #841: People surreptitiously study Shay when they're with her. Given the opportunity, people will watch Shay's eyelashes flick shadows across the high ridge of her cheekbones. They will watch her long lips part to reveal perfectly scalloped white teeth. They will watch her short sweet nose wrinkle up when she laughs. They will watch her Tiffany-blue eyes express all her expensive emotions.

"This whole thing is turning into a real mess," she says suddenly. "I mean, I was home free before that goddam car got stolen. The whole thing was a wrap. It was in the can. It was just a question of distribution. And then—"

"I'm going to report that my car was stolen to the police," I interrupt her.

Shay looks at me with a sour expression. "What is it with you, Nat? *If it ain't broke, don't fix it.* Either the FBI or the CIA took the car. We're not talking any of your basic everyday street hoods here. We're talking about the Big Boys."

I help myself to one of Shay's cigarettes. I am furious. I hate when she lectures me in that know-it-all tone of voice, as if she's got the inside track on the truth. That tone in her voice tortures me like the scratch of a fingernail on a blackboard.

But Shay has to think big. She has to think CIA or FBI. She always has to go top-of-the-line: Cartier, Concorde, Harvard, Mercedes, the Plaza, Trump Tower, La Grenouille, Canyon Ranch, Chanel, Gstaad, Louis Vuitton, Dom Pérignon, Sotheby's, Petrossian, Corsica, Chase Manhattan, Sister Parrish, Leo Castelli or Mary Boone.

She can't help it. She programmed herself to process life that way. Chic is Shay's Higher Power.

My sister, the "recovering" Quaker.

My sister, the Neiman Marxist.

"To tell you the truth," I say with a sudden surge of venom, "my only interest in this now is how to get my car back. I work too, Shay, remember? I *need* a car. It doesn't matter who took it, but when the cops find it, they'll think it's weird I never reported it stolen."

"I wish you'd lighten up, Natalie," Shay hisses. "Chill out a little."

Suddenly Eli smacks the palm of his hand on the marble tabletop. Our wine goblets shake atop their long stems like tulips in a spring breeze.

"Okay, let's get this over with *right now*," he orders. "I can't stand this kind of fighting. You *both* acted like schmucks—Nat for leaving her keys in the car and Shay for leaving the goddam papers. You both acted like flakes. Airheads. Turkeys. So enough with the blaming already, all right? You were both wrong, but it's a hundred degrees out here, we've got a real problem on our hands, and you're squabbling like kids. Do me a favor and knock off that crap, *right now*, wouldja? I'd really appreciate it."

It's like when our father used to yell at us.

First we are stunned.

Then we fall silent.

Grieve.

Repent.

Turn over a new leaf.

I could never bear it when my (her? our?) father got angry at either of us. I would instantly start to panic.

Cringe. Cower. Collapse.

S N A P S H O T

That's Shay in her cap and gown after her high school graduation. I am the only one in the football stadium who knows that under her gown Shay is wearing a slim gold ankle bracelet—expressly forbidden by *her* mother—two hickeys on one breast and no underwear. At nine that night, she left with her date for the senior prom and didn't return or even telephone until the next evening. *My* parents called half the city trying to locate her. At noon, Dad called the police. Marge was so hysterical that at one point in the afternoon she fainted. It was already getting dark when Shay, still wearing her pink strapless prom gown with its matching wrist corsage, sauntered in through the back door, as high as a kite. I then witnessed a fight between her and Dad that knocked my socks off. Dad kept yelling that Shay was grounded for the entire summer and she just kept laughing in his face. Dad saw Shay's behavior as distinct from her character, while I saw all her actions as expressions of her megalomania. Because I wasn't a problem to him, Dad didn't engage with me the way he did with Shay. He didn't have enough time to.

But Shay has never scared easily and she is certainly not frightened now. Oh, no. She is simply eager to make some amends, some minor adjustments, so she'll look good again. That's all that interests her—looking good.

But I cannot bear to have Eli angry at me. It breaks my heart. It makes me remember when Dad used to yell at me all the time for not playing better tennis.

SNAPSHOT

That's Dad on one of the courts at North Commons. He coached Shay and me several times a week and at least twice on weekends. Here's how he taught us strategy: He saved all the cardboard stiffeners from inside his laundered shirts, numbered them with a marking pen and then put them in strategic places on his side of the net. Shay and I would stand in the opposite court drop-serving balls until we could hit each cardboard marker three times in a row. Shay had better aim than I did and quickly got the hang of this exercise; Dad took great pride in her prowess. He could never understand why this practice was hard for me, why I lacked Shay's coordination—or was it concentration? Or was it her keen sense of competition?

Curbside, little sports cars roar at each other like animals in a forest. The street is a military motor pool of cars, trucks, Domino's Pizza delivery vans and #90 Metrobuses that ferry maids home from their daylong cleaning jobs in Maryland before taking aliens, without green cards, off to their nighttime jobs. Because I've turned my back on Shay, I'm the first to see a District taxi stop at the curb and launch a large but agile man from its backseat. The man is carrying an overnight bag and a Valpack. Like a heat-seeking missile, he sights us and starts to cross the sidewalk. The crowd parts in front of him like the Red Sea.

This has got to be Mickey Teardash. He's blond and handsome, early Burt Lancaster-ish. Clearly a high roller from the Big Apple. A great hard-on of a man, a high-IQ *Fortune* 500 jock.

"Hey!" he calls, striding toward our table.

I can see him inhaling the essence of this club like a line of coke, drawing it inward and upward to his brain, so he can get off on the hot restless crowd milling around looking for action.

"This is terrific. Great bar! Hey, Shay!" He throws a hefty arm around her shoulders. "No wonder you like this place."

Now he is nuzzling her long lean neck, dipping down to drink a patch of brown shoulder exposed by the stretched-out neckline of her skimpy little dress. Shay smiles and blushes, lowers her eyes. She's acting or *actually feeling* shy. Shay shy? Shy Shay?

Shi-it.

A second later Mickey Teardash is pumping Eli's hand and smiling across the table at me.

"You have *got* to be Shay's sister. No way around it. You're like two peas in a pod."

"Yeah," I say. "Split peas."

Shay is visually devouring Mickey Teardash. Shay worships anyone with style, and this guy oozes it. This man is style incarnate. A world-class stylist. He's a mixture of myths. Daddy Warbucks, Ernest Hemingway, Jack Kennedy, Robin Hood, Richard Cory, King Midas, Dick Tracy, Sonny Crockett, Davy Crockett, Dirty Harry, the Lone Ranger. He's a star, a superstar, a golden prince, a great lover. Sexcess, like strobe lights, radiates around him.

Mickey Teardash is a hard-core showman. A male Auntie Mame. He's got caramel eyes and butterscotch hair. He's a sweet sundae of a ladies' man, younger than Shay, maybe in his mid-thirties. His eyes don't pause for a second. They dart around, deliberately tasting everything, skimming across surfaces— speedy, greedy. This is a guy who knows what he wants and waits for it to come to him. I don't like him. I am too tired to deal with him, too weary even to try. He's too much for me at this moment.

"Find yourself a seat, Teardash," Shay says in a smoky, sexy voice. "It's time for the eleven o'clock news and you're not going to like what you hear."

He cops a stool that belongs to someone temporarily away from a nearby table. Then he sits down close beside Shay. He is savoring the razzmatazz setting, emotionally trolling for new sensations. He watches Shay's face as she speaks. When she tells him my car was stolen with all her luggage inside, he looks properly concerned. He is Sir Launcelot, a knight inspired by his lady's distress. He lays hot eyes on her.

"I'll help you shop for some new stuff," he promises.

He is Mr. Fixit. Harry Homeowner. Dr. Feelgood.

"Mickey," she says, "the Fawn Hall papers were in the car too."

"Whaaaat," he yodels, genuinely stunned. "Whaaaat are you *say*ing? Where was the car? Where were you?"

Shay gives him the details.

"Well, don't say I didn't warn you this was gonna get you in big trouble, Shay. It was wrong from the get-go. You knew Jerry'd done some work for me and that I didn't want to piss him off. I told you that. And stealing from a friend . . . Shit. I can't believe you did this."

"It wasn't my fault, Mickey."

"Damn it, Shay, you're so careless. Jerry Russo is not a guy to mess around with. I warned you—he's connected to people who take care of business. They protect their own. You just don't know what you've gotten yourself into."

"It wasn't my fault," Shay repeats wearily. "Natalie left her keys in the car. It's all her fault."

Mickey turns around to flag a waitress. This allows him to ignore Shay's charge against me and remain neutral. It's hard to tell whether he's acting like a gentleman or a politician.

My stomach is churning so violently I am unable to speak. The injustice of her accusation makes me dizzy.

"Hey, waidaminute," Eli says. Although he missed the first bounce, he's got the rebound. "Nat has done a lot for you, Shay— why don't you give her a break once in a while?"

I lower my eyes, overwhelmed by Eli's defense. It's almost as if he still loved me.

S N A P S H O T

I took this picture of Eli. We were in England, staying at an inn near Blenheim Castle, and had spent the night in a fever of sexual excitement—probably because we were so elated to be in England. Actually I had been hemming a dirndl skirt when Eli asked me if I would sit on him while I sewed. Drunk with happiness, I climbed aboard him, where I sat sewing with a slanty overhand hemming stitch that's as distinctive as my signature. He enjoyed this sex a lot because it was a *very* full skirt. The next day we went out for a walk and when Eli came through the doorway I snapped this photo. He has that sheepish, bearish, shit-eating grin on his face and I was dizzy with love for him, deliriously happy that we were married.

"Anyway, what's the drill for tonight?" Eli asks, standing up. His voice sounds removed. Remote. Receding. Clearly he's had suspicions from the very beginning that Shay was going to invade our lives for the weekend. "Are you folks coming home with us or what?"

"Would that be okay?" Shay asks in an elevated, innocent tone of voice.

"It's okay with me, but let's get outta here right now," Eli says decisively. "I'll make some drinks back at our place. C'mon."

Mickey Teardash stands up. He has absorbed everything. Already he knows about me and Eli and the estrangement between us. Already he knows about Shay and me and the rage between us. He's wickedly quick. Dropping some bills on the table, Teardash picks up his stool and carries it over to the young guy standing nearby with a bewildered expression on his face.

"Sorry about that, old man," Teardash says, with Jay Gatsby charm. "Here's your chair back."

Then we all walk back to the parking lot to reclaim Eli's car and drive home.

I love my house.

The more insecure I feel about Eli and our marriage, the more I love our house.

S N A P S H O T

That's Eli and me standing in front of our home on the day of the final closing in 1976. He has his arm around my shoulders and is smiling one of those sloppy grins that spills all over his face. We both feel very grown up to have bought such a distinctive home.

Eli is happy because we have purchased a handsome two-story stone *farmhouse* on Adams Mill Road only three blocks beyond the hot skillet of Eighteenth and Columbia. Some family actually moved it in from Virginia to this urban site in 1899. While one branch of Adams Mill Road accesses the National Zoo, which is nestled inside Rock Creek Park, the other branch winds along a thickly wooded bluff that juts away from the edge of Adams-Morgan like a long fingernail. It is atop this hilly slice of wilderness that five gnarled old homesteads sit. Eli and I bought the last house, the one closest to the zoo.

At night, lying in bed, Eli and I can hear the lions and tigers roar, the elephants trumpet and the hyenas scream. Some of our friends can't stand the wild cries that rip through the fabric of night silence. Fear of the untamed is a common sign of the White Man's Disease. Several times, in the middle of the night, I have found visibly shaken houseguests sitting in our living room, fully dressed and ready to flee. These are often brave people who do brave work. I have come to believe that what frightens people is not what is savage in those jungle soundings but what is encaged and enraged.

Eli and I love the jungle music to which we dance away our nights. The roars of the lions always lent a "Snows of Kilimanjaro" strain to our sex. Fun and game. That's what Eli used to call it. The shrieks of jungle animals became as integral a part of our existence as did the screams from the urban jungle, three blocks away in the opposite direction; human cries also cut the edges of our dark nights like a pair of pinking shears.

Virgin cooled air, soft as a silk kimono, wraps itself around us when we enter the front hall. Stashing Shay's and Teardash's gear near the stairs, we walk toward the rear of the house, which hugs the tree-covered slope that scrambles down into Rock Creek Park. I have made our three-hundred-square-foot cathedral-ceilinged kitchen the centerpiece of our home. It is furnished with turn-of-the-century and mission-oak pieces that I rescued from yard sales in rural Maryland, Virginia and West Virginia. I restored all of them with a great deal of time and effort.

I had the time because I didn't have a child.

When Eli turns on the recessed lighting, Mickey Teardash emits a shrill, showy whistle. Shaking off his jacket, he walks around the kitchen, carefully studying my various antiques. Shay wanders off to the powder room, which we created from a butler's pantry adjacent to the kitchen.

"Not too shabby," Teardash finally says, grinning at me with genuine appreciation and admiration.

I give him a four-star smile and start to like him a little better.

"What'll you have to drink?" Eli asks, opening the signed Stickley corner hutch where we keep our liquor.

"A beer," Mickey says, loosening the collar of his shirt and rolling up the sleeves. The recessed lighting lacquers his blond hair from above. "I always drink beer when I'm in the tropics. It helps fight off swamp fever."

Now Shay reappears, kicking off her sandals to pad across the oak floorboards. Like Clark Kent, she is changing her identity— from embattled journalist to late-night siren. Even barefoot, Shay looks expensive.

"Well, it's getting late," she observes. "I know the whole drill about the guest room, so don't worry about us. It's a good thing I'm too tired to boogie tonight," she says to Mickey. "All our condoms were in the El Al flight bag I left in the car."

Although Mickey Teardash looks embarrassed by her comment, he lifts his beer can as a good-night salute to us, and then follows Shay toward the entry hall. Eli flicks off the lights and we go up the rear staircase to our bedroom.

Since Eli sleeps in his boxer shorts, as soon as he peels off his shirt and trousers, he's ready for bed. I sit down at the oak writing desk I use as my dressing table and stare at myself in the wall mirror.

I am a prose statement of a woman. I am like Michael Dukakis. What you see is what you get. Nothing glamorous, swift or shimmering. Nothing to inspire passion or cause any craziness. Like Dukakis, I radiate sturdy, solid decency, which turns out to be more boring than either wimphood or nerddom. Men will kill for a California-type hard-bellied woman like Shay; I am not one of the female players men pursue.

Eli lies down. I go over to the bed, put my mouth on his forehead and cover his face with soft kisses, quiet as questions. He's tired. Even though he can do what we do in his sleep, he doesn't want to bother.

Over the years, we unavoidably domesticated our orgasms.

We tamed them like wild beasts trapped in the jungle and brought back alive to be kept in captivity. Like zookeepers who train their animals to appear at feeding time, we conditioned our orgasms to arrive by command on demand. Marriage made our lovemaking dependable, but relieved it of either savagery or surprise. We wore down our own passions, used them up greedily until they suffered inevitable erosion. Now Eli and I no longer share the pleasure of stalking our satisfaction on long, dark safaris; we simply summon our climaxes in from the wilderness.

"Go take your bath," Eli says softly, brushing my hair away from my face. "Wake me when you're finished. In case I fall asleep."

He doesn't mean what he's said.

Our bathroom was photographed for the Thursday home supplement of *The Washington Post.* We kept all the old Victorian fixtures—tub, sink, toilet and shower stall—but had them reglazed a fire-engine red. A magician of a plumber got them all working again.

I turn on the water, spill in some bubble bath and then fold myself inside the curvy cup of the claw-footed tub. It is not until I turn off the brass faucets that I realize I can hear Shay and Mickey Teardash talking. For some reason they are directly beneath my bathroom. Instead of sleeping in the first-floor guest room, they are in the den. They must have opened the sofa bed.

This is the first time I've ever heard pillow talk in my own home.

"I'm not your toy-boy."

"Oh come on, Mickey. Just be nice tonight."

"I'm always nice."

"Yeah, nice and hard."

"Move down here."

"No, I don't want to tonight."

There are some muffled sounds.

My sister laughs.

"We don't have any condoms, Mick," she whines.

"We don't need any. I bought you a present."

Silence.

"Oh my God. Where'd you get that?"

"Pleasure Chest."

"Jeez, it's huge."

"Flesh pink and battery-run."

A dildo.

All in good fun.

Soon I hear Shay moan.

All women make the same sounds. Like the deep hum of sea mammals. Shay's initial moan signals penetration, an ambivalent mix of relish and reluctance, surprise and surrender. Any woman can tell where another woman is being touched from the sounds she makes. Each internal pressure point releases its own unique song.

Oh, yes.

Shay is on her way. Now she is an audible time bomb ticking toward detonation. I hear all the sequential sounds of abdication, the delicious shrugging off and loss of self, before the ultimate dissolution.

I sink lower into my bathwater.

I remember sex . . . like a sweet, almost forgotten, rain that touches every surface before sluicing off into secret spaces, filling canals and channels, rushing forward to spill over a waterfall. I hear my sister's soundings of pleasure and I feel a wild despair stir me. Stark deprivation stalks my heart. I feel as if I'm dying and have only one second left in which to mourn the loss of love. Life without sexual pleasure is like the earth without rain, withering as it waits for relief.

S N A P S H O T

That's the Loring apartment building. Those stones were brought from Europe and the cupolas are copies of some famous ones in Rome. When we lived in the Loring, having sex made me feel important. In the morning, when I walked outside, I thought everyone who saw me *knew* what Eli and I had done in that first double bed of ours. Back then I believed sex was serious, that those liberties we took with each other's bodies were important. I thought we did things no one else had ever dreamed of doing or dared to try. I felt as if what we did was significant in the larger realm of things . . . an important social statement about freedom and passion and love. There's that much to say for innocence: It makes everything feel like a first. In those early years, before I learned I couldn't get pregnant, I was scrupulous about using my diaphragm. I still regret using that damn thing when I didn't even need it. It always slowed me down when I most wanted to hold Eli in my arms.

Eli is sleeping when I return to our bedroom. I do not wake him. If our marriage ends in divorce it won't be a no-fault divorce. It will be a default.

Eli is defaulting on me.

5

It is three o'clock Saturday afternoon. Wearing a demure cotton dress and leather sandals, I leave my house and walk past our private wilderness area toward the congestion of Columbia Road.

The midafternoon heat is circling overhead like a troubled airplane.

I walk east on California for three blocks to reach the Third Precinct, which I consider *my* police station just as I think of the Safeway on Columbia Road as *my* Safeway. However, the fact that I view the V Street station possessively does not mean anyone there is glad to see me. Of the five black police officers behind the room-length counter, none makes any sign of noticing me enter. They do not see me approach the counter any more than I saw the unemployed black men plastered like posters against the storefronts on Eighteenth Street.

Selective blindness is a popular means of doing business in Adams-Morgan.

I lean against the counter for a long time while the police

continue whatever they were or were not doing before I arrived. The two women officers are talking about a strip search they performed on a female suspect the previous night. I do not want to hear the details, so I go deaf. Selective hearing is another negotiable neighborhood instrument. Taunts, threats and racial or sexual slurs are best left unheard.

A young cop is writing in a large ledger not far from where I'm standing. Behind him an old-fashioned wall clock clucks its tongue disapprovingly during our long standoff. After stretching his insolence to the max, the young man finally relents and asks me what I want.

"I'd like to speak to a detective," I say.

Then all five of them turn around to look at me.

Of course the White European Lady would like to speak to a detective.

Why would she want to speak with a plain, ordinary, not to mention black, cop? Why would she bother speaking to a rookie when she has been trained to speak only with management—to deal exclusively with supervisors and higher executive authorities?

"Whaddabout?"

"My car was stolen."

Silent exasperation escapes and floats up toward the ceiling like a helium balloon.

"Didja report it?"

"No." I let a little white-woman edginess creep into my voice. "That's why I want to see a detective."

Hooked now, the cop sidles along the counter toward where I'm standing.

"How do you know it's a detective you need ta see?"

The two women officers have now returned to their desks and are trying to look busy while listening to our strained dialogue. Eventually, *my* cop slides a mimeographed paper toward me and says I should fill out a stolen-car report.

I take the form, but let my irritation shift into a higher gear. Again I ask to see a detective. Now my voice is sharply petulant.

I have introduced the threat of hysteria into the room like someone advancing a political candidate. The effect is equally disruptive. After a few more moments, the cop releases a reluctant sigh, picks up an intercom and speaks to someone in an inaudible but aggrieved mumble.

"Okay," he says to me. "He'll be right down."

Now everyone gets busy. Very busy.

And quiet. Very quiet.

Washington is one of the few American cities where a white person can feel what it's like to be the Other. The Outsider. An intimidated member of a disliked minority group.

Racial hatred is sizzling through the room.

They hate me.

I am the White European Woman. I am the enemy. I am a *colon.* I am a Brit during the Raj. I am a Boer in Johannesburg. I am a settler come to rape Rhodesia. I am a White European Woman who drinks hot tea in the midday sun and sips late-afternoon mint juleps seated on a veranda from where I watch the natives working my land. At night I dress for dinner in lacy white Victorian frocks, get drunk and go off to shoot antelopes by moonlight in an open Daimler.

Now a slow burn, like a long snake, hisses and crawls on its belly across the floor.

I recognize it immediately. I know too well the heat of *any* resentment fueled by injustice. Because of my incendiary relationship with Shay, I know there is nothing hotter than a slow burn. A slow burn will destroy the host that harbors it. A slow burn will scorch the earth and the entire environment enveloping it.

I walk over to an oak bench shoved against the wall and sit down. From the lockup behind a barred gate there come some troublesome noises I prefer not to sort out. I look at the stolen-car form. I take a pen out of my purse. The only blank I fill in is SEX?, where I write: "Infrequent." When I see the stairwell door open I shove the paper and pen back in my purse.

"You waiting to see a detective?"

A black man wearing sport clothes is walking toward me.

The guy's maybe fifty. Overweight with a mini–beer belly that begins beneath the middle button of his short-sleeved madras shirt. He's handsome. Very handsome. His skin is the color of an emery board. He has gray-edged close-cropped hair, a well-trimmed Vandyke and teeth a white for which there is no English adjective. Maybe the Eskimos, with all their words for snow, could come up with one.

His moves are street-smart. Slow, but steady, sort of premeditated. He looks like he's seen it all but can still forget about it when he wants to. He looks like he might have been the guy who spray-painted last Thanksgiving's harsh messages on the brick wall of the Eighteenth Street parking lot:

SAVE A TURKEY—EAT THE RICH and

TOO FEW HAVE TOO MUCH—DOWN WITH YUPPIE VALUES.

"You waiting for a detective?" he asks again.

"Yes, I am," I answer in precise standard English.

At least I don't succumb to counterfeit street talk, to any slurred hipster accent, which is a common symptom of the ethnic nervousness often accompanying the onslaught of the White Man's Disease. I do, however, involuntarily rise to my feet in deference to an officer.

"Well, what can I do for you?"

Flat. Uninflected. Unfriendly. Uninterested.

"My car was stolen last night."

"Yeah?"

"*Yeah.*"

I did that good. A quick return close to the baseline. I didn't get suckered into playing net. Twenty years as a *colon,* you learn some moves.

"Come up to my office."

He jerks his head at me to follow him through the doorway marked EXIT and up a set of cement stairs. When he brushes past me, I can smell a lot of Lagerfeld cologne. From behind, I can see his muscular back straining against his shirt. His love handles jiggle a bit, creasing his style. He has missed one of the belt loops on the back of his trousers, which makes me smile a little despite the practiced disdain he dumped on me back downstairs.

A white woman in a black city has got to accept her punishment. Even though I didn't commit the original crime or even very many subsequent ones, I've got to take some shit for the sake of history. It's the old Calvinist tradition. Guilty by virtue of original sin, further compounded by additional insults.

On the second floor the detective leads me into a small bare office where he sits down, completely filling the round desk chair parked beside a table. Then he hands over a little white name card with a gold police-department emblem embossed on it.

"I'm Lieutenant Bo Culver. Where was your car when it was stolen?"

I sit down in the only other chair.

"In Georgetown. In a driveway on Reservoir Road. Between Thirty-eighth and Thirty-ninth."

I watch impatience travel across his face.

"Maybe you should be over at the Second Precinct," he says with genuine boredom.

"But I live *here*," I protest.

"Where?"

"Adams Mill Road."

"What kinda car was it?"

"A Ford Escort."

"You drive an Escort?"

His surprise is a backhanded compliment.

We both smile.

"Even on *my* salary I can put a lady in a better car than that," he says.

I laugh.

Now at least our problem is on the table.

Upper-middle-class white lady meets black police officer. Lots of shit going down. Lots of history. Even though my silent collaboration with his joke betrayed a few feminist principles, I've made a little peace with this guy. I've acknowledged that my white man hasn't done all that well by me, which means that I, the White European Woman, haven't done all that well for myself. This acknowledgment also produces a slight sexual ripple that doesn't hurt my case.

Long pause.

Now my tongue, shy and heavy, remains grounded.

I look above Lieutenant Culver's head at a framed photograph of Marion Barry, Washington's once-promising black mayor, a sixties radical who lost his innocence amidst the fast-track vices of the eighties. Marion Barry is the man whose former wife, current mistress and best friend all served concurrent prison sentences without adversely affecting his reelection to a third term. This is a man who chases women, gets drunk in public, runs with drug dealers and gives the finger to *The Washington Post* even after eleven of his top aides have been convicted on corruption charges.

Marion Barry is the man who threw the political World Series.

When Lieutenant Culver looks up I immediately lower my gaze.

I certainly do not want to appear critical of our mayor.

Washington whites keep their anger about Marion Barry to themselves. The white tom-toms beat only at night. The white minority only whisper jokes about D.C.'s Mayor-for-Life in the privacy of their homes, and then only among trusted friends. I certainly do not want to discuss the rise and fall of the District's mayor with Lieutenant Culver at this time.

White liberal lady keeps her mouth shut.

But this detective ain't dumb.

"Yep, ol' Marion," he says with a slow smile. "Doesn't know which side he's fighting on. Keeps getting caught behind enemy lines in the war on drugs. In our war on thugs."

"Well," I say with a shrug, "you know what they say about power."

I hope he doesn't, since I feel sorry about the mayor; I once liked Barry a lot and even worked for him back in 1978, when he was bucking the white establishment and the black bourgeoisie.

"Yeah, well." Now the detective shrugs. "You want to get your car back, I need to get some information, okay?"

I give him my name, my address and my telephone, driver's license, car-registration and license-plate numbers. He inscribes all of them in a grade school–like notebook and then puts down his pencil.

"Took you quite a while to get over here," he says. "You got enough other cars you didn't need this one very bad or what?"

I giggle.

But he's serious.

"Why didn't you report this last night, Ms. . . . Myers? Whose house were you visiting when you got ripped off?"

Idly he eyes my bod while waiting for an answer.

I make a move to get out of my chair.

"Whoa. Waidaminute. Siddown."

I sink back down again.

"You got a special friend, Ms. Myers?"

"What?"

"You got a boyfriend you were maybe visiting last night?"

High indignation: "Of course not!"

"So then what were you doing in Georgetown?"

"God," I murmur, with heavy disgust. "I was over at my brother-in-law's house."

Lieutenant Culver frowns.

"Let's get real," he says. "We can save a lotta time. Your husband know you were over there? Visiting your brother-in-law?"

"He was there with me," I say, choking with anger.

Then Lieutenant Culver begins to question me. He wants to know the whole scenario, plus a lot of details. I have to tell him how I went out to the airport to pick up my sister. As soon as I mention Shay by name, Lieutenant Culver gets even more interested.

"Shay?" he repeats. "Shay Karavan? That's your sister?"

I nod reluctantly.

Impressed, he looks me over again.

"Well, now that you mention it, I do see some family resemblance. Yup. Two good-looking sisters."

I blush and smile.

"She's a foxy lady, Shay Karavan. A real tough cookie."

Then he makes me go through the whole thing from the moment we arrived at Christopher's until we discovered the car missing from his driveway. Of course, I omit any mention of the papers and simply say Shay's luggage was in the backseat. Lieutenant Culver also knows who Barney Yellen is. When he learns Shay was once married to Barney, Lieutenant Culver really gets turned on. He asks when and how long they were married. He asks if I know what Barney's working on at the present time. He asks me if it's common for Shay's first husband to visit her second husband.

I give him some inane answers. I feel hot and disheveled. Uneasy. Endangered.

"What she bring in on the plane this time?" Lieutenant Culver asks. "More MIAs?"

I shake my head and try to adjust my attitude so as to produce an appropriate smile.

"Still," he muses, looking at his watch, "it's almost eighteen hours since you lost your car. You don't look like a procrastinating kind of lady to me."

Briefly I consider calling Eli and asking him to come over to the police station. But instead I try to steady myself with a mental mantra: Be cool, be cool, be cool. Act like Shay. Think what she'd do. Think how she'd protect herself and throw everyone else to the wolves. Be cool. Be cruel.

The detective is on a fishing expedition. I know he's thinking drugs. He is suspicious about everyone—my husband, my sister, both my brothers-in-law, me. At least he's heard of my shelter, which gives me a couple brownie points. A Home Away from

Home has a good rep. But Lieutenant Culver seems a bit too conversant with Barney's notorious past. I do not think this is to my advantage.

It's always hard to tell if Barney is good or bad for the Jews.

S N A P S H O T

This is a picture of Barney from the *Minneapolis Tribune* when he was on trial in his hometown of Chicago. Barney is your basic American bad boy, a radical who observes no party lines. As a left-wing folk hero, he embodies certain movement campaigns and confrontations that make him greater than the sum of his own private experiences. Having fulfilled the mythic requirements for becoming a movement symbol—organizer in Chicago, Mississippi Delta voter-registration worker, conspiracy defendant in Chicago, law student at Berkeley and storefront lawyer in D.C.—he has achieved a limited immortality. His is a name people use as a code word for a 1960s kind of commitment. For women, Barney's name also evokes images of old-style druggy nights and lewd love. Because Barney loves women, women instinctively gravitate toward him.

I cannot believe the turn this interview has taken. I also cannot regain control of it. For the next half hour I continue answering questions. I end up telling Lieutenant Culver more about myself and my family than I'd ever want anyone to know. He's not dumb. He knows how to question a suspect. And that's what I've become.

A suspect.

When he's done interrogating me, Lieutenant Culver stands up.

"Okay, I'm going to put out a stolen-car bulletin. But don't get your hopes up. We lose quite a few cars every day here in the District. Anything else you wanna tell me, Ms. Myers?"

Without waiting for an answer, he leads me out into the hall. I have to walk quickly to keep up with him because he's light on his feet and moves the mountain of his body with surprising grace. He's heavy but somehow weightless. So are his moves. All his moves are relaxed.

Deliberately lazy.

But effective.

Suggestive.

Back on the first floor he gives the people behind the counter a look that says "shape up." They do. All five of them are sitting or standing sort of at attention as I leave.

Then I hurry back up V Street toward Eighteenth.

Walking through the ghetto areas of Adams-Morgan is always an adventure in not seeing anything either too sad or too threatening. Here's what I don't see:

- Skinny run-down row houses, their front stairs splashed with tired children baking like cookies in the sun.
- Weary women sprawled across their front stoops, soaking up the overheated scene like soft absorbent sponges.
- Teenagers, splattered up against the fenders of rusted-out cars, listening to music leak out of boom boxes balanced atop the stove-hot car hoods.

Near the Reed School playground, I lean against a stop sign while I fix the strap of my sandal. Every sign in Adams-Morgan has the word "war" written in under STOP. It's what the old hippies still like to do—go around ordering people to stop making wars.

The steaming heat is a thick presence all around me. There is a gamy jungle smell, spawned by the heat, spicing the air. The humidity is an insistent throbbing presence beating like a drum. Our weather is on the warpath.

By the time I reach home at six o'clock, I am exhausted, but my kitchen looks like a downtown disco during happy hour. Eli, Shay, Mickey, Barney, Barney's slinky girlfriend, Victoria Lang, and sweet little Amelia are drifting about drinking wine, beer, vodka with grapefruit juice, Scotch, champagne and decaffeinated A & W root beer, respectively. Everyone is dressed for tropical temperatures in cotton shorts, shirts and sandals. I am quickly informed that Barney and Victoria took Amelia to the zoo before bringing her here to deposit with Shay.

My small Sony radio has been switched to Shay's favorite FM hard-rock station, which is playing "Sexual Healing." I wonder if someone called in and requested that tune for me and Eli. Every time the rhythm kicks in, Shay twitches her tail and does a little bump and grind in front of my double-sized restaurant stove, where she is making a big mess with a couple of eggs.

Shay always likes a loud sound track when she plays her indoor scenes.

I sit down at the table and pull Amelia up on my lap. She is dressed in a too-small striped T-shirt and dusty white shorts that push her palm-sized tummy above the elasticized waistband. Near the back door is the little yellow flowered suitcase that accompanies Amelia every time she makes a move somewhere new.

"Want a cold beer?" Eli asks, coming over to give me a peck on the cheek.

I nod and smile at my husband, who looks quite attractive in his cutoff Levi's and a sweat-dampened T-shirt that Marge sent him for his birthday. The shirt says: HUG A SWEDE.

While scrambling eggs for Amelia's supper, Shay is regaling everyone with Hollywood gossip garnered last month at the Cannes Film Festival where she has Class-A hotel reservations (probably comped) for the rest of her life. Her fast-track chatter is meant to impress Victoria, who is languidly sipping champagne from a Redskins beer mug. Victoria is thirtysomething, a good-looking blonde wearing a one-piece denim sunsuit with a bib that doesn't quite cover the fleshy side folds of her breasts. She is a feature writer for the Style section of *The Washington Post*, which stirs Shay's competitive feelings. Predictably, Victoria appears unaffected by Shay's performance. Shay experiences Victoria's indifference as a challenge.

So she begins to escalate, telling nastier stories in greater detail at a faster pace.

"Did you know Peter Bogdanovich just married Dorothy Stratten's kid sister? You know, *Star 80?* That *Playboy* bunny who was doing Bogdanovich and got murdered by her husband when she asked for a divorce? Don't you think it's weird? Him marrying her sister? Also I heard Tom Hayden is just furious at Jane for apologizing to those Vietnam vets the way she did. It's going to be splitsville there soon. And Debra Winger's dating her old flame, that governor from Nebraska who's a senator now . . ."

My sister Scheherazade is playing tag with herself.

Dad always used to say Shay was like the heavyweight boxer who knocked himself out while alone in the ring.

When Mickey Teardash sits down between me and Victoria at the table, Shay gets even more hyper. Honing her instinct for malice, she mockingly catalogs the items Bess Myerson was caught shoplifting from a small-town department store near the state penitentiary where she was visiting her lover.

"Flashlight batteries. Six bottles of nail polish. Five pairs of earrings! Gimme a break!"

Then she names some of the celebrities expected to be in Atlanta. Mort Zuckerman has rented a gym and invited all the superstars like Jane Pauley and Judy Woodruff and Diane Sawyer to work out with him in the mornings. The Hollywood bratpackers, led by Ally Sheedy, who's become Jane Fonda's political protégée, are also scheduled to make appearances.

I watch in petrified silence as my sister the love junkie starts to go nuts. She is desperate for a reaction. Any sort of reaction, any response to her performance. But nobody is reacting and she is becoming hysterical. She can't stop. Mickey is clearly suffering from her off-key performance. Superbly uncomfortable, he has begun poking Amelia in the tummy with a rigid forefinger, giving her a few seconds after each poke to try to catch his finger. Her squeals of excitement start to voice-over Shay's performance.

Barney is also edgy. He is embarrassed both for and about Shay in front of Vicky. He is drinking fast. He is drinking up a storm. Seldom does Barney have an excuse as good as this event to get roaring drunk.

"Amelia," Barney calls out in the singsong voice he always uses with her, "tell Auntie Nattie what you saw at the zoo."

Amelia immediately turns shy in response to this clichéd approach. I squeeze her a little and change the subject.

"What have you been learning at nursery school, honey?" I ask.

"Blue and puple," she answers solemnly, turning her bright little face upward like a spotlight.

This drives Shay crazy.

Already flushed from the strain of her floor show, she whirls around, squealing with delight.

"But you *know* all your colors," she trills. "You're even learning your alphabet."

Amelia stares at her grandmother. "Jimmy don't know puple. Asley don't know lellow," she says,

"Oh, aren't you a nice little girl?"

Shay smiles emphatically to reinforce Amelia's social conscience while flashing Barney a coded look regarding the miseducation of gifted children.

"See? That's why I think she should go to the Montessori school," she says in a preachy voice.

Already half-drunk, Barney is ready for a fight.

"Jesus. A *private nursery* for thirty-eight hundred dollars a year?"

On principle, Barney abhors private education. He and Shay battled about Steven's schooling for twelve years and now both seem ready and eager to start again.

But suddenly the contents of the frying pan begin to smoke and Shay rushes back to the stove to scoop the scrambled eggs onto a dish before addressing herself to the toaster oven. Right away she begins messing around with the light-dark dial. Always frantically impatient, Shay tends to undercook foods and tan, rather than toast, bread. Finally she brings the plate to the table.

Automatically, I begin spooning eggs into Amelia's cherry-red mouth.

That's when Barney adopts a more adversarial posture.

"Hey," he begins. "I was thinking that just because the damn hard copy of the interview is lost doesn't mean the story's dead. Eli, you've got great connections inside the bureaucracy. You should be able to spring loose another copy. I don't think we should just let this story die on us. Losing Nat's car was a bad break, but we shouldn't deep-six the whole story."

"Listen," Eli says in his down-country voice, "releasing that story's not going to change anything. The whole Iran-contra exposé hasn't had any real impact on the public. People don't care anymore."

"I do," Barney snorts.

"You're not people."

"Hey," Barney growls at Eli.

The Scotch has painted his nose pink and illuminated the broken veins in his shallow cheeks.

"You can break all the scandals you want and provide all the necessary evidence, but it's not gonna matter," Eli continues. "The people love Ronnie Reagan; that's the bottom line. That's why Dukakis is modeling himself after him. Anyway, I'm off to cover the convention starting tomorrow. I'm the only one from my bureau going, so I'm out of this mess."

"We could still *give* the story to someone over at the *Post*," Barney insists. "Vicky knows all the good guys there. We'll just decide who to give it to and let them spring it."

"Sure," Victoria says, nodding. "We can give it to Carioca. He'd kill for it."

But then Mickey Teardash stands up.

"Look," he says. "What's the net result of releasing this story? Who's gonna gain what from it and what's it gonna cost?"

"This isn't a leveraged buyout we're talking here," Barney says. "Net gains and costs and that sort of jazz don't apply. This is politics, not business. What we've got here is information about people who are fucking up our country. So let's just put it out there so the public knows what's happening. It's a sin to sit on a story like this one."

"But what good can come from releasing it?" Mickey asks again.

"Well, to start off, it'll hurt the Republicans in the election," Barney answers.

Uh-oh. Big confrontation. We've got the Greed King and the Bad Rad in the ring together. Mucho fireworks.

"Is there someone you're trying to protect or something?" Barney asks, stalking Mickey around the kitchen.

"No. I know Jerry Russo, just like Shay does," Mickey answers. "I've got no reason to protect him. What I'm asking is what's the big deal if Fawn Hall does coke? Everyone does. If Shay publishes that story, twenty people around town can say they've seen her do coke too. There's no big story in this because everyone does drugs."

"Yeah, but not everyone works in the White House," Barney argues. "Not everyone who snorts coke has access to top-secret documents."

"Who cares? Jesus." Teardash shakes his head wearily. "This is why the Democrats can't win an election. You guys always get sidetracked by some miniscandal. You always go off on some cockamamy tangent that no one else cares about."

In his exasperation, Barney turns around and looks accusingly at Shay. His old friend Shay. His former wife and once great ally.

Shay flushes and shifts her gaze away before making a wadda-ya-gonna-do? kind of shrug.

Translation: *Big handsome billionaire who's good in bed has funny politics. So sue me.*

A little before seven someone turns on NBC and we watch Connie Chung deliver the news, which consists almost exclusively of weather-related stories.

- The first five months of 1988 were the hottest on record for the United States. One-hundred-degree temperatures dominated the country. Washington, D.C., along with twenty-two other states, reached a three-digit temperature peak several weeks ago and plateaued there.
- Corn, soybeans and spring wheat crops have already failed. Drought fears have sent prices soaring for wheat and wheat futures. Economic analysts say cake, cookie, bread and cereal prices will rise considerably this winter.
- The incidence of skin cancer is skyrocketing due to an insufficient layer of ozone to screen out ultraviolet sun rays. The camera scans sun worshipers on the beach and then shows close-ups of faces covered with fresh malignant tumors.

Commercial break. Next:

- Prisoners in various federal penitentiaries have begun rioting for air conditioners in their cells, and several wardens have capitulated to the demands.
- A spokesman for a New York City Merchants' Association claims there are no longer any window AC units available for sale in any of the five boroughs.
- Washington, D.C., which has not had to enact any water restrictions, last week mailed to its residents a self-congratulatory letter noting how well the city has handled the drought.

I received one of these letters. It was signed "Wally Water."

What doesn't get in the news is the fact that D.C. has started to smell like flowers decomposing in a vase.

After the news, I go upstairs with Eli to help him pack.

What I feel is the beginning of a deep depression plus a jittery kind of neediness. This is not a recipe for seduction. This is a bad way to feel since any sort of upset turns Eli off. He can't stand it when I'm depressed. He can't stand it when I'm agitated.

Sitting on the edge of our bed, I watch him ferry his clothes between the bureau and his suitcase. He is systematically disorganized. He rumples his clothes the same way he rumples his face with conflicting expressions.

"I didn't want to ask downstairs, but what happened at the police station?"

Eli hikes his glasses up higher on the bridge of his nose with his middle finger. A hundred times a day Eli gives his finger to the world.

"Nothing much. I filled out a car-theft report."

Eli is nervous. His body language has developed a stutter. I know he's feeling guilty because he didn't invite me to Atlanta. Before Eli lost interest in me, he often converted business trips into holidays for the two of us. But now he no longer feels any impetus to be with me in a new and different setting. All the romance inspired by his overseas assignments has evaporated. The fact he's not trying to restore it is simply a sin of omission.

It is part of the sign language used by people falling out of love.

Tentatively Eli presses down the top of his suitcase to see if it will close. Then he walks over to the bed, pulls me up and envelops me in a big bear hug.

"I hate like hell leaving you home alone with all this mess," he says.

Gratefully, I smear myself against the geography of his body. I can feel the friendly warmth of his breath on the crown of my head. I concentrate on not giving off any negative vibes.

"You think we're going to have to feed that crowd downstairs?" he asks, effectively jamming reception of any emotional message from me.

"I don't know," I whisper, pressing my pubic bone against the corresponding hollow above his groin.

"We could order in," he suggests. "Chinese. From the Empress."

I arch my back so I can apply more low-body pressure and also see his face. Eli gives me one of his long, slow smiles while his hands inch down my backside. Eli has slow hands. For me, slow is always better. I don't like being startled by sudden moves in unexpected places. When some of the movable flesh on my buttocks slides out of his grasp, he politely corrals it in again.

I laugh. He laughs. He almost kisses me. Instead he says:

"I've got something for you later."

Although Eli has responded to my pelvic pressure with a sweet hardness, he now pats me on my backside, like Kareem Abdul-Jabbar encouraging some fellow Laker to hang in there. Then I'm released from his hug.

It is almost dark before Eli orders our dinner. As usual, he orders too much. I will be eating Chinese for the rest of my life. After Shay puts Amelia to bed, everyone helps clean the kitchen while I make coffee. Finally Barney and Victoria Lang leave. Around ten o'clock I say good night and go upstairs to my bedroom. I take off my clothes and pull on an old shirt of Eli's.

No bath tonight. No repeat of last night.

Eli comes into our room.

After twenty years, conjugal love is like brushing our teeth at bedtime. It doesn't necessarily make us feel *better,* but not doing it invariably makes us feel worse. A quick once-over is our common compromise. But that's exactly what I don't want tonight. I do not want a slapdash lickety-split encounter. I do not want a sexual non sequitur. I want a coupling that has consciousness and cognizance. It has to feel important, not just like a pun on all four-letter words including l-o-v-e. I don't want to screw just because we both know it's good for our relationship and that we'll feel better afterward. I don't want Eli to feel *virtuous* for screwing me.

"Eli," I begin, sitting down at my dressing table and adopting a certain tone of voice about which there is no confusion, "we've got to talk."

"I know," he says after a heavy, reluctant pause that's as emphatic as a groan.

"Eli, what's happening to us?"

My question establishes a direct confrontation. Of course

what's happening between us is the most compelling subject we share. It's the big R-word. We're talking texture here. Density. Compulsion. Quality time.

"I don't know," Eli says, dread making each word grate abrasively against the next. "But I know it's my fault. You haven't done anything wrong, Nat. You've been terrific. Really patient."

"Eli, are you involved with someone else?"

"No, there's no one else. I'm just out of it, Nat. Burned out. Stressed out. Bummed out. I'm stuck in a rut over at work. I can't seem to bust loose over there."

I rest my elbows on my dressing table so I can prop up my head, which has suddenly become as heavy as my heart.

P O L A R O I D
S N A P S H O T

This faded, creamy yellow Polaroid print is a nudie Eli took one hot (in both senses of that word) summer night. It is not in my album; I keep it in a dresser drawer. Eli always claimed legitimate film-processing labs wouldn't develop nude or explicitly sexual negatives. I don't know whether or not that's true, but when the spirit—or better yet, the flesh—moved him, Eli would encourage me to attempt various poses for him and our old Polaroid. Men are weird about visuals. Women are not into *looking* the way men are. Anyway, great sex is habit-forming. Sometimes, for fairly long periods of time, Eli and I forget about sex. But when we're *into* it, it's all I can think about. Doing IT. DOING it. IT, in ITself, is mind-boggling. Eli knows how to spin me off into a sensuality that frees me from gravity (in both meanings of that word). Once accustomed to sex on a steady basis, I suffer withdrawal symptoms when it's withheld. My sexual hold on Eli is simply my own addiction to sex. That's what turns him on.

"So . . . is it all over?" I ask in what I hope sounds like a reasonable tone of voice. "Are we finished?"

His silence grows like seeds in a garden, impacted in soil, struggling to break through the earth's surface to reach the light.

"I don't know," he finally manages to say. And then to be nice he adds, "I sure *hope* not."

"Well, what's the deal, Eli? If *you* don't know, who does?"

"No one," he answers sadly. "No one but me. That's why I think maybe I should spend some time alone. To think things through."

"I wish I had the residuals on that line of dialogue," I say bitterly.

Silence.

Then he says:

"Listen. I don't know what I'm thinking right now. I mean, to talk about breaking up after twenty years is like discussing whether or not to cut off your arm or your leg. You *know* you'll miss it."

He seems oblivious to how that comment pierces me. I am speechless.

"What we should try to do is set aside some time for discussing things, Nat. If not this week, then soon."

"Great," I say sarcastically. "I can get behind that."

Thick silence once again. I can sense his kindness struggling to break through barriers of other feelings.

We are both stymied. Paralyzed. I turn off the lamp on my table and walk back to bed. Lying next to each other, we listen to the animals in the zoo. Tonight the gibbons are going crazy. They are chattering wildly, as if they sense danger approaching. I know how they feel. I also feel imperiled. Eli extends one of his arms across my midriff. But there is no buzz between us. No magic to inspire us. No electricity to spark a connection.

"Auntie Nattie?"

I separate myself from Eli in one smooth, fluid motion.

"What, Amelia? Why are you up?"

"Can I sheep with you and Uncle Eli?"

"Not tonight, sweetie," Eli answers, but Amelia is already crawling over me, tumbling between us, giggling nervously.

Eli groans. "Why don't you go find your grandmother and your Uncle Mickey?" he asks in a droll voice.

"I want to shtay here," Amelia responds.

And stay she does.

"Okay, Eli," I whisper over the little girl lying between us. "Go to sleep. Don't worry. We'll talk when you get home from Atlanta. Everything will be okay."

I don't cry until much later, when both of them are sleeping.

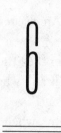

The next morning at seven-thirty I drive Eli to the airport in his Honda. In the car we barely speak. We are both mentally too busy. I am focused on his imminent and symbolic departure. He can't wait to be gone. I do not want to crumble in front of him. He doesn't want to appear overeager to leave.

I am back home again at eight.

By eight-thirty I am drinking my third cup of coffee and taking a second pass at the Sunday *New York Times* crossword puzzle, when Shay appears in the kitchen doorway.

"Good morning," she says amiably.

As usual she's camera-ready.

What she has on is the white shirt Mickey wore yesterday and her silver bracelets. Her hair is a mess; she has "bed-head," our childhood word for hair pressed flat in back from sleeping. Shay's problem was most likely caused by sex rather than sleep. Although she claimed she was too tired to boogie on Friday night, she seems to have gotten a second wind.

Barefoot, she makes her move on the coffeepot.

"Mickey's taking Amelia for a walk," she says. "Our plane's not until three."

Sitting down in a chair across from me, she starts to sip her coffee.

"If you only did crossword puzzles you'd think James Agee and Erle Stanley Gardner were the only American writers who ever lived," I say. "These clowns always need an E-R-L-E for some reason. Do you know a four-letter word for addict?"

"Natalie, listen," Shay says. "I was a real asshole Friday night. I'm sorry. I don't know why I came down so hard on you. It was stupid of me to leave those papers in the car. And now I'm taking off and leaving you with all these problems on your hands."

I start going through the Acrosses again.

A four-letter word for addict?

"But I have to ask you to help me get through the rest of this thing, Nat. I'm not saying it's your fault, but before the car got ripped off, things were really going great for me. I mean, this Fawn Hall story would have been a big feather in my cap. And I think Mickey was—*is*—planning to ask me to move in with him. He has a fabulous apartment on Park Avenue. Five bedrooms. And after we get settled I'm going to bring Amelia up there to live with us. Get a full-time nanny. You know. The whole schmear."

A four-letter word for addict?

A four-letter word for addict?

"But now everything's up for grabs," Shay continues. "I mean, chances are if those papers are found the DEA will bring charges against me."

"Maybe not." I shrug. "Maybe they won't want the publicity."

Shay sips her coffee. "The thing is, everything can be traced right back to you through the car registration."

"Good morning, Sasha," I say sarcastically.

Translation: *As usual you're a day late and a dollar short catching on to anyone else's reality.*

The telephone rings. It is Christopher asking for Shay, so I

hand her the receiver. She says hello and then listens silently for
a while. When she finally speaks her voice is quivering.

"Listen, Christopher, I'm not going to Atlanta for a *vacation*.
This is a *working* trip. *Nooooo!* How am I supposed to find a
baby-sitter in a city where I don't even know anybody? *Jesus!*
This's quite a stunt for you to pull at the last minute. What the
hell do you have to go to Atlanta for, anyway? Even if you got
a plane reservation, you'll never find a hotel room. *No!* No, you
can't stay with me. *No!* This is *not* gonna be a second honeymoon!"

She is clawing for her cigarette pack in the breast pocket of
Teardash's wrinkled white shirt.

"This is really a shitty thing for you to do, Christopher. But if
you *have* to act like an asshole, I'll just ask Barney to keep her.
Believe me, I'm really pissed off. *Nooooo!* I have other things to
do this afternoon. I have to buy another laptop for one thing."
Now she changes her tone of voice. "Listen. Is it okay if I charge
a Toshiba laptop to your Visa card and pay you back as soon as
the insurance company reimburses me? We still have that floater
on our homeowner's policy, don't we? To cover personal property
outside the house? Great, thanks. *No, I don't know which hotel
I'll be staying at.*"

She slams down the receiver, lights a cigarette and looks at me
with despair in her velvet-blue eyes.

"Oh, God. Now Christopher's going to Atlanta and his maid's
going on vacation and I know Barney won't be able to take care
of Amelia. He's got a big case in court this week and Victoria
works. What am I going to do? Everything's coming apart."

She drains the remaining coffee from her cup and then makes
her pitch.

"Do you think there's any possible way you could keep Amelia
here with you? Just until Friday? I mean, as long as Eli's out of
town and you're on vacation anyway? She's crazy about you and
she's been pushed around so much lately."

Shay begins to cry.

Holding her heavy hair back away from her face, she lets hot tears drizzle down her face. They slide off her cheeks and fall into the deep V opening of Mickey's shirt. During this crying jag, it is clear that the thought of Amelia's distress tortures her. She looks ravaged, like a caged animal.

"Could you, Nat? Would you? I'll never ever ask you for anything ever again. Really. The rest of my life. I promise. Just this one last thing? It'll make up for leaving your keys in the car. I'll never ask you for anything else. I *mean* it this time."

Yeah, sure.

What a bunch of *ca-ca.*

This is really too much. First she plants stolen documents in my car and then she asks me to take care of her granddaughter while I plow through the shit she's piled on me. I am breathless with indignation at what a user she is.

User! The four-letter word for addict is "user."

"When is this going to end, Shay?"

"What?"

"This addiction to using people."

"What do you *mean*?" Her entire face puckers up with consternation. "Why are you attacking me, Natalie? I didn't mean for this to happen. And, besides, you were as careless as I was."

The tears start cascading down her face again. There is a wild expression in her eyes.

Quietly I write U-S-E-R into #24 Down and look to see what new opportunities this opens up for me.

"I should think you'd have a little bit of compassion," she sobs. "First I had to raise Steven all by myself . . ."

I look at my sister reproachfully. Mom, Dad, Barney, Eli and I took care of Steven almost as much as she did.

". . . and now I've got Amelia on my hands while I'm still free-lancing. I don't see how it would hurt you to take care of her for five days. Really. You *are* her great-aunt, you know."

"Oh, *all right,*" I say. "All right." My words are like broken dishes with ragged edges. "She can stay here, but *don't* ask me to cover for you with the cops or your famous FBI or CIA, because I won't do it, Shay. I mean it. I really won't."

"Oh, Natalie, thank you!"

Shay hurtles herself at me, knotting her arms around my neck. I inhale her essence. Her pretense.

Sometimes when we were in high school Shay would wear one of my sweaters and then deny it. But I could always smell her spicy odor on my clothes. I once read somewhere about two sisters who shared a bedroom and years later discovered each had been devirginated on the other's bed. I thought about that a lot, about what it really meant. But I could never decide if it was a story about love or loathing.

Sometimes I hate myself more than I hate Shay.

Mickey Teardash at least shows enough grace to call a taxi to take him and Shay out to Dulles. I have to admit he has more sensitivity to other people than Shay does. She's a user; he's just a taker. Amelia and I stand on the front stairs and wave good-bye until long after their cab has turned the corner and disappeared into Rock Creek Park.

By four o'clock Sunday afternoon the city feels deserted. Most of the media elite and Democratic leaders have left for Atlanta. The familiar crowd of people who power-lunch at Duke's, dine at Germaine's, take tennis lessons from Kathy Kemper at Mount Vernon Junior College and shop at the Georgetown Safeway have disappeared. Washington's political types are like little children who can sense immediately if their parents aren't home. When the president goes to Camp David for a weekend, lots of Washingtonians remain uneasy until he returns to the city.

After her nap I take Amelia for a walk up Columbia Road to Kalorama Park. When Steven was young I used to bring him there frequently, but now the city has abandoned the park because of an infestation of rodents. Indeed the Recreation Department has simply bequeathed this park to the homeless, the dealers, the winos, the junkies and the rats. The grass is knee-high. The benches are all missing slats from either their seats or their backs.

On one bench, close to the sidewalk, sits my client Hannah, with her shapeless body, faded eyes and torn shopping bag stuffed full of seasonal costumes. She has been crippled by arthritis. The lower parts of both thumbs are gone, actually devoured by the disease, and her fingers are frozen into contorted claws. She is holding on to the Safeway shopping cart she shares with a friend, who actually boosted it from the supermarket and thus holds majority control. The cart looks like a piece of found art. Each mesh square is stuffed with a prized possession: scraps of material, papers, cooking utensils, washcloths, used soap and empty containers.

My first concern is whether or not Hannah will frighten Amelia, but my little grandniece shows no alarm. She seems to view Hannah as some sort of street performer trying to act funny. Today, with the temperature over 100 degrees, Hannah is wearing an old bus driver's jacket that doesn't quite button, a large white apron tied around her middle, baggy pantyhose and two mismatched shoes. Although elsewhere she has been busted for indecent exposure, in Adams-Morgan the cops are sort of soft on Hannah. Last year one of them gave her his old police cap for Christmas—definitely a no-no.

"Whaddaya got?" Hannah asks in her ear-piercing squeal. "Whozat doll baby?"

"This is Amelia," I say begrudgingly.

"Hi-hi!" Hannah says.

She smiles at Amelia in her usual harmless, empty way. Hannah has a full round face, splotches of broken veins in each cheek, a Dutch Boy–cleanser hairdo and a walleye similar to Jean-Paul Sartre's. But this is not the reason it is difficult to meet Hannah's gaze. Hannah never looks directly at anyone. She tilts and turns her head, as if protecting her bad eye, successfully avoiding any eye contact with anyone.

"How you doin', Hannah?"

"The shelter's closed."

"Yes, I know. We'll open up again in September."

Slowly Hannah raises her arms to inspect her clawlike hands.

"Bad. It's so bad today," she says. "In Sarasota when I couldn't get the groceries in the Winn-Dixie bags no more, the customers bagged their own, but the manager fired me anyhow."

I am shocked. Seldom does Hannah mention anything about herself or her past, and now in one sentence she has given me the name of a city, a job and even a skeletal explanation for her situation. So. Hannah was a Winn-Dixie clerk. From bagger to bag lady.

"I didn't know you were a checkout clerk," I say carefully. "Come on—let's go over to McDonald's and I'll buy you something to eat."

But Hannah doesn't like restaurants. She does not like going inside any building. Twice, in defiance of city regulations, I took her home with me for a proper bath, but she would only sit on the front steps. My fantasy is that I'll finally find out enough about Hannah to discover she has a devoted sister somewhere who's been seeking her for decades and who will quickly come to this corner near Eighteenth and Columbia Road to reclaim Hannah when notified of her whereabouts.

"I didn't know you were a bagger," I probe again.

But now Hannah is spent. She's produced so many words she doesn't feel like talking anymore. Picking up her Lord & Taylor bag, she stuffs it inside the Safeway shopping cart, wobbles to her feet and trudges off toward a more secluded bench.

I pause for a moment and then go after her with Amelia trotting behind me.

"Hannah, do you want to go to the House of Rachel?"

She looks at me glumly. "I like your shelter," she says accusingly.

I think of the keys to the padlocked door, which are sitting on my bedroom bureau.

"I'll get it reopened by September, Hannah. Really."

I think about the shelter. Because there are no showers, the storefront always smells foul in the summertime. In the winter, when I draw the old sheets we use as curtains across the front windows, there is an elemental cavelike quality to the place that stirs some strong, primitive feelings in both me and Angie, my friend and unpaid volunteer assistant.

Hannah makes several strange snorting sounds through her nostrils, shakes her head and then turns and walks away again.

S N A P S H O T

I have always kept this picture of my Bubbie among my important papers—our wedding certificate, my B.A. and M.S.W. diplomas, the titles to our house and cars. It is mounted in one of those heavy cardboard folders European photographers used in the early twentieth century. My Bubbie is maybe twenty years old here. She is wearing a high-collared dress with a brooch at the neck. Her dark hair is brushed back into a coil and her blue eyes are bright. Sometimes I feel that I knew her best when she was twenty—a wild political firebrand, stirred by the murder of her father and by her socialist dreams. At eighteen she joined some revolutionary cell, met my Zadie, fought in the streets and finally walked across Poland en route to America. I know this: If that young woman, Melunah, came to me now, looking as she does in this beige, tawny-tinted print, she would say: "So? This is your great America? With women living in the streets, sleeping in boxes, begging for food? This is your great democracy? Your golden dream? *Feh,*" she would shrill mockingly. *"Feh!"*

Amelia and I have just returned home and are ransacking the kitchen in search of a snack when the telephone rings.

"Ms. Myers?"

"Yes?"

"Lieutenant Culver here."

"Oh! Hi."

"Your car's been recovered."

"Oh! Great. Was . . . my sister's luggage inside?"

My voice is at least an octave higher than usual.

"Nope. Sorry 'bout that. Nothing but a bunch of papers spilled out all over the floor in the backseat."

"Oh?" Be still my heart. "So what do I have to do?"

"Are you alone over there?"

"Yes." Weird question. Unless he's coming here to arrest me. Panic begins panting inside my rib cage, where I keep it chained. "Except for my little grandniece. I'm taking care of her this week."

"Look," Lieutenant Culver says. "A few questions have come up that I'd like to discuss with you. In private. Since I have to make a quick run in my car, how 'bout I stop by there for a few minutes?"

"Sure."

There is a drought developing in my mouth. I begin to dehydrate as soon as I envision the pleasure of the precinct cops seeing me brought back to the station house in handcuffs—stoop-shouldered, shuffling along as if wearing hospital-issue paper slippers. Me. With all my white ways and means.

I'll have to find Barney, I think. They'll have to let me phone my lawyer. He'll come and take Amelia. If I can't find him, I'll try to reach Victoria at the *Post.* They'll have to let me find someone to take care of Amelia. She's only three. Both Angie and Helen, my most dependable friends, are up on Martha's Vineyard.

"You got your car registration there with you?"

"Yes."

"Okay. So I'll see you in about twenty minutes. Five-eight-one-five Adams Mill Road, right?"

"Right."

Amelia is standing on one of the kitchen chairs straightening out my silverware drawer for the second time today. Earlier I had removed the knives so she could put the forks and spoons in their proper molded spaces. She seems totally absorbed, but when I walk over to her she stops her work and looks up at me expectantly.

"Whasa matta, Auntie Nattie?" she asks sympathetically.

Amelia has long been programmed to acknowledge, even anticipate, adult moods. It was her mother, Yvonne, who taught her how to gauge degrees of distress and despair, to determine the differential between fear and panic. Watching her mother disintegrate, Amelia learned lots of diagnostic skills.

Now she can interpret adult faces like pictures in a storybook.

"Nothing's wrong, honey." I give her a hug. "I'm just going to put on some makeup."

In the powder-room mirror I see a moving still of myself, an implicit story etched on my face. My eyes, which change colors like a mood ring, are a light hazel-gray color right now. I know that means I'm afraid. In fact, I'm terrified.

Amelia will freak out if I leave her. After all my promises, half a day goes by and I will disappear like all the other adults in her life.

I'll call Shay. If she refuses to come back, I'll tell the police to pick her up in Atlanta. She's the felon here. I'm not my sister's keeper. I'm just her sister. Or Mickey Teardash can come back. He's not covering the convention. He just went down there to be at the Democratic-party party with my sister the party girl.

Boola, boola.

I fix my hair, blot my face with a damp hand towel and use the cosmetics I leave on the sink for crash-makeup campaigns.

Then the doorbell rings.

"Hello, Lieutenant."

He is wearing vanilla-colored linen slacks, another madras sport shirt and white loafers with no socks. In one hand he is swinging Shay's Big Brown Bag stuffed with messy, badly wrinkled papers.

"Always wanted to see the inside of one of these houses," he claims, looking around as he follows me into the kitchen. "It's a great block. Great-looking houses. And that's your little . . . granddaughter?"

I don't correct him.

It feels sweet to be mistaken for a grandmother, as if that makes me a nice person by definition. Shay told me Jackie Onassis was ecstatic about becoming a grandmother this summer. Ellen Gilchrist on NPR is always raving about her grandchildren. Ditto Lena Horne, who lives a few blocks away, on Connecticut Avenue. Grandmotherhood is definitely an identity a woman can wrap around herself like a shawl to keep warm.

"Would you like some iced coffee? Or tea?"

"Iced coffee'd be great," he says, sitting down at the table.

Amelia continues working on the silverware.

I fill a large glass with ice and pour this morning's coffee over it. My hands are quivering.

I know I've got to get a grip on myself. All I have to do is tell the truth and I'm home free. So why am I freaking out? Why do I feel as if I'm in free-fall?

It is clear Lieutenant Bo Culver has come to arrest me.

Me! I am just like poor Sherman McCoy. I did not mean to do anything wrong, to go astray. I did not *mean* to break the law. I do not want to get arrested.

"Where'd you find my car?" I ask in a chatty voice.

"Badly parked on MacArthur Boulevard. Squad car noticed it this A.M. and called in the license number. I went over to check it out. With my partner. It was my partner collected all these papers thrown around the backseat."

He accepts the glass of iced coffee from me and helps himself to three heaping spoonfuls of sugar. Lieutenant Culver clearly has a sweet tooth. He is also probably a high-cholesterol man. He might possibly score in the top 200's or even low 300's.

"My partner . . . was sorta suspicious about those papers." He nods toward the bag parked near his feet. "For some reason he thought they were government property. Classified documents. So I said I'd check that out with you. Since we'd already talked. Which is why I came past."

"Came past" is a black Washington expression. I would have said "came over."

I sit down.

I am about to betray my sister. Turn her in. Let her be punished for all the crimes of the heart she's committed. And for all her sins of omission.

"What do you mean?" I ask.

"Which word you having trouble with?"

"What do you mean by . . . government property?"

"Whaddaya think that means?"

"Well, I don't know."

Amelia, sensing my nervousness, suddenly abandons her silverware job and wanders over to the table. Backing up, she wedges herself between my knees so she can keep the detective under surveillance.

Lieutenant Culver smiles down at her. In fact, he actually looks into her eyes, showing some capacity for relating to little people. This is a good sign. Amelia looks back at him with a great deal of solemnity and suspicion. Clearly she knows that men can disappear women just as adults know fascist South American governments can disappear leftists.

"I mean," I begin again, "how would *I* come in contact with government property?"

"Well, that's hard for *me* to say," Lieutenant Culver responds, returning his attention to me. His eyes, the color of apple butter, have hardened with determination. "Maybe some lawyer friend of yours left them in your car," he suggests. "Maybe even . . . your former brother-in-law, Barney Yellen?"

Cool out, I tell myself. Stay calm. Think. What would Shay do now? She'd probably opt for ambiguity. For space. For keeping her options open. And she wouldn't hesitate to dump on Barney.

"We've got a lot of lawyer friends," I say, rumpling Amelia's hair and tugging at her bangs to make them droop lower across her forehead.

The detective nods toward the Big Brown Bag again. "That stuff in there *is* sorta weird, though. Like . . . I guess you'd have to say they're Grade-A, VIP-type documents."

"I wanna ice cream cone," Amelia announces in a last-ditch effort to defuse the tension.

Detective Culver smiles down at her.

"I scream, you scream, we all scream for ice cream," he recites slowly. "Okay. Let's go get a treat. Out on the street. How 'bout that?" He smiles. "I'm-a-poet-but-I-just-don't-know-it."

Then he drains his coffee, tilting the glass so high on his face that it encloses his nose. When he's finished, he smiles. His smile has different levels of brightness, like a three-way bulb.

"I'll just leave the bag here for the time being."

I go to find my purse. My panic is blinking on and off like the digital clock on my coffeepot.

"Really. These are great houses," Lieutenant Culver says again after we're outside.

He walks along, nodding at the gingerbread house next door to mine, the old Tudor-looking castle beyond it and the Hänsel and Gretel cottage beside the old-fashioned apartment building on the corner. When we pass People's Park, Lieutenant Culver stops to survey some of the urban debris trapped in the chain link fence.

"Lookin' good," he comments with satisfaction. "Condoms all over the place. *Somebody*'s practicing safe sex." Then he glances down at his wristwatch. "I just went off duty. How 'bout I buy us a drink?"

At noon a newscaster had excitedly announced that this was the hottest day of the year to date. The temperature at twelve was 104 degrees. We maneuver through the heat and cross the jazzy intersection of Eighteenth and Columbia Road, skirting the jolly fat kiosk covered with layers—generations—of leftist fliers. This Adams-Morgan kiosk could compete with any in Managua as a kaleidoscope of local color, chaos and political enthusiasm.

The jarring juxtapositions on Eighteenth Street mirror my mood. The boomtown stores, feverishly renovated when the yuppies invaded the neighborhood, wear facades, like false smiles, to hide the sad, shabby truths lurking behind them. Their duplicity reflects my own. Our neighborhood McDonald's, squeezed inside a totally incongruous gingerbread Victorian building, is not like its swift suburban cousins. Here winos, bag ladies, beggars, down-and-outers, street psychos and latchkey kids stand in unruly lines waiting to be served by reluctant and surly counter attendants.

Walking beside this handsome black out-of-uniform cop, I feel dangerously conspicuous. Even in Adams-Morgan a white woman with a black man still causes some consternation. Neither the blacks nor the whites of D.C. are crazy about miscegenation. This is a racially sophisticated, but basically separatist, city.

"Fourteen Ethiopian restaurants on this block," Lieutenant Culver brags, squinting into the white-hot sunshine. "That's both sides of the street. *Fourteen!* You hungry?"

"No."

"Okay. Let's just have a drink at Café au Lait. But first we'll pick her up a cone."

Amelia's ice cream begins to melt as soon as we leave the Inside Scoop. Back on the sidewalk, I jog along beside her, trying to stem the flow and keep the drippings off her T-shirt. Some chocolate drops onto her beloved pink plastic jellies, which I know hurt her feet, and she stoops over to wipe them clean. The cone is still drooling as we take a sheltered table inside Café au Lait, away from the heat of the street.

Lieutenant Culver and I order beers.

I am nervous and unfocused. I am fearful Amelia will slip off the backless stool. Watching her breaks my concentration. The marble tabletop is covered with melted ice cream and flies are crash-diving toward the sweet drippings. Stickiness prevails.

From our table I can see the street. Suddenly I feel a new affinity with all the outsiders—all the immigrants walking aimlessly along the sidewalk, looking at wares in store windows that trifle with their desires. Because I am now on the wrong side of the law, I feel peril all around me. It is producing a panic that pounds inside my chest, pummeling my heart.

D.C. is a dangerous city, a toxic city. Hazardous waste products, dumped by both the federal and district governments, pollute the environment. Political corruption has corroded the administrative infrastructures so that everything reeks of rot. Rats run rampant through the alleys and children call them squirrels. Cars carrying Chicago-style mobsters pursue their targets in broad daylight. Drugs determine who will live and who will die.

"So? Tell me. You're still married to your original husband?"

"Yup," I nod.

"Wish I could say the same thing."

"How many?" I ask, knowing what he wants to tell me.

"Three marriages, two divorces, one separation. No kids, no property. I've got a learning disability. I'm sexually dyslexic."

I give a hoot.

He's funny, this guy. And nice, even though he doesn't seem to notice that Amelia is in danger of falling off her stool. Clearly one or all of his wives did some good groundwork on him. America's women are embarked upon a male reeducation project similar in intensity to Castro's literacy campaign in the backlands and mountains of Cuba.

"Didja know the second largest settlement of Salvadorans in the country lives here in Adams-Morgan?"

I nod amiably, indicating that I wasn't aware of the precise statistic, but that I could *feel* the truth of it. I am waiting for him to finish warming up. I am waiting for him to come at me.

It takes only another minute.

"Their kids are getting hooked on crack same as black kids. Since the street prices dropped, more of them can afford to try it. They get hooked fast. That damn shit is powerful. It's going to kill off our next generation. It's a"—he looks at me cautiously—"holocaust. A goddam holocaust."

I wet a paper napkin on the tip of my tongue and make a move to clean Amelia's face.

"Don't put shpit on me," Amelia protests urgently.

Lieutenant Culver erupts with laughter.

"She's smart," he roars. "Who wants someone else's smelly spit rubbed on their face? My mother used to do that to us kids all the time. Anyway, Ms. Myers, tell me how you got those papers. The whole story."

This is it.

Once again my mind begins flailing about. I don't know if I want to protect Shay or just tell the truth. I don't know if I should pretend to have no knowledge of the papers, and thus perjure myself, or if I should simply recite what I know. I decide to proffer a stripped-down version of the truth.

"Well, my sister was a houseguest out on Long Island and she somehow saw this testimony lying around in her host's study and I guess she just stuffed it in her purse or something. Being a journalist and all that."

Lieutenant Culver elevates his eyebrows in wonderment at my *chutzpah* and begins to look a little impatient.

I drink some beer.

"We're going to have to do better than that," he prompts. "We're not playing Twenty Questions."

I flush. "Well, lemme think. I don't know those people. He's a D.C. lawyer, I guess, but they have a summer place out on Long Island."

"Jerry Russo?" Lieutenant Culver asks. "Is it Jerry Russo?"

A furious blush scalds my face. "Yes, I think that's maybe right. Do you know him?"

"Yeah—Jerry Russo represents a lot of rich Hispanics here in D.C. and he's been involved in some very big and very shady deals. He works for a couple of the big contras who live here or float in and out of town. Guys like Cruz. In fact, I'm kinda excited that he had a copy of Hall's testimony at his place. I like that. It plugs him right into the network I've been tracking." Lieutenant Culver takes a few gulps of beer. "I'd like to talk to your sister."

"She's out of town until Friday."

"What about your husband?"

"He's gone until Friday too."

He is silent for several minutes.

"I was just appointed the Third Precinct drug czar," he says.

"That's my job now. Which gives me about as much power as the Channel Four weatherman—what's his name? I'm spending three quarters of my time tracking the different drug-importation routes into D.C. Anyway, I should probably go up to Long Island and have a little chat with Mr. Russo because I'm thinking he knows about some things I'm real interested in." He sighs and smiles. "If I'm talking too fast or if you don't understand something, Ms. Myers, just say so. Because it seems to me you might be in a sort of precarious position. Those papers name some of our local talent who'd be very upset if they knew you had them. I'm gonna make sure the guys patrolling your area keep an eye on your house. Just as a precaution. But I want you to stay alert to anything that feels suspicious to you."

I place my hand on Amelia's knee so she'll stop kicking the wrought-iron base of our table, which is wobbly enough without her assaulting it.

Lieutenant Culver strokes his beard thoughtfully. "We have a homicide a day now, as you probably know, and half the victims are kids. This damn city is out of control. It's a goddam zoo here at night. The drugs in Adams-Morgan are controlled by an organization of contra *jefes*. It's a Nicaraguan Cosa Nostra, and they run a tight ship. Real tight. They own some cops in this town and some politicians too. You hear what I'm saying?"

I nod.

"I get sick when I see those kids' corpses. I puke."

I nod again.

"All I've learned so far is just one thing. If there are drugs around, kids will use them. Now I got no kids of my own, but my first wife, Bernice, had a little boy I helped raise up. At least partway. But she found him dead three weeks ago with—excuse me—his penis cut off and stuffed in his mouth. His body was out on her back porch. I got there about twenty minutes later. Ronald'd gotten into a turf struggle with some dealers. So you see why I'm pissed off at the Feds and the DEA and the FBI and everyone else who's fucking up around here?"

I realize something important is happening, but Amelia has a hammerlock on my attention. I am fanning flies away from her face and watching so she doesn't lean back too far and tip over her stool. A fall from that height onto the cement floor would fracture her skull. In just three hours I have become a mother.

"Now the way I've got you people figured—"

"Who's 'you people'?" I echo him.

"You and your husband and your sister and all her husbands. I figure you for Sandinista fans, right? And you're pissed off because Ollie North and his crew have been funding the contras, right? You figure that a lot of drug dollars have been buying guns for the wrong team. Well, I don't have any problem with that. I suppose that's why your sister took the testimony in the first place. If you blow the whistle on North, you might blow the cover off the Columbia Road crew, and I'd like that a lot. But I'm only interested in this for drug reasons. That's all. I'm not interested in nailing Ronald Reagan or Ollie North or any of those jokers. I just want the guys who are importing the drugs into D.C. Anyway, at the moment, my interests correspond with yours. See, the contra crack-cocaine dealers operating on Columbia Road are being protected by some federal . . ."

Amelia begins to rock precariously atop her stool.

Lieutenant Culver reaches out to steady her. The fact that he moved faster than I did makes me like him enormously.

But now that I am fully informed about my situation, I realize how vulnerable I am. Finally all the vague anxieties that populate my mind are magically brought to life. Like suddenly animated statues, they assume attack positions and spring into action. Finally real men are plotting my demise, lurking in the dark, pursuing me like death itself.

Bo Culver finishes his beer, signals the waitress to bring over the check and hands her some dollar bills. Then he stands up, lifts Amelia down from her stool and smiles at me.

"Okay, let me walk you ladies back home."

"Oh, really," I protest, "you don't have to bother."

"You think I need a white grandmother bludgeoned to death in an alley eight blocks from my station house? You're wrong."

There is a small fissure in the heat outside. Maybe a possibility of rain. We walk slowly. Now Eighteenth Street doesn't seem as threatening as it did before. The stores look friendlier and less menacing now that I feel less felonious.

As we pass McDonald's, I see Hannah standing near the trash bin. From that receptacle, on a good day, Hannah can recover enough thrown-away food to fill her stomach. Spotting us, she begins waving vigorously.

"Oh," I say. "That's a client of mine over there. I want to go talk to her."

Still watching us, Hannah continues searching through the trash can with her twisted hands. When she finally recovers a Big Mac carton, she shakes it until one remaining piece of sandwich falls to the ground. Then she quickly bends over to reclaim the scrap from the sidewalk.

"Uh-oh, Auntie Nattie," Amelia says, watching this forbidden act with wide and anxious eyes.

We have a crisis.

"Hannah has ow-ows in her hands," I say as if that explains her eating off the dirty sidewalk.

"Bad. It's so bad today," Hannah says, chewing the morsel she's recovered.

Then Hannah turns and trudges off, back toward Kalorama Park.

Amelia watches her disappear before reaching out to take my hand.

"Hannah sick?" she asks me.

"No. She has to go someplace."

"Bag lady," Amelia hums happily. "Bag lady, bag lady."

"How do you know about a 'bag lady,' Amelia?" I ask her sharply.

"Shaysie told me."

Of course. Leave it to my sister.

At our front door, Lieutenant Culver puts his hand atop Amelia's head for a moment and ruffles her hair.

"Now you keep a sharp eye open," he says to me. "You got that card I gave you with my number? Anyway, here's another. You call me if anything seems out of the ordinary to you. Okay?"

He turns back toward the sidewalk.

"Hey! What about my car?"

He stops and turns around, laughing.

"Call the Motor Vehicle Department. They'll tell you where to pick it up. It's probably out on Bladensburg Road Northeast."

Then he's gone.

I park Amelia in front of the television set in the den and then I sit in the kitchen while I read the Fawn Hall document.

She's a ballsy little dame, Fawn. It sounds as if she views herself the way Shay does: outside and above the law. She doesn't sound particularly contrite and she certainly doesn't sound worried that her coke use might be a breach of government security. Having access to top-secret documents doesn't mean she can't date contras or do blow in Georgetown. Raked by my own outrage, I get Shay's hotel number from Atlanta information and then call her room. She answers in a husky, whiskey, having-sex kind of voice.

"Shay! The police found my car. They called right after you left. Everything was gone *except* the papers. They were spilled all over the backseat. Whoever stole the car couldn't have cared less about the papers; they just wanted your luggage and computer and shit."

A squelched silence.

"So then this detective came over here because he'd read the papers and was real interested in investigating the drug dealers Fawn Hall mentioned and also your friend Mr. Russo. Actually, he *guessed* you'd taken the papers from Jerry Russo. Anyway, he returned them to me and I just finished reading them. They're really wild, Shay. You've got to get this story out right away. Before the convention's over. They're *really* incriminating. You were right. This'll blow the Republicans right out of the water.

Bush can forget the whole thing. The Reagan administration has dirty hands up to the elbows. There's been a real big cover-up here, and it could cause a *big* splash."

Shay's voice sounds very distant. "Listen, Nat. Things have changed a little. Mickey and I've talked to some of Dukakis's top people and they're not interested in any explosive news stories coming out right now. The Duke wants to keep his campaign pretty neutral."

The *Duke?*

"He just wants to focus on his administrative ability. He wants to rest on his good-Massachusetts-government laurels. Nothing explosive. So I've decided to let the whole thing drop. At least for a while. I'll just hold on to it and wait for a better time."

"Shay! That's insane. There won't ever *be* a better time than right now."

"Listen, Nat, I've got to get ready to go back over to the Omni. Tom Hayden's having a book party for *Reunion.* Is Amelia doing okay?"

"Yes. But look, Shay. If you don't want to write the story, can Eli do it? He could use a boost like that right now. And, of course, he'd put a totally different slant on things. He'll—"

"No way, Nat. Just forget it. I mean it. Don't mess around. Now I've *got* to go. I'll call you tomorrow. Thanks a million. Ciao."

Ciao?

No one in North America has used that expression in the last twenty years. It's as passé as thin gold chains.

Shay's starting to slip a little.

1

Around eight o'clock that evening, while I am bathing Amelia in my bathroom, I hear the sound of glass shattering.

A scream flies up into my throat but I trap it there. It flutters inside my neck like a warm-breasted bird, pulsing vibrations toward my temples. As an older sister, I was trained to take charge, to trade fun for authority, to offer leadership during crises. Now my first concern is that Amelia not be frightened.

But what could have happened? Did a picture drop off a wall? A window fall shut and break? A burglar smash some pane to gain entry after dark?

I lock the bathroom door and find some empty plastic bottles beneath the sink to convert into toys for Amelia. When ten minutes pass without any further noise, I take her out of the tub, put on her shorty pajamas and lead her out into the hallway.

I am ready to sense the presence of an intruder in my home. But the house feels empty to me.

Safe.

We walk down the hallway and I kick open the door to my bedroom. That's when I first smell the smoke. The white muslin curtains on the windows beside my bed are burned. One panel hangs like a dehydrated tongue, scorched and blackened along the edges. Another has inexplicably been trimmed short and hemmed in brown lace. There are burn holes in three of my four curtains.

I do not understand.

How could my curtains catch on fire? What would make them burn?

"Auntie Nattie, I'm afraid," Amelia whimpers.

There are holes in the windowpanes.

There is broken glass on the sills.

There are also small hills of white powder on my carpet in the center of the room. I don't know what they are. Flour, sugar, salt? Cocaine? I don't understand how the powder got there when my carpet had been clean.

Amelia and I remain standing in the bedroom doorway as if seeking shelter during an earthquake. She slides the soft petals of her fingers into my hand. Then I feel them curl into a fearful fist of emotions.

"Everything's okay, honey," I lie.

Without thinking, I lift my eyes toward the ceiling. And that's when I see the holes. Three deep round holes in my clean white ceiling.

Suddenly I understand.

The piles of white powder on my carpet are plaster dust. Something smashed through my windows and set my curtains on fire. Someone shot *bullets* through my windows. They set the curtains on fire before smashing up into the ceiling, leaving behind charred fabric, broken glass and plaster dust on the carpet.

I press Amelia gently back into the hallway.

Alone I would be hysterical, but being responsible for Amelia keeps me calm. I take her down the back staircase to the kitchen. It is beginning to get dark but I don't turn on the lights. Instead I stand against the wall and dial information to get the number of the Third Precinct. Then I ask the switchboard operator for Lieutenant Culver before I remember he went off duty.

But he's there.

He answers his extension. I tell him about the bullet holes and he says he'll be right over. Then I sit down at the kitchen table and hold Amelia on my lap while I place a call to the Atlanta Omni. Eli isn't in his room; I leave a message for him to call me. I telephone Barney. He says he'll be right over. While we wait, I tell Amelia a story. I tell her "Snow White and Rose Red," the first fairy tale that floats into my head.

In less than ten minutes, Lieutenant Culver appears at my front door with a uniformed policeman. I unlock the safety bolt and they both come inside. Without speaking, Lieutenant Culver runs upstairs and I hear him walking around in my bedroom. After a while I hear the sounds of furniture being moved and then some pounding noises. When he comes back downstairs, he is holding two bullets, rolling them around like dice on the pale palm of his hand.

"What happened?" I ask.

"You were right. Someone fired into your bedroom with a semiautomatic."

The other policeman goes upstairs. Lieutenant Culver, Amelia and I remain standing in the hallway.

"But what's *happening*?" I persist.

"What's happening is that someone's mixed you up with your sister."

"He must be from Mars," I say obliquely so Amelia won't know I'm criticizing her grandmother.

"There's probably more than just *one* Martian," Lieutenant Culver says dryly. "I'll bet it was some of Jerry Russo's friends from Columbia Road. He must've told them Shay stole the Fawn Hall papers and they should shake her up a little."

"I don't think I can handle this," I say in a small, precise voice.

Lieutenant Culver gives me a strange look. It is sort of a blank look. No. A *black* look. It's to remind me what a sweet simple white life I've led up until now. It's a look that challenges me to get tough. But I resist being mau-maued. That's too retro. I am not responsible for the violence in the black community. I abhor violence. It is not my fault that D.C. has become a shooting gallery.

"This is really a wild thing Shay's done," I say, profoundly exasperated. "Those damn papers are going to get someone murdered."

Lieutenant Culver doesn't look all that happy about what's happening either. He looks like he would rather be doing something other than chasing criminals in a completely corrupt city. He looks like he'd rather be out in the countryside somewhere, maybe skimming along some sleek highway to a friend's farm in a four-wheel drive listening to his favorite tapes, not digging bullets out of some stranger's ceiling.

Turning around, he looks into the den.

"Where is it your husband went?"

"Atlanta."

"Your sister?"

"She's there too."

"Jesus Christ."

"They're both covering the Democratic Convention."

"Tell me about it," he complains. "I'm starting to think you and your sister are thick as thieves."

"Listen," I say. "Shay went down there with her boyfriend. Also her second husband's there. Not to worry."

"I'm not worried about your sister." His mouth slides into a half-smile. "Sounds like she knows how to take pretty good care of herself. You're the one I'm worried about."

"Oh, shit. Just what I needed." Now hysteria begins pinching me as it scales the ladder of my spine. "Why do you wanna think everybody in my family is doing everybody else? As far as I know, nobody's gotten laid around here in a long, long time."

At first I can't believe I said that. I am stunned. I have never said anything like that in my entire life. I feel like a puppet, as if someone else is pulling my strings, jerking my chain. I clutch Amelia's hand, hoping she hasn't caught on to anything I'm saying. I look sorrowfully at Lieutenant Culver.

"Well, okay. Let's start over," he suggests kindly.

"Not right now. First I have to put Amelia to bed."

Then I make another big mistake.

Bending over solicitously, I ask Amelia if she would like to sleep in the guest room near the kitchen where Shaysie sometimes sleeps.

Never offer a child a choice.

My mistake leads into a lengthy negotiation, ending with my promising to read *The Five Hundred Hats of Bartholomew Cubbins*—the *War and Peace* of children's literature—to Amelia before she goes to sleep. By the time I bed her down, read the book and rejoin Lieutenant Culver in the den, I am exhausted.

"Look," he begins again. "I know it's hard to believe something like this, but you're in some big trouble here."

"Yeah?"

"Yeah."

"Well, what should I do?" I ask.

"You asking me what *I* think?"

"Yes."

"Okay. Take the little girl and get out of here. Go to a hotel or move into some friend's house. This place just became a practice range."

"You mean right now, tonight?"

"Well, by tomorrow morning. I can provide you with protection for the night. But I expect you'll be hearing from the complainant again. Real soon. He wants you to know you should keep your mouth shut. The truth is, you're probably going to bring a lot of rats out of their holes. That's good for the D.C.P.D., but not so hot for you."

Suddenly I feel compelled to say everything I'm feeling. I tell him how I feel misused, abused, manipulated. I tell him how vulnerable my family is, how unprepared we are to defend ourselves against armed criminals. I tell him that we're inexperienced and untrained. That we own no guns. That I've never even *touched* a gun. That we're different.

I don't say from whom.

He hears me, but he doesn't offer any real consolation. Indeed, he says rather gently that there's no way for him to avert what's going to come down upon me, that he can't guarantee my safety.

"Listen," he says, leaning against the arm of the sofa. "This shooting puts a lot of pressure on me because it puts you in a real precarious place. I've got to find whoever did it before he finds you again. And if it was Jerry Russo who sicced those guys on you, they'll be back. I can put some surveillance on you for a while, a couple days or so, but not forever. And these guys don't go away. That I can promise."

Now I become his confidante. His partner. He begins talking to me the way Eli does when he's on a story, strategizing aloud, using me as a sounding board. Men love to bounce their ideas off women. It empowers them to proceed. I go into automatic pilot and make confirmational nods and noises.

"Did Jerry Russo know Shay would be staying here?"

I shrug my ignorance.

"Well, who else knew about Fawn Hall's testimony? Your husband, your sister's two husbands . . ."

He pronounces "husbands" so it sounds like "has-beens."

"And her boyfriend," I say. "That's it. I think that's all."

"Well, someone wants to keep Shay quiet. It might even be someone from the White House. Someone who knows you all want to discredit Ollie North and hurt the administration. Or it could be one of the contra capitans. Or one of the dealers Fawn mentioned in her interview. Or the FBI or CIA or DEA. It could be a lot of folks. It could be *all* of them. Anyway, it's clear people think Shay's staying at your house. Or else they think *you're* Shay."

I shake my head at the irony. "Look, Lieutenant—"

"Call me Bo," he says. "Here's what probably happened.

Someone came over here to get the papers and couldn't get inside so they decided to put you on notice. Shooting up your windows was a warning for you to keep your mouth shut. To show they mean business." He sighs heavily. "Still, you're gonna need some protection. I'll leave my man here with you for the night. But that's clearly not a permanent solution."

"Listen," I say more to myself than to him. "I'm going to call Shay and tell her to get back up here. I said I'd be a baby-sitter, not a sitting duck. She got us into all this and now she doesn't even want to release the damn interview anymore."

"Why not?"

"Because it's no longer politically expedient," I say, sticking burrs of bitterness into my words. "*The Duke* wants to run on *competence,* not *ideology.*"

"Can't your husband do it?"

"I don't know. A few days ago he said he wasn't interested. He's sort of disillusioned, my husband. Actually, he's gotten kinda cynical. Politically, I mean."

"As long as it isn't personal," Bo mumbles.

I flush. This man puts a little English on everything he says, a spin that makes his words sound super-suggestive.

"Now *I* want to check out the house," he says, moving down the hallway to the kitchen.

I watch him walk away.

He's a come-on kind of guy.

He looks like the kind of man who prefers nooners to nocturnal sex. He looks like the kind of man who doesn't bother to rest his weight on his elbows or wait for his partner on the first go-round. He looks like the kind of guy who says exactly what he's doing right while he's doing it. He looks like the kind of guy who's done it in a sleeping bag and on a sandy beach without a blanket.

As for me, it suddenly seems I'm going to guest-star in a rerun of *Charlie's Angels.* Or better yet, *Mod Squad.* That was more my speed. My biggest problem at the moment is making myself believe that this kind of melodrama is real. I've got to reprogram myself to remember drug smuggling and semiautomatic weapons and cops and robbers are not just TV pap, but play on the big screen of real life as well.

A few minutes later Barney arrives. He gives me a quick hug, asks about Amelia and then runs upstairs to my bedroom. When he returns, he looks shaken.

"This is wild," he says, shaking his head in disbelief. "I think you and Amelia should come stay over at our place."

I say no so definitively that he looks insulted.

"Well, then, I'll stay here with you. That's probably better than waking Amelia up and moving her in the middle of the night."

"I'm too freaked out to leave right now," I explain apologetically. "But it'd be great if you stayed here."

Then, to distract him, I repeat Bo's theory about Jerry Russo's friends being responsible for the shooting.

When Bo returns to the den I introduce the two men and right away they start exchanging Jerry Russo stories.

"Natalie said you think Russo set this up," Barney begins. "He's a real lowlife, but I don't think he'd go this far, shooting up someone's house. He's a front man. I know he's totally corrupt, maybe ninety percent of his clients are illegal, but I don't think he'd do anything like this."

"Don't kid yourself," Bo counters. "He might not actually do it himself, but he wouldn't have any qualms about sending out someone else to do it. Don't forget, that interview could get him in a world of trouble. It was careless of him to leave it somewhere that it could get stolen. I don't know how he came into possession of it but it had to be illegally. He'd be in a lot of trouble if the government traced the document back to him."

"You know, the D.C. Bar Association started disbarment proceedings against Russo this spring for mismanagement of an estate he was handling," Barney says.

Bo begins making departure moves. "I'd like to hear about that. Can I give you a call sometime?"

"Sure."

"Barney's offered to spend the night with me," I tell Bo.

"Okay. Then I'll just have a squad car make periodic checks on the house. That should do it, with Mr. Yellen here inside."

But Bo doesn't look at me as he speaks and his voice has changed noticeably. I should have known. Bo is touchy. He doesn't like people going over his head or behind his back. He doesn't like it that I made my own arrangements. Now he probably thinks I was afraid to stay alone with a black cop all night. Now he's looking at me like I'm your basic White Woman, totally prejudiced, totally predictable. Totally fucked.

After Bo and the other policeman leave, I sit down with Barney in the den.

"What'd he say you should do?" Barney asks.

"He thinks I should leave town."

"I think he's right. It's dangerous for Amelia and you because those guys think Shay's here."

"Maybe I should take Amelia out to Marge's," I suggest.

"Well, I can't help out with her this week. I'm tied up with a big case that's finally coming to trial tomorrow. But why the hell can't Shay come back here and take care of her? Why do *you* have to do it? Too bad you can't just get a divorce from her like I did. End the misery."

I shrug. "Listen, Barney. Right before this happened I called Shay down in Atlanta, and she said she'd changed her mind about releasing the interview. She said the Dukakis people don't want any issues like that raised right now. They don't want any scandals; they don't even want any ideology. No nothing. Dukakis is planning a campaign based totally on his administrative competence in order to look like the logical successor to Reagan. So Shay jumped right on the bandwagon and promised to kill her own story. The one she was ready to kill for, right?"

"That's my girl," Barney says, shaking his head with *faux* pride. "What a turkey."

We look at each other for a while, each of us thinking about Shay. When Barney speaks again he sounds regretful.

"You know, this Fawn Hall cocaine story could hurt Ollie

North a lot. It could undermine his whole Boy Scout defense. Shay's a flake to drop it right now."

When we both begin to fade, I go upstairs to find some clean linens. After helping Barney make up the sofa bed, I go back to the guest room and crawl in beside Amelia. Then I lie wide-eyed in the darkness, thinking about the attack on my home. My rage at Shay grows exponentially as I envision what might have happened to Amelia and me; I sleep only intermittently throughout the night.

Barney has already left when Amelia and I get up the next morning. By eight-thirty we finish breakfast. Eli still hasn't called. I phone the Omni again; he's not in. I leave another message saying something urgent has come up. But I feel ill. Weak. Faint. I suspect I have stumbled upon evidence of adultery.

The ache I begin to feel about my marriage starts hovering somewhere around 9.5 on a scale of 10. It would hit 8.7 on an Olympics scoreboard and maybe 7.6 on the Richter. A mood ring would turn a serious blue; the Minnesota Multiphasic would register high levels of both depression and anxiety. If my discomfort were a movie star, it would have to be Bette Midler.

Finally I settle down enough to call the glazier company with the largest ad in the Yellow Pages. A dispatcher promises to send out repair people within two hours. At nine o'clock I telephone Shay. She answers the phone sluggishly.

"Shay, something's happened."

Pause.

"To Amelia?" There is panic in her voice.

"Oh, no. Sorry. Didn't mean to scare you like that. No, what happened is that after I talked to you last night I went upstairs to give Amelia a bath and while we were in the bathroom someone fired a gun through my bedroom windows."

"What? Are you kidding?"

"No."

"I can't believe it. Who did it? Why?"

"Well, Bo—Bo's the detective on our case—thinks Jerry Russo

told the drug dealers you took Fawn's interview and that you were staying here at my house. That's his theory. But Barney says Jerry would never do anything like that. He says you guys have known Georgia for years and that—"

"I can't believe this." Shay sounds desperate, wild. "Really, this is too much. I just can't believe it. Poor Amelia. Poor *you.*"

"So?" I prompt.

"I can't think what to do right this second," she says. "Give me a few minutes to talk to Mickey and I'll call you right back."

Five minutes later the phone rings.

"Okay," Shay says. "How about you taking Amelia and going out to the Hamptons?"

"Oh, great. So Jerry Russo can get a better bead on me? So he won't have to use one of those telephoto lenses to kill us? You're nuts, Shay."

"No. No. Listen. Mickey's got this huge house in East Hampton. Jerry Russo lives in *South*ampton. But that's not the point, Nat. They're looking for *me.* You'll be safe there. Anyway, here's the deal. Mickey wants to return the papers to Jerry. To stop all this craziness. To put an end to the whole thing. So he'll catch the first plane to New York and meet you out on Long Island. That way you and Amelia will be safe and you'll even get a half-assed vacation out of it. That asshole Christopher is down here traipsing around with absolutely nothing to do. Everything would have been okay if he'd just stayed home. Have you ever been to the Hamptons, Nat? You'll just love it out there. When I call you back with the directions, I'll tell you who all to phone while you're out there. You'll have a blast—and just remind me to reimburse you for the plane tickets."

"Yeah, fine," I say.

I'd say "fine" to anything right now because, frankly, I don't give a damn anymore.

"Anyway, let me just say hi to Amelia."

Amelia holds the receiver haphazardly against her cheek and listens listlessly to her grandmother. When I start to hear the dial tone drooling out of the receiver, I replace it in its cradle. Instantly it rings again. This time it's Bo Culver, checking up on us, asking how I feel.

"I'm a little shaky this morning," I say. "But I'm going to take Amelia and go up to the Hamptons this afternoon to meet my sister's . . . boyfriend, Mickey Teardash. I'm going to give him the papers so he can return them to Jerry Russo. He thinks he can make some kind of deal with Russo so they'll leave us alone."

"Are you sure that's what you want to do?" Bo asks.

"What do you mean?"

"Well, you'll be throwing away a big opportunity. All that political leverage you talked about at Café au Lait. Remember?"

"Bo, they're trying to kill us."

"Whose decision was it? To give back the interview, I mean."

Now I feel embarrassed because I let Shay get me into all this trouble in the first place and then let her decide how and when to end it. In fact, I'm too ashamed to admit the truth.

"We all decided," I lie. "It's obvious what we have to do. It's too dangerous any other way."

"Would you give me a chance to talk to Russo before you return the papers?"

"About what, Bo? Gee, I don't know. Mickey and Shay want us to get them back as fast as we can."

"Well, would you mind if I go up there with you? I can provide some security. A little show of force won't hurt your case with Russo at all."

"I'd like that more than I can tell you."

I mean what I say and he knows it.

So we end up flying to Islip on USAir at one o'clock that afternoon. Before we leave I oversee the replacement of my bedroom windows, pack for me and Amelia, roll and fold the Fawn Hall papers so that they fit like a lining on the bottom and up the sides of my big shoulder bag, and close up the house.

Eli doesn't call. He clearly did not get the messages I left late last night or first thing this morning. He clearly did not spend the

night in his own hotel room. In that closet of my consciousness
where my sense of Eli resides, there rages a firestorm of anger
and grief upon which I close the door.

Bo Culver picks us up in his own beat-up Pontiac to go to the
airport. I feel a lot more secure with him back in the picture. By
the time we've parked, shuttled to the terminal and checked in,
I realize what a weird combo we are: middle-aged black man and
white woman clearly not the parents of the little girl they have
in tow. But it's nice to be with Bo. Pretty soon I hardly notice
people noticing us. Pretty soon I stop wondering what they're
wondering.

From ten thousand feet, it is difficult to distinguish between
the highways and the dried-out riverbeds below, except that the
man-made scars are straighter. The Greenhouse Effect has laid a
yellow blanket over most of the farmland. The drought will have
killed off all the crops before August.

Amelia naps during the flight. I am too revved up to sleep.
Unaccustomed to the company of a child, I am exhausted just
from *being* with Amelia, even when we're not doing anything.
Recent events have turned me into an anxiety queen. I can't seem
to swallow my own saliva, much less food from the dry earth. I
seem to have given up both eating and sleeping.

With Amelia between us, Bo and I maintain our private
thoughts for a long while. Then I begin to wonder if he thinks
I'm rude for not taking this opportunity to get to know him. So
I ask him some questions and, with just a shade of impatience,
he tells me he was raised in D.C., went to Howard for a year,
joined the army, spent eighteen months in Vietnam, used the
G.I. Bill to get a degree at the University of Massachusetts and
then, after a year of law school at Georgetown University, joined
the D.C. police force.

That's that. When he changes the subject I know enough not
to press him for any more personal information.

"Here's my thinking on all this at the moment. However Russo
got that DEA document, it was illegal. It's stolen federal prop-

erty. Maybe he got it from some corrupt DEA agent, I don't know. But I figure he wanted it to use as some sort of shield in case any of his big contra clients got indicted. Then he could make a deal by threatening to show the DEA suppressed information about Fawn Hall to protect Colonel North. Or maybe he was going to use it to keep them from being indicted in the first place. Either way, it's been working like a charm, I can tell you that. You following me?"

I nod.

"It was illegal for him to have it, but it was really dangerous for him to let it get ripped off. Over at the precinct, word was that one of the Columbia Road coke capitans went up to the Hamptons to read Jerry Russo the riot act about getting so sloppy. That's one of the reasons I'm flying up here with you today. The guy they say went up, Pepe Alfonso, is a killer. Anyway, that heist your sister pulled off clearly shook up the contras. They don't like it that government papers naming their local distributors are floating around D.C. That's why they got trigger-happy at your house."

Bo rests his head against his seat back.

"Look," he begins again. "I'm figuring I can force Russo to call off his dogs. I'm going to tell him I've got enough evidence to bust him for possession of stolen government property. I'm going to tell him that unless his boys cut the crap, I'm going to let out the word that he's given some dealers' names to the news media. That could really jeopardize his practice," he chuckles. "And, if that doesn't work, I'm going to make him an offer he can't refuse. I'll tell him that I'm holding him personally responsible for your family's safety. The thing is, Nat, I think it would just be a damn shame to give those papers back to that lowlife. I mean, you'd still like to link North and Poindexter and the rest of those White House honchos to the contras, wouldn't you? And I'd still love you to blow their cover so I could get a crack at them."

He squints at me, waiting for my answer.

"I guess I'd still like to see it released," I say. "It hurts to watch Ollie North get away with everything he's done. But it's much more dangerous than I thought it was, Bo. I didn't know there was so much drug money involved. I suppose that's why Mickey Teardash is coming up here to return the papers. I don't think either you or I could change his plans now."

"Maybe, maybe not. But how'd you feel if I went to see Russo alone as soon as we get there? I'd treat my visit as completely independent from whatever Teardash sees as his mission."

I look out the window at the blue ocean below the clouds. Now I understand that Bo didn't volunteer to be my bodyguard. He has his own agenda; apparently everyone does except me. Bo wants the Fawn Hall interview released, come hell or high water. He's not along to protect me, he's here to pressure me into releasing the papers. He's going to do his own thing. He'll make Mickey crazy by acting on his own and undermining Mickey's efforts to cut a deal with Jerry Russo.

There're going to be some fireworks out on Long Island.

Bo has reserved a rental car at MacArthur Airport. Amelia is cranky. I have to half drag her along as we hunt through the Hertz parking lot. The leather strap of my shoulder bag has begun cutting into the flesh of my shoulder while the leather straps of my sandals sand the skin off the back of my heels. I am edgy. Amelia starts to cry and says she wants to go home, though I can't imagine where she means. I probe a little and finally determine that it's Christopher's house and housekeeper that she sees as home base. Poor little thing. I'd telephone Steven so she could talk to him except I don't want to alarm him about our situation. I won't call him until I can tell him everything's okay.

Bo drives us to East Hampton in a two-door Oldsmobile. Mickey's house, an astonishing late-nineteenth-century mansion set back from the beach, is near the Amagansett town line. I feel terribly conspicuous as we pull into the driveway. The neighboring houses are not close, but I am sure people are watching us as we walk up to the house. The key is beneath the welcome mat, just as Mickey had promised during our long directions-and-instructions telephone conversation.

An aura of romance, stored inside the closed beach house, wafts against me the minute the door swings open. The hallway has a faint sweet odor of old money and lost summers. There is a pale layer of sand dusting the floor. Through the living-room archway I can see that all the furnishings belong to the grand period in which the house was built. Everything is quietly expensive. A large antique armoire conceals the television so that it can't mar the mood set by the pale chintz-covered chaises and chairs. Sheer sun-bleached curtains follow the contours of the bay windows, veiling a wraparound porch furnished exclusively in wicker.

I am impressed despite myself.

Amelia is immediately infected with excitement. She runs through the living room, dining room, kitchen and then back along a side hallway to the front door. It is the emptiness that excites her. Vacant rooms. Unused furnishings. Absent people. She likes the place because it's empty; I like it because it's full of the past. I am moved by the magnitude of memories left behind by previous residents.

The kitchen smells slightly swampy. A glass salt shaker and sugar dispenser sitting on the handsome refectory table display kernels of white rice used to protect the contents from seashore dampness.

"Pretty nice place," Bo says, coming up behind me. "Shay's boyfriend's not hurting for money."

"No one ever said he was."

"Where's the oshum, Auntie Nattie?"

"I'll show you pretty soon, Amelia."

"I'm going to drive over to Southampton now," Bo says, studying the Hertz map. "I want to lay down some ground rules with Russo before Teardash talks to him."

I don't answer. I'm not sure Mickey Teardash is going to welcome Bo's assistance.

It feels strange invading this beach house with a man and a child who don't belong to me. But, instinctively, we adopt the attitudes and motions of a family. Bo brings in the luggage from the trunk before he leaves for Southampton. I find our swimsuits, our towels, our flip-flops. It is close to five o'clock and the sun is subsiding. Amelia and I follow a winding lane to the dunes and then splash through the sand down to the beach.

Amelia has never seen the ocean before. Stunned by her first view of the water and the sound of the surf, she takes my hand, shrinking back from the glare and the glory. The Atlantic is too much for her to process all at once. She has to stand still until she can acclimate herself.

Fiction writers often try to describe human emotions by equating them with elements or acts of nature. Using the language and idioms of the sea, they compare feelings of abandonment to damp desolate beaches. Today my loneliness is like a fog sneaking in to erase the beige beach properties clinging to the dunes. Feeling forsaken is like a beach-gray day that rinses the seashore, dissolving solid objects as easily as sand slipping through a sieve.

Jean Rhys wrote that she remembered the ocean pounding against the shores of her distant island homeland as sounding like doors opening and shutting. That's how I perceive the surf today—one ending after another, endings after endings that never stop happening.

"Okay, Amelia," I say as I spread out our blanket. "Sit down and I'll show you how to build a sand castle."

"But I want to go in the oshum."

"You can't, sweetie."

"Whyyyyyy, Auntie Nattie?"

"Because the water is . . . dirty."

"Auntie Nattie," she says in the preachy voice she uses to educate me, "I got a book—"

"The ocean's not like it used to be, Amelia. It's not the way it was in your book."

"But—"

"Somebody put some dirty things in the water, Amelia. When it's cleaned up, I'll take you in. Maybe next year."

"Next year," she whispers without comprehension. "But can I *look* at it, Auntie Nattie?"

Something squeezes my throat and makes tears shoot into my eyes. Never much of an environmentalist, I suddenly feel a poignant sense of ecological loss. Although I've always been more interested in the welfare of the people than the land, I now see they are not really separate. Like an invalid sinking back against a nest of pillows, I collapse upon the blanket.

Then I retreat into my obsession with Eli once again. I actually feel cozy cocooning inside this obsession, snuggling deep into my misery, transported by pain into another dimension. I obsess, therefore I am. The thought of another woman receiving Eli's sexual affection makes me cringe; I enjoy concentrating on that internal sensation. I shift between the beach and my melancholy mood with dreamy indifference.

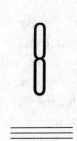

About half an hour later, I see Mickey Teardash appear atop the dune we'd just scaled and begin walking across the beach toward us.

The red sun ignites him like a bonfire.

Unexpectedly devilish expectation dances up inside me.

I watch him approach Amelia and hand her a package that contains a huge rubber beach ball. She shrieks with pleasure when he finally gets it blown up and bounces it toward her. Then, without speaking, he folds himself down beside me on our blanket. He is wearing neon green trunks, a striped T-shirt, orange rubber thongs and a carny barker's come-on grin.

Totally self-conscious in my snug blue maillot, I simultaneously begin to pull it higher up at the top and lower down around my thighs.

"How'd you get here so fast?" I ask.

"My Range Rover was here already, so I just took a helicopter from LaGuardia."

"How was Atlanta?"

"Crazy. Big party scene. Dukakis is looking pretty good. But now we've got this other problem," he says soberly. "Looks like Shay plopped us right down in the middle of a goddam drug war or something. I'm thinking maybe we should all just pack it in and go to the south of France for the rest of the summer. Whaddaya say? Or, more important, what do the police say?"

"They think we're in big trouble."

"Sounds like they're right."

"The detective who's on our case flew up here with us. A black guy. He's actually been acting like our bodyguard."

"That's good and bad news all rolled up together. Good that you got him and bad that you need him. Where is he?"

"He drove into town, but he'll come back to your place later. Do you think we should ask him to stay over?"

The slightest pause.

"Sure. Why not? Police protection right on the premises? We could use it."

He gives me a cocky smile, pulls off his T-shirt and flattens out beside me on the blanket.

It's as if we're in a bed.

Hmmmmmm, I think, surprised by a soft stirring in the central valley of my body.

Something has begun to excite me. I think this man is sexy simply because he's rich. Rich is a whole new dimension. Being near big money is exciting. Wealth might be the real Big Easy. Anyway, it puts an entirely new spin on things.

But guess what we talk about?

Shay.

Mickey apparently doesn't find it all that easy being Shay's lover. He sings a rhapsody of complaints. She is difficult, especially when she's working. Moody. Impulsive. Self-centered. Erratic. Impatient. Short-tempered. Her interests, obligations and preferences always come first. She is frequently thoughtless and totally impractical. She runs hot and cold. She is restless. No matter how busy their social life, she always craves more excitement. She is endlessly competitive, forever measuring herself against other high-profile women. She is sexually demanding and judgmental.

The list goes on and on.

Gently I suggest that Shay might not be the right companion for him.

"Well, it's not as if she's a member of the Baader-Meinhof," he laughs. "Maybe she's not your basic Jewish grandmother, but she's not really *all* that far out. She's not a Muslim fundamentalist or anything like that."

I think for a while and then I ask:

"Well, why are you with her?"

"I have an addictive personality."

"Come on," I chide. "That's too simple."

But I know how easy it is to get hooked on Shay. She's a hot ticket to any fantasy a person fancies. Still, on this issue there's no winning side for me, so I change the subject.

"Look, Mickey. I've been thinking about Shay dropping the Fawn Hall story and returning the papers to Russo. Maybe that's a mistake. Fawn Hall is the first really dramatic link between Ollie North and the contras, and there won't ever be a better time than right now to go public with it."

"Hey!" Mickey says, raising his head. "It's stupid to spend another minute discussing that interview. Shay was out of her mind to steal it. You see how she put everyone in jeopardy for no damn good reason? Having people shooting up your house wasn't a lot of fun, was it?"

"You should read that interview, though," I counter. "It's wild. These people have no respect for the law. Here they start an anti-drug frenzy in the country and then they spend their Saturday nights snorting blow in Georgetown toilets."

"I did read it, Natalie, and I still say, Who cares? I said the same thing Saturday afternoon in your kitchen. Who the fuck cares if someone else parties it up a little? I use coke. Everyone uses coke. It's no big fucking deal."

"But it's not about partying," I insist. "Bo says it's the contras who are bringing all the crack cocaine into D.C. They're bumping off the Nicaraguans with guns and the Americans with drugs. And Fawn Hall is the shortest, straightest line between the White House and the contras' cocaine scene. That bleached-blond space cadet is the *connection.*"

"What's with you, Natalie? Why can't you forget it? I happen to know this guy Russo, and he's not someone to mess around with."

"How well do you know him?"

"Well enough to know it'd be better for everyone concerned to forget this whole cockamamy caper you and your nutty sister dreamed up. As soon as we get back to the house I'm going to call him and ask if I can come over to see him. Then I'm going to tell him that Shay acted nuts and now she's sorry. I'm going to apologize. I'm going to eat shit. And then I'm going to promise we'll keep our mouths shut from here to eternity if he'll call off his thugs—assuming he's the one who sent them. Then I'm going to give him back the fucking interview and get the hell out of there. In other words, I'm going to try to save as many Karavans as I can and salvage the rest of the summer, if possible."

"Why should he trust you, Mickey? Why should he believe we won't talk about it later?"

"Because if the story gets out, he'll know we're responsible for it, and then we'll have to face the consequences. You've already gotten a little taste of that, haven't you? These drug guys don't monkey around. They're like any other businessmen when it comes to money and image. Hey!" he says irritably. "It's really not that complicated, you know?"

"But what if the D.C. dealers come after us anyway?"

"They won't if they have their damn interview back. Those papers are like an insurance policy for them. It's protection. You take away their protection and they get real upset. It's also got their names in it, for chrissake. They don't appreciate that kind of publicity, Natalie."

I get up then, angry that he won't really listen to what I'm saying, angry that he knows so much but feels so little. It's all so easy for him; this man wants peace, not justice. I walk slowly through the still-warm sand and lure Amelia into playing catch with me. After a while, Mickey joins us. Then we play running bases, with Amelia hurtling back and forth, trying not to be thrown out. At the end of the game, she collapses in a laughing heap upon the sand.

By the time we get back to the house, Bo is sitting on the front stairs of the porch. I introduce the men and toss Bo a cautionary look that he quietly absorbs. It is clear Bo and Mickey are on a collision course. Mickey wants an armistice while Bo still wants to win the war. Fresh from his first, still-secret engagement, Bo looks satisfied with himself.

We sit on the porch as the sun makes its glorious descent.

"Mind telling me your plan," Bo asks Mickey, "vis-à-vis Jerry Russo?"

"Sure." Mickey nods. "I know exactly what we should do."

Bo gives Mickey a "Who's we, white man?" look that Mickey misses completely.

"I'm going to phone him in a little while," Mickey says. "We've met socially out here over the years. Then I'm going to tell him I'm in possession of some property of his that I'd like very much to return to him tomorrow. No questions asked. Then, when I see him, I'm going to ask him to guarantee our safety in exchange for the papers. End of story. A gentleman's agreement."

"That simple, huh?" Bo stirs the high-backed rocking chair in which he chose to sit.

"That simple," Mickey confirms.

"And what do we get out of it?" Bo asks, putting a little twist on the word "we."

"We?" Mickey repeats, holding Bo's look. "We get some peace and quiet. We get some safety. We get out of the way of the fucking train that's about to run us over."

Bo is quiet. I lower my eyes, pretending to study the cover of a *New Yorker* parked on the wicker table beside my chair. Amelia runs inside, letting the door slam behind her.

"I wouldn't do that," Bo says, looking at Mickey.

"What? You wouldn't do *what?*"

"Trust him."

"Why not?"

"For the same reason you shouldn't get into a pissing contest with a skunk. Given the odds, you can't win. Even if he wants to keep his word, his buddies can decide to free-lance and go after you on their own."

"I'll work it out," Mickey grunts, rearranging himself into a rich kid's kind of sprawl on the glider. His body spreads out greedily, filling more space than it actually requires. "He wouldn't double-cross me. I know how to cut a deal."

"I don't think you're right," Bo says. "I've already gone to see him. I talked to him for more than an hour. I told him he'd better call off his pit bulls because even if he has protection from his Republican pals in the Justice Department, he's got no goddam protection from me. I also told him that if anyone hurt Natalie or her sister I would hold him personally responsible. That I would come and get him. Like this."

Bo puts an extended index finger next to an imaginary temple and makes the sound of a gunshot.

"You *what?*" Mickey groans. "You're out of your fucking mind. Who asked you to do a stupid thing like that? I wanted to give him those papers back and end this thing."

"Forget it," Bo repeats. "Russo said it was out of his hands. He said he couldn't stop the dealers from chasing you down while that DEA document was floating around out there."

"But wasn't he saying everything would be all right if he got his papers back?" Mickey asks.

"Maybe. But I told him I didn't know anything about that and it wasn't his property anyway."

"You've got a real intelligent friend here, Natalie." Mickey settles back into the glider again. "I had the whole fucking thing worked out and now he's gone and blown it for us."

"It'll be okay, Mickey," I say nervously. "I'm the one who should be scared, and I'm not sorry Bo did what he did. That interview is a powerful piece of evidence. It could blow the lid off Contragate and the whole drug scene in D.C. It's too important to trade away for some unguaranteed promise by a shyster lawyer that his thugs might leave us alone."

"Whatever," Mickey says disgustedly. "I'm out of it."

We sit silently in our seats watching the purple sky turn black, hearing night insects slapping against the screens, feeling mired in this impasse.

"Well, just forget about it for a while," Mickey finally says. "We'll see what happens tomorrow."

"Good idea," I say gratefully.

Mickey's on his feet, headed into the house, when suddenly he stops and turns around.

"Why don't you stay here while you're on the Island?" he asks Bo. "Plenty of room, as you can see."

"Well, thanks. That'd be very convenient. Nice of you to ask."

Later Mickey drives into town to buy pizzas for dinner. After we eat, I take Amelia upstairs to choose a bedroom. She selects a small stuffy dormer room with two prim twin beds and one little window. I try to persuade her to choose again, but she refuses. Then she starts begging me to stay with her until she falls asleep. I finally agree and, pulling off my dress, lie down in my bra and panties. Amelia is on her tummy in the next bed, her arms and legs stretched out like butterfly wings. She is watching me closely so I don't escape.

I close my eyes.

The sun is up before I am the next morning and Amelia is not in her bed. I hurtle down the stairs.

Mickey, wearing a woman's small white terry-cloth robe, is reading *The New York Times* at the kitchen table. Amelia is seated beside him wearing her lavender bathing suit inside out. When she sees me, she starts acting silly and begins picking

Cheerios, one at a time, out of her bowl, biting each one as if it's a doughnut.

I feel an enormous rush of relief that she's okay and that Mickey's been taking care of her.

"Good morning," Mickey says, smiling at my frantic arrival.

Since he's wearing boxer shorts, he takes off the robe and holds it open for me. I back into the arc of his arms, slip into the robe and tie it shut before turning around again.

"Good morning, Amelia," I say like a cheery Mary Tyler Moore, bending over to kiss the crown of her head. "Where's Bo?" I ask Mickey.

"Went to work," Mickey says, walking over to the counter. "Hunting and gathering again. What do you like in your coffee?"

"Bourbon."

He smiles. He likes that. He nods that I should sit down. He brings me a cup of black coffee.

Amelia watches us silently, expectantly. A little drop of milk trickles down her chin and falls into the scooped neckline of her "ba-ling" suit, as she calls it.

"Looks like a great beach day," Mickey predicts like a recreational director at the start of a luxury cruise.

I have been married long enough to be suspicious of good humor in the morning.

"The *Times* says the temperature of the ocean this year is the highest ever recorded. Right when swimming's been outlawed. Who says there isn't a God? Or that She doesn't know what She's doing?"

Uh-oh! He is clearly loaded for bear.

"What did you do last night?" I ask, tasting my coffee.

"Bo and I played Nintendo. And discussed Russo some more—"

"Let's go to the oshum," Amelia suggests sweetly, letting her spoon slide inside the bowl to a milky grave.

So we do.

Amelia makes friends with a little boy on a nearby blanket.

All I have to do is reoil her every few hours.

Mickey and I begin to get acquainted. He's been married twice and has three middle-sized children, two from his first wife, one from the second. He claims to have been politicized at Swarthmore ("Michael Dukakis's alma mater") during the early seventies and then socially traumatized by New York's nouvelle society during the roaring eighties. He claims to be a maverick, a renegade, a traitor to his class. From what I've read about him and seen in the last few days I can't imagine why he thinks so, but that's clearly the bottom line of his self-image.

We return home around one o'clock. Bo is still not back. Amelia eats lunch and naps until three-thirty. Then we drive to Southampton, park the Rover and walk along Main Street. By now I am so tanned I feel as if I've been cast in bronze. I am wearing old shorts and a faded T-shirt that assert I am an Amagansett economy-class person just popping wheelies among the wealthy for an afternoon.

Today the world looks like an acid trip to me, totally repainted in primary colors. The Southampton street scenes seem to have been sketched in broad chalky strokes, the sky and horizon with a bright blue marker. The sidewalks are filled with casual summer people. Too rich to care how they look, they are, nonetheless, perfectly tanned 10's, A-list lean and limber. They're feeling good, too, happy to exhibit their summer styles, their seasonal goodwill.

A few people toss quick glances in our direction, recognizing Mickey despite his claim of having long ago abdicated his place in their social scene. Regardless of how *he* feels, he is, of course, really one of them. Indeed, he's more than that. He's a hero of theirs, admired more for not playing strictly by the rules. He is the unorthodox, unconventional super-rich stud-scion of the Teardash family. Maybe a prodigal son, but still *their* prodigal son.

Walking beside him across this perfect stage set makes me feel like Cinderella. Amelia scoots ahead of us in spurts of excitement before stopping to wait until we catch up. Again and again we pause to study shop windows that offer whimsical togs and toys for the rich. People can vacation in this greater New York over-charge area confident its pricey stores will produce the extravagant luxuries they need.

The salt smell of the sea perfumes the atmosphere.

A dicey breeze ruffles well-coiffed hair.

The late-afternoon sun strokes flawless complexions.

My arm bumps against Mickey's as we walk. I am getting a contact high off him and his shadow—that open line of credit which he drags along behind him like the broken leash of a frisky puppy. In truth, Eli's rejection of me and my sense of sexual humiliation is turning me on to Mickey. Or maybe it's his wealth—which has the same allure as freedom.

My superego starts doing a Q-and-A with me.

Q. What are you thinking?

A. I'm not thinking; I'm just playing with matches.

Q. What are you going to do?

A. Probably act like a moth.

Q. Are you thinking about getting involved with your sister's main squeeze?

A. I'm *not* thinking; I'm just feeling that deliciously bloated sensation in the lowlands south of my tummy, which feels surprisingly taut. Everything's been so crazy I've actually begun losing weight.

I keep walking, but now I begin to think about Eli. He doesn't know where I am. This is probably the first time in two decades he doesn't know exactly where I am, who's with me and what I'm doing. Maybe he's been trying to find me. Maybe not. Maybe he's feeling that same unfastened, flimsy sensation I get when I think about him and wonder what he's doing and to whom he's doing it.

"I wish I'd brought my credit cards," I say, a touch of Shay in my voice. "I'd love to get my hair done."

"Here," says Mickey. "Try using dollars. They might still take them here. Amelia and I can go see that movie across the street there. The Steven Spielberg, *An American Tail.*"

"Really?" I ask, thoroughly delighted. "Okay. I'll pay you back."

He opens his wallet, extracts some bills and folds them inside my hand without looking.

I feel like David Stockman.

I've started stockpiling debts.

The downside of this beautiful buzz I've got going is knowing that I am purposefully fueling and fanning it. I am throwing dry kindling on a burning fire. I am compromising myself to the point that I'll have to come across if and when he sticks it to me. We have reached a steamy point in this day of teasing, where a refusal would constitute coitus interruptus.

In front of the theater I kiss Amelia good-bye and give Mickey a thumbs-up signal. Then I run back to Elizabeth Arden's. Once behind the Red Door, I open my fist to see three one-hundred-dollar bills. At first I feel a stab of alarm about how I'll repay it, but then a recklessness possesses me and I tell the receptionist I want the works. I have never done this before. If I'd ever thought about it, I would have rejected it on the premise I would feel too guilty spending money so frivolously. But now, having somehow suppressed my own moral objections, I simply turn myself in, surrender to the beauty technicians. I don't have to say anything. They take one look at me, wonder how long I've been on the loose and start to work.

The Fairy Godmother does her number on me.

Two and a half hours later, I pay the bill, leave ten-dollar tips for everyone and walk outside, immediately missing the familiar ribbons of hair that always danced on my neck. Instead I now have a slick Joan-of-Arc head, a close, tight, shining cap that takes years off my face and smudges my gender. It's interesting. I feel at once more boyish and more sexy. I'm on an androgynous roll.

Amelia is jumping up and down outside the movie theater. Thrilled by the film, she starts telling me about it. So does

Mickey. He says it's a Marxist film for babies. The two of them are tight from having seen it together.

"Great haircut," Mickey says. "Let's go shopping. I'll buy you a new dress for a total . . . whaddayacallit? Makeover?"

Translation: *So! There's someone home inside there, huh? Inter-est-ing. Maybe blood really is thicker than water. You're not exactly the spitting image of your sister, but you're sure coming on stronger now than you did before. Okay, so show me your stuff.*

"Well, we can look a little," I say.

Translation: *I might be up for a little fooling around.*

Unconsciously, I am trying to remember the plot of *Hannah and Her Sisters,* which I'd seen but now can't seem to remember. I know that somehow it relates to what's happening to me. Maybe it's because I've become part of another strange new trio. Saleswomen behind their counters comment quietly about us because Mickey Teardash is obviously much too *into* me to be my husband. But I don't care. I am Queen for a Day. Shopping with Mickey Teardash is like having sex. Every moment it's happening is outrageously exciting.

Implicit in his act of buying clothes for me is his right to remove them at, and for, his pleasure. Being outfitted by this man is a form of public foreplay. The saleswomen understand our silent sexual negotiations and treat me respectfully because clearly this man wants to stick it to me. At least he's giving it his best shot; this makes me one of the chosen.

Price, formerly an elemental component of shopping, is no longer a factor. There are no limits, restraints or curtailments. Anything—no, *everything*—is possible. This is recreational shopping. I let the saleswomen flatter me. It's like being licked, inside and out. These are totally different strokes—slow and steady.

Act natural, I tell myself, studying the clothes produced for our consideration in an elegant fitting room while a younger salesclerk entertains Amelia in the front of the store. Pretend you're Shay Karavan, I coach myself, looking over my shoulder to see *my* American tail in the three-way mirror. Now I have begun to resemble one of those mysterious models who lounge across expensive full-page magazine spreads, promoting designer jeans for postcoital wear. Ads for ids.

It's just like in the movies. I am a Before and an After. A *Mademoiselle* makeover. I am the ugly duckling suddenly transformed into a swan. I have a new body, new hair, new skin. Best of all, I have a new self-image. My new cap of hair caresses my head like the hand of my father, which used to descend from above to crown me with love when I least expected it.

I no longer feel docile, dumpy or depressed. No. This is your basic Hollywood fantasy and, for once, I have the starring role. I am on the top deck of the *Love Boat*. This is the American way. Beauty is but another frontier. Another fresh start. Another beginning.

I buy so many outfits I can't remember which ones I've chosen. I am making a ballsy statement. I am saying both to Mickey and myself, "Let's go crazy." What I realize halfway through the experience, right about the time Amelia begins to get fretful and overtired, is that in all the years I've been with Eli, I never asked (nor would have allowed) him to treat me to such an orgy of expenditure. I would never have wasted his salary in such an extravagant way.

But that, too, is another American tale.

Walking back through town with our bulky shopping bags and packages, we stop to buy ice cream cones. I feel great. I feel like I finally have a date for the prom with a BMOC. Driving home in Mickey's enormous beast of a Rover, dripping chocolate down the fronts of our shirts, we laugh and giggle, drunk on anticipation, excited about the silent promises we've exchanged, the banns we have published.

An hour later I am sitting on the porch watching the sunset. Amelia and Mickey are in the house somewhere and I am enjoying my solitude, feeling like a toasted marshmallow. My arms have turned a dark-rum color. My nose and cheeks tingle so that I feel like a bright, shining penny. I feel pretty. Pleasing. Pleased. I am lighter than I have been in years; I am able to feel the friendly protuberances of forgotten bones.

I actually experience a splash of resentment when I hear the screen door slam and Bo's footsteps on the porch. He is wearing an ivory-colored linen suit that makes him look professorial, even ambassadorial. The gray in his beard and hair blend with the beige of his suit.

"So?"

I smile at him, expecting a compliment, some low-key acknowledgment of how I look. But he just shakes his head.

"What?" I ask.

"Bad news."

"Wha-at?"

I start to stand up as if to deflect what's coming.

"Jerry Russo got shot this morning."

I sink back into the chair, my heart thundering.

Suddenly wet patches of sweat paste my clothes to my skin. My mouth feels parched. A dry but gummy substance has begun forming in the corners of my lips. My tongue feels swollen. It bats against the ridged roof of my mouth and sticks there momentarily before breaking away. It makes a *tac* sound as it comes loose.

Bo walks back to the side door and summons Mickey outside.

"What's the matter?" Mickey asks, looking back and forth between Bo and me. "What's wrong?"

"Jerry Russo got shot this morning. In his own driveway. While he was getting into his car. He's in the hospital. One bullet made only a flesh wound, but the other one shattered his elbow. The cops have no leads, no witnesses, no nothing."

"Jesus," Mickey whistles through his teeth. "Who do you think did it?"

"I think it was the same guys who were trying to find Shay. Alfonso and his crew. They're really pissed. Jerry was a fool to be so careless with those papers. I'm telling you, these guys don't fuck around. Alfonso doesn't give a damn if he shoots his own lawyer. These guys live in a different world."

Suddenly chilled, I hug my arms around myself.

"Do you think they know *we're* up here?" I ask.

"I don't know," Bo answers. "Those guys might still be wandering around. You better take Amelia and get off the Island. Go to your mother's in Minneapolis or something. Let's see if I can get you on a plane out of here tonight."

But in the next instant, as we hear a car pull up and park in front of the house, we lose our cool. I see the color drain out of Mickey's face. I see Bo reach for the gun in the holster under his jacket. He tells us to go inside before he walks toward the front of the porch.

From the window, we watch him talking to someone in a car. When he returns he's with two large, deeply tanned young men wearing summer business suits. He leads them into the side porch, where Mickey and I join them. The men are from the Southampton Police Department. They do not offer to shake hands. One of them gives me a perfunctory nod.

They ask Bo if he'd rather talk to them inside, meaning alone, but he shakes his head so the two men sit down next to each other in an antique wicker loveseat. I feel a dangerous urge to laugh at the Norman Rockwell aspect of two hefty cops jammed together in a fancy loveseat. Bo fills his usual rocking chair. Mickey and I sit side by side on the glider.

It is quickly apparent the men are going to play good cop/bad cop. Good Cop begins by saying they've been briefed by their captain about Bo's early-morning arrival at the Russo house. He says the captain appreciated Bo identifying himself. He says that now the captain wants Bo to sign a statement that reiterates his earlier explanation for being in the area the previous night and at the scene of the shooting this morning. The captain also wants Bo's badge number and the name of his superior officer.

"What exactly's the problem here?" Bo asks evenly.

Bad Cop leans forward. "No one in the Long Island P.D. can understand why a D.C. cop would be so interested in Jerry Russo. Or why that interest should happen to peak on the night before

the guy gets shot. We can't seem to get a straight answer from
your captain and we also think it's somewhat unusual that you
would arrive here in Southampton without the courtesy of a
phone call or any kind of advance notice. That's not our style."

"I didn't shoot that lowlife lawyer," Bo laughs. "I've got better
things to do with my time. I'm a cop, not a hit man."

Good Cop intervenes. "You're not a suspect, Lieutenant
Culver, but we need an explanation for your presence in Southampton. You understand that, of course. This is a little out of the
ordinary. Also, you may know something more about Russo than
we do. About the whole situation, in fact."

"That's probably true," Bo mutters.

Bad Cop loses his temper. His speech is crude. His tone is rude.
He is unimpressed by Bo's credentials. He treats him like some
lower form of life. Several times he points out that Bo's jurisdic-
tion does not extend to the State of New York.

I cannot, will not, look at Bo. I will not witness his humiliation.
In my nervousness I somehow launch the glider into motion.

"We don't wanna tie up your dinner hour," Good Cop says
with just an edge of impatience. "We just want you to sign this
statement explaining what brought you here. It's exactly what you
told the captain earlier today."

Suddenly Amelia flings open the French doors leading from the
sitting room. The squawk of television cartoon characters wafts
outside as she studies the unexpected strangers. Then she makes
a lunge for my lap as if catapulted from a missile launch pad.

"I explained my interest in Jerry Russo to Captain Bennett,"
Bo says. Beads of sweat have erupted on his forehead. His eyes
have dilated and seem to be protruding from the pressure of his
contained rage. "He certainly had no difficulty understanding
what I told him."

Good Cop: "You're quite right about that, Detective. But since
this morning, the commissioner appointed a special investigator
to take over this case. He's the one who wants the statement from
you."

"Well, you should know about some other D.C. folks who're

interested in Jerry Russo," Bo says. "By no means am I the only one. I already mentioned to Captain Bennett a possible DEA entanglement. But there's also a White House interest and a National Security Council interest and a CIA interest and an FBI interest. Lots of folks are interested in Jerry Russo apart from whoever shot him."

"Well, that's very reassuring," Good Cop says. "But at the moment we just want to take care of this one particular affidavit."

"Tell you what's pissing me off," Bo says flatly. "You guys see a cop on his own and decide to hit on him 'cause he looks easy, right? Well, get smart. Most of Russo's clients are illegit. Any one of them could have taken a hit at him. Or the government could have done it. You know who they use for problems like this one: indicted dealers or anyone else they got goods on. They offer 'em a deal. A convicted felon will do anything to get off doing time. So the federal government's got a private army of experienced killers at their disposal."

"Detective Culver, why don't you just read the statement and sign it for us, huh? So we can get the hell outta here?"

Bo reads the paper once, twice. Then, quietly, he signs his name.

The two men get up without saying good-bye and walk back through the porch and out the front door. The screen slams hard. The summer sound of a slamming screen suddenly takes on more ominous meanings.

Bo is frozen in his rocking chair. His rage is so raw he can't speak. Irrationally I feel responsible for the way the white men trashed him. Abjectly apologetic, I can't think of anything to say. It's hard for me to know if the cops gave Bo the business because he's black or because he's trespassing on their turf. Maybe only blacks can make such nice discriminations.

I clutch Amelia against my chest and rock back and forth. I feel sick. Sullied. Like I've done some despicable thing that I can't undo. Guilt is wrapping itself around me like a boa constrictor. My mind is darting about. A man has been shot because of my sister. I am ashamed that my sister has caused all this trouble. I am ashamed that my sister betrayed Georgia and Jerry Russo while staying in their home. I am sorry that she defiled the ancient role of a guest and made everybody's life uncertain and unsafe.

This is as close to the edge as I've ever been and it seems corny to me, phony, a low-budget episode of *Miami Vice* moved north into a false setting far from the pale pastel Art Deco hotels of lower Collins Avenue. It is easier to believe in fictive mayhem than in real violence when it occurs. It is easier to swallow television make-believe than the reality of two white cops bullying a black detective from D.C.

"Let's call Northwest Airlines and see when we can get you out of New York," Bo says.

We all walk into the kitchen.

The next three hours are a blur. I telephone Marge to say I'm bringing Amelia home for a short visit and that we'll reach Minneapolis at ten-thirty her time. She is so thrilled I feel guilty, and as soon as I begin packing I have an anxiety attack. Mickey hangs around trying to be helpful but his nearness sets off sporadic alarms throughout my system. Our all-day flirtation seems tacky now after hearing about Jerry Russo's shooting. There is even something sinister about our frivolity, in retrospect.

I carefully avoid being alone with him before we leave.

Bo struggles and finally gets me plane connections to Minneapolis. Then he locates a flight to D.C. for himself. Mickey decides to remain on Long Island. Bo drives us back to Islip's MacArthur Airport at an outrageously illegal speed. We barely speak. I am totally inhibited by the fact I saw the Southampton cops bully him. I can neither mention the good cop–bad cop episode nor forget it.

At the airport Bo helps me schlepp Amelia and our luggage into the small movie-set terminal. Inside the airport restaurant we order Diet Pepsis and Bo says he'll stay in touch with me, that I don't have to be frightened while I'm in Minneapolis, and that he'll let me know about any new developments. He waits while we board a prop plane to fly to Kennedy and is still standing at our departure gate when we take off.

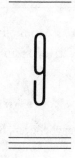

A melia sleeps throughout the flight to Minneapolis. I watch
the darkness outside the window, sorry I'm not able to see the
Mississippi slithering through Minneapolis on its journey south.
Last week I read in the *Post* that the river is at its lowest level
in 115 years of recorded history. Big barges have begun traveling
in convoys to provide assistance if one runs aground. Long-lost
ships have begun to emerge from the once-muddy Mississippi
riverbed. Hulks of hundred-year-old barges, ancient steamboats
and even skeletons of prehistoric animals have begun surfacing.
At Vicksburg, Mississippi, three Confederate steamers—the
Charm, the *Dot* and the *Paul Jones*—have staged a reappear-
ance.

Weird.

The craziness Shay has unleashed upon us is as strange as our
recent weather and its varied repercussions. Last week officials
announced that they had closed the Mississippi River—whatever
that means. Still, I believed they could do it. Why not? If we can
punch a hole in the ozone atmosphere three times the size of the

United States and as deep as Mount Everest is high, we should be able to stop a silly little river from running.

S N A P S H O T

That's the four of us. I'm maybe seven, Shay five. Our parents had taken us up to Bemidji, where we all jumped across the small natural spring that is the source of the Mississippi. That was a nice day. It had inherent drama. We grilled hot dogs and marshmallows in a picnic area near the river and played with some children eating at a nearby table. Afterward our two families organized a baseball game with real sandbags for the bases. When Shay hit a home run in the top of the ninth, Dad picked her up and triumphantly carried her on his shoulders back to the car. On the ride home to Minneapolis, I sat in the backseat beside my little sister, shivering from too much sun and not enough attention.

Minneapolis is to Washington as country girls are to their city cousins—simpler and shier but growing more feisty by the moment. Recently Minnesotans have begun to pay a lot of attention to the cultural quotient and quality of life their cities offer. In the upper Midwest, Minneapolis has always been the acknowledged homecoming queen, sitting alone in the first open convertible. Iowa and the Dakotas are only her attendants, crowded together in the next car, smiling and waving with runner-up resignation.

Marge is waiting at the gate for us, standing on tiptoe to see above the heads of people in front of her. Always introverted, at seventy-one she has embraced her senior years with a bear hug of relief. Tonight she is wearing a pink Polo golfing shirt tucked inside size-eight kelly-green culottes, neat white anklets, pink-and-white tennis shoes. Her hair, once thick and dark like Shay's, has turned gray and begun to thin.

Psychologically unable to press her way through a crowd, Marge waits for us to reach her. She embraces me quickly before kneeling to hug Amelia, clearly overjoyed to see the little girl for the first time since Easter. Amelia strains to manufacture some toddler mix of respect and affection, but then regresses into a bashful babyish mode.

"This was almost too sudden for me." Marge smiles, cupping Amelia's hand in her own. "A few hours' notice? I didn't have a bit of food in the house and the man still hasn't come to fix the air conditioner in the den. I didn't even have a chance to go out to buy any toys for Amelia. But we'll do that tomorrow."

Amelia flushes with pleasure but is still unable to look directly into Marge's face. Her eyelids flutter as if she is watching the sun.

We begin the now-familiar trek toward the baggage-claim area. What I would like to do is fall upon my mother and let my hot tears stain the front of her shirt like I used to do when I was little and aching from some insult Shay had inflicted upon me. Only Marge knows how Shay has shaped and shaded my life. Now I want to tell her that I feel bereft, that my marriage is a sad and useless thing, that my sister still abuses me in a million different ways, that I have been shot at and chased and uprooted and terrorized. I want her soft sympathy to enfold me like a baby blanket.

But these are selfish feelings because now my mother is needier than I. I am not yet forty-three and she is already past seventy. She misses Dad and has been hurt by Shay's neglect. She is the aging one, living a solitary life, with real health complaints. I have no right to crave sympathy from her. So I adopt a cheerful voice. By pretending to feel "on," I stay up.

I load all our luggage, including the suitcase I borrowed from Mickey to hold my Southampton loot, onto a baggage cart, which I then push to the underground garage. The thought of all my expensive and totally unnecessary new clothes makes me nervous; I will hide them from my mother. Without waiting to be asked, I slide into the driver's seat of Dad's last Cadillac and take the beltway that winds toward St. Louis Park. This highway skirts all the city lakes, where I spent most of my childhood.

PICTURE POSTCARD
MINNEAPOLIS:
THE CITY OF LAKES

This is an aerial view of Glenwood, Cedar, Calhoun, Lake of the Isles and Lake Harriet. From our house we could bike to all five of these lakes. Each was distinctly different. My favorite was Glenwood—the smallest and shabbiest lake of all. Along its shaggy shoreline, islands of lily pads floated atop the murky waters, attracting insects and algae. Even near the roped-off bathing area, clusters of weeds waved above the water. Below the twelve-foot diving platform, just beyond the dropoff, the surface of the water looked green instead of blue. On its narrow pebbly beach, people of different colors and classes mingled. This was what probably gave Glenwood its bad rep. When we were little, Marge told us that during the big Minneapolis polio epidemic, Glenwood was the first beach closed—as if its shabbiness spread germs, as if its multiracial swimmers were infectious.

Mom's apartment building is situated right off the highway on a preposterously thin slice of land alongside the exit ramp. It looks like a beached whale but it feels only like a tired hotel when we walk inside. There are long, long corridors filled with an infinity of slammed doors. It used to be that only a certain class of French women lived in this kind of isolation. Now their American counterparts do also. Instead of staying in shabby hotels, the lucky ones among America's forgotten women live in small, L-shaped apartments with bars on their windows.

Marge's apartment doesn't feel permanent. Maybe it's not. The furniture looks rented, which it isn't. My mother looks uncomfortable, which is not necessarily the case all the time. She moves around tentatively, using only a small portion of the available space because she's spent her life trying not to take up too much room, not to make any disturbance. It's easy to have everything you need when you no longer want much of anything.

She is trying to make her life come out even, like a piece of chocolate cake with a glass of milk.

"Now, Amelia, where shall I put your suitcase?" she asks as

seriously as if she were questioning an adult. "Would you like to share my room with me so Aunt Nattie can have the guest room to herself?"

This is a tough call for Amelia, but she finally accepts Marge's invitation, looking toward me for some acknowledgment of her bravery. I give her a wink and she smiles proudly. Now we are far from danger, back to basics again—room-and-board decisions, maintenance requirements, the planning of meals, the execution of domestic chores.

S N A P S H O T

This is a picture of Marge and me when I was about five. I am on roller skates and she is holding my hand so I won't roll away out of camera range. This picture tells much more than it shows— truths more real than factual. Marge lived her life in a land of fear and trembling. Anxiety stained every hour of her days and nights. Her fears for Shay and me were endless—babyhood diseases, child molesters, car accidents, academic troubles, popularity problems. I once heard Marge tell a friend of hers that she thought she could handle me, but knew she could never control Shay. Indeed, the real dangers were psychological, not physical. Each year, when we went on our summer fishing vacations to Brainerd, Minnesota, it became progressively obvious how different Shay and I were. I was Mama's Little Helper, Shay was Daddy's Little Girl. Because she got in trouble so often, Shay won the major share of our parents' attention, which turned her into a love junkie. What I learned was that it's *awful* to have to compete for love. When the competition became too keen, love didn't seem worth the trouble and I'd just drop out of the running.

After Mom puts Amelia to sleep, she returns to make us tea. Then we sit down at the table for our traditional catch-up talk. First Marge tells me I look great, remarking upon my weight loss, haircut and tan. I return the compliments and then ask about her friends. One by one. Each by name. She gives me a complete account of all recently diagnosed illnesses and deaths, and the psychological conditions of surviving spouses. Then she discusses her finances. In detail. Dollar by dollar. In the year since Dad died, Marge has learned a great deal about personal bookkeeping.

I ask about Yvonne. Marge is our point person for Yvonne, picking up the slack in this area by visiting her once a week. Although Yvonne is currently drug-free, no one yet feels confident about her chances for survival in the outside world.

"Hazelden's great," Marge says. "If Yvonne's got a chance, it's only because she's there."

"Do you think we should take Amelia to see her?"

"I don't know," Marge says doubtfully. "We should ask Steven. And Yvonne's doctor. Or her counselor."

"Well, I'll call Steven right now," I say.

"That's a good idea."

S N A P S H O T

This is Shay and Steven on his eighteenth birthday. I had stopped by their (Christopher's) house to drop off a gift, but Steven was on his way to the Georgetown post office to register for the draft. I knew he had had long serious talks, with both Barney and Eli, about possibly registering as a conscientious objector. Finally, however, not wanting to jeopardize his chances for admission to medical school, he decided to comply. In this picture, Steven, who looks like Tony Perkins, has his arm around Shay's waist. It is astonishing that the slim, young-looking woman beside him is actually his mother. Right after I snapped the camera, he gave us a nervous smile and waved good-bye. As he started down the front stairs, Shay opened her purse and ran after him with a five-dollar bill. "Honey, can you buy me a book of stamps as long as you'll be at the post office?" Really. My sister should have gotten the Mother of the Year Award for 1987.

I pick up the telephone and dial Steven's number.

"Hello?"

"Steven? It's Aunt Nattie."

"Where've you been? I've been calling your house for days.

And Christopher's and my dad's. I couldn't find anyone. Where're Shay and Amelia?"

"Amelia's here with me, Steve. In Minneapolis. Your mom asked me to keep her while she went to Atlanta for the convention. So I brought her out here to visit Marge."

"Aunt Nattie, what the hell is going on?" Steven wails. "I've gotta know where my daughter is. I know it's not *your* fault, but I can't believe the way my mother leaves Amelia all the time. With *anybody*. I don't mean *you*, Aunt Nattie, but I gotta know when someone takes her out of Washington!"

"Honey, I'm sorry. But, really, she's fine. She's been having a great time the last few days."

"Thanks, but . . . shit, what's Shay's problem?"

"You'll have to talk to her about that, Steven. It's certainly not a new one." Steven's anger at Shay has grown with the years. "So? How are your classes going?"

"Chemistry's a bitch." Steven's voice is becoming sulky, just as it did during his childhood. "I'm hanging in, though."

"What would you think about Granny and me taking Amelia to visit Yvonne?" I ask hesitantly.

"No way! I don't want her to see Yvonne in a hospital and I don't want Yvonne to see her. *At all.* No way, Aunt Nattie. *Please.*"

"Steven, calm down. Of course we won't do it if you don't want us to—that's why I called."

Silence.

"I can't believe this," he finally says wearily.

"Look, don't worry. We'll be back in place in Washington in a few days. Have you been able to watch any of the convention?"

"A little. Well, listen—say hello to Granny for me and I'll call Amelia tomorrow morning."

"Great. Good night, honey."

"So how's Steven sound to you?" Marge asks as soon as I've hung up the receiver. "When he called me last week he seemed very tired."

Translation: *Premed students are supposed to be exhausted.* This is actually a great diagnosis from a Jewish grandmother.

"He's working hard," I agree. "He'd never have been able to do this if he'd taken Amelia up there with him. She's a handful."

Marge shrugs. Medical school versus being a good parent is a tough call for a Jewish grandmother. But being a father at nineteen puts Steven in a special category.

"And how's Eli?"

Translation: *How's your marriage, or, in other words, your life? Are you doing all the things a wife should do to hold things together? Marriage is the center; are you making sure that your center will hold?*

"He's fine. Working too hard, as usual."

Translation: *He's bored stiff with me, Mom. We're coming to the end of our road together.*

"Can't he take some time off?"

Translation: *Can't you provide him with a home life that will keep him happy? Can't you be a helpmate to him in a way that would make you indispensable?*

I am giving her the same rote answers I always produce over the telephone, but Marge likes to see my face when I deliver my lines. Saying the same things about the same people in the same way for decades is an important part of our relationship. My recitation is reassuring to Marge. It makes her feel close to me. Of life's many mysteries, intimacy is the most profound one for her. But now she segues into her favorite subject, one so loaded with stress that she sometimes can't even initiate it.

"So. Have you seen much of Shay lately?"

Translation: *Has she been behaving herself?*

"Pretty often. She's been traveling a lot, but she and Amelia spent last weekend at our house."

"Oh really? Goodness. How nice."

Our mother smiles.

Our Demand-Feeding Mother of Eternal Forgiveness.

Our Mah-Jongg Champ of Confucian Confusion.

Our Hadassah Mother of Megacontradictions. Our Canasta

Club Player, Our Beth El Women's Auxiliary Vice President, Our Jewish Country Club Geisha, who tiptoes past the 19th Hole Men-Only Game Room so as not to disturb the male members playing cards, and who turns away so as not to see the combination when some lady opens her locker in the women's dressing room.

Although Marge still doesn't believe she spawned Shay, she is genuinely happy when her daughters spend time together. In her eyes, I offer Shay a legitimacy that no one else can bestow upon her.

"Is she . . . seeing anyone?"

Translation I: *Has she been sleeping around?*

Translation II: *How can she bear to be so intimate, so close, with so many different men, so many different . . . bodies?*

Now Marge dons the facial expression that means Shay's sex life makes her feel ill, dizzy, weak in the knees.

Where did Daddy and I go wrong? her eyes ask me.

What do people think of our family, of *me,* for having raised such a nonconformist, a person who observes none of our observances, who values none of our values? How did we raise such a promiscuous, totally unconventional, out-of-control hellion? What is going to become of her? From Marge's perspective Shay did *everything* wrong from the very beginning. Marge saw Shay's low birth weight as a preternatural prenatal act of defiance that set them at odds from Day One.

"No. Not anyone special," I say in a particular tone of voice.

Translation: *If she's sleeping around it isn't public knowledge.*

"Do you have any wine, Mom?"

"I think so."

In an instant she's up and rummaging around in Dad's old liquor cabinet. Eventually she produces a bottle of Clos Robert Chardonnay and a corkscrew.

"That should be a good bottle," she says, which is what Dad would have said. "Do you want something to eat?"

"Nope."

"I don't think it's good to drink wine without eating something."

As soon as I lose a little weight I gain a lot of self-control because I don't want to lose my new "lightness of being." I've probably dropped five or six pounds in these last, long days. I'm feeling lean and much too good about myself to indulge in a midnight snack. Uncorking the bottle, I pour myself a glass of wine.

S N A P S H O T

This is the last picture I took of Dad before he died. He's standing in his leathery law office in front of his shelf of ivory Buddhas. We had just returned from a lunch during which he'd asked me so many questions about Shay I became furious. Back in his office, I continued to berate him for having focused on Shay, almost exclusively, during our teenage years. He defended his behavior, his struggle to contain her wildness. I said that he encouraged her acting out by paying so much attention to it. I said that by letting Shay sub for Marge at various country-club events, by entering the mixed-doubles tournament with his daughter rather than his wife, he'd inflated Shay's sense of importance. I said, "Dad, you played *a lot* of mixed doubles together. Too much!" Then he came over, put his arm around my shoulders and pressed my head against his chest.

"And how's . . . poor Christopher?" Marge asks.

His name emerges haltingly from between her thin lips. It is a difficult name for Marge to muster because it sounds so much like *Christian*.

"He's doing better," I answer, deciding to change my testimony. "Actually, Shay *is* seeing someone. Someone sort of famous. Mickey Teardash. From the—"

"Teardash tobacco family? My goodness. That is a *very* rich family. It's maybe the richest Jewish family in America." Marge seems to shrink a little at the contemplation of such great wealth. "I read somewhere that they own their own island off Greece. They bought it from the Greek government after the war."

Marge means the Second World War.

"Like Aristotle."

Marge means Aristotle as in Onassis, not Aristotle as in Plato.

"They are very rich," I agree.

"So? Does it look . . . serious?"

Marge has begun to flush a little. But this time it is not embarrassment that is coloring her face; it is excitement. I am shocked that Marge is so impressed. Although she always encouraged my stability, seriousness and sobriety, at this moment she seems charmed by Shay's *chutzpah,* by our *Fortune* 500 hunter successfully landing a millionaire. Suddenly it appears that Marge, my main ally in life, is like everyone else when it comes to the rich and famous. She's like my friend Angie, a serious political person who loves to hear stories about Shay's frantic antics and extravagant escapades.

But is it possible Marge has secretly been a Shay-supporter all along? Are all her condemnations of Shay's unconventional behavior really only a cover for her vicarious pride in Shay's outrageous deeds? Is Mom secretly getting off on Shay's love affair and possible merger into the Teardash family? Doesn't Mom, like everyone else, love a winner? And didn't I experience the same sort of thrill from being in Mickey Teardash's company?

Who am I kidding?

Still, this hurts. Marge seems to have shifted her emotional shekels from me to Shay. Perhaps my mother believes that if Shay's sins are grand enough, sufficiently grandiose, they are more acceptable. Suddenly it seems that the thrill-seeking daughter is more interesting to the mother than the daughter she made in her own image.

Like mother, like daughter.

Maybe Marge and I are both boring.

Feeling a soft flutter of panic in my throat, I refill the goblet.

Is this the same Marge Karavan I've always known? Is this Marge Karavan the same consummate consumer who carried carefully scissored discount coupons to the supermarket and asked the meat department for special cuts of lamb and veal? Is this the woman who would never wear brown with navy or silver with gold, who would never don white heels before Memorial Day or be caught dead in them after Labor Day weekend? Is this the woman who'd never appear in public without an "important piece of jewelry" and who carried colorless nail polish in her purse to stop runs in her nylons?

Is this my mother?

Is this the woman who decorated our shower curtain rod with fragile undies every night before she went to bed and who rinsed out new hose *before* wearing them? Is this the same Marge Karavan whose leather belts matched her leather shoes, which matched her leather purses, which she changed to match each different outfit? Is this the woman who never let her orange Pan-Cake makeup cake around her nose and who never rubbed her upper and lower lips together after applying lipstick because she knew their shapes were different? Is this the same woman who sent out thank-you notes for get-well cards, who never tried out a new recipe on company or wore brand-new shoes on an important occasion? Is this the same woman who safety-pinned Dad's socks together before putting them in the washing machine and who'd never put a bra in the dryer?

Had I been bamboozled, brainwashed and programmed into believing that good was better than bad just so I'd clean up after Shay, mop up her messes, just like I'd hung up the clothes she left drooling off the chair in our bedroom for nearly twenty years? And if Shay *wasn't* the wicked sister, did that mean I'd been an altruistic asshole all my life?

Marge stands up, walks around the table for no practical reason, returns to her chair and sits down again. She's clearly winding herself up to say something.

"Nat, I've always meant to ask if you'd ever discussed your

. . . problem . . . your condition, with a specialist," she says quietly.

I have now finished my second glass of wine.

"My problem?" I echo, filling the glass again at a measured pace so as not to attract her attention. "Wouldn't you like a little sip of wine, Mom?"

"No, not really. Well," she says, flushing, "your problem of being . . . sterile."

I am beginning to feel the same sense of disbelief I experienced when I saw the burned curtains in my bedroom.

"Whaddaya talking about, Mom?"

Never before, not once, has Marge ever even alluded to the fact I have no children. Silence on this subject was par for the course since anything even distantly related to sex is a taboo topic for her. But now there is an expression on her face which announces that, after twenty-some years, she has learned about my abortion and the perforation of my uterus that sterilized me.

My blood starts going crazy. Rushing through narrowed arteries like large lumbering trucks inside the Holland Tunnel, it is leaping and roaring toward my brain.

S N A P S H O T

That's Shay and me standing beside the 1964 Ford Fairlane Dad bought us for commuting to the U. of M. Whenever I remember those distant days, I am seized by ancient spasms of alienation. Every afternoon I would wait for Shay in the student union and watch the smooth Scandinavian coeds come gliding in from the cold. With snowflakes clinging to their lashes and the mouton-trimmed collars of their storm coats, they would pause in the entranceway, full of charming expectation, as they searched the vast open lounge for signs of their mates. Then, singly or in pairs, the girls who let their straight blond hair rest like royal mantles upon their shoulders would approach the terrace, where a herd of tall, muscular young men from St. Paul or White Bear Lake huddled together like burly sheep in their darker-colored storm coats. There they would all come together and I would quicken and stiffen with a sweet-sour jealousy as the crowd shifted into couples and disappeared, strolling down toward the riverbanks to reclaim their snowcapped convertibles from newly plowed parking lots.

"You *know*," Marge insists. "What happened because of that . . . abortion."

"What did Shay tell you, Mom?" I ask in a pseudo-patient voice. "I mean, when did you two discuss this?"

"Let me see. Maybe a month or so ago."

"How in the hell did it come up? I mean, that was twenty-one years ago. What reason was there to bring it up? I mean, *why* do you think she told you, Ma? Don't you see she told you to put me *down* and stir you *up*?"

Marge looks thoughtful. "Well, I guess she knew that I've always wondered why you and Eli didn't have any children. I suppose she wanted me to understand you *would* have, if you *could* have."

"Mom, can't you see she was only trying to make me look bad? Make you feel bad *for* me and *about* me?"

Marge smiles uncertainly.

Her sweet passivity is a red flag to me.

"Mom," I say, feeling the wine stir up old stubborn feelings, "what exactly did Shay tell you?"

Then I fold my arms on the table and lower my head into the dark secret cavern created by my bent elbows.

Oh, Mama, I never wanted you to know. I never wanted you to know I'd lost my virginity—voluntarily, eagerly—way back then. It's so hard to explain why I wanted to have sex, why I wanted to own that experience. But I'd felt deprived for so long, about so many things, sex seemed like a dazzling, sweet solution. I didn't know that a few minutes of confused pleasure would result in a situation that effectively took my past, my present and my future, crumpled them up like a sheet of typing paper and tossed them into a wastebasket. You might have expected Shay to need an abortion, but it would have killed you to know that I did. That's why I never had the heart to tell you. So then I could never explain what my barrenness had done to me, what it felt like never having children. You'd only have felt worse about it, knowing how it happened. But I've felt so bereaved all these years, so useless. Because the truth is that Shay—for all her wild and wicked ways—at least produced Steven, who's now produced beautiful little Amelia for you to love.

My Abortion
Act I

There is no photo from that day, only the memory of a moody winter afternoon in February 1967, when I emerged from the Department of Social Work to encounter a strong icy wind rising off the Mississippi River flats. Slicing between the buildings, the wind slashed along the open quad, creating a gale-strength force that tried to rip the notebooks from my arms and a windchill factor that burned my face. So I'd retreated into the basement of Folwell Hall, where I entered a garage that led into a labyrinth of tunnels beneath the University of Minnesota campus.

This subterranean chain of furnace-hot parking lots, filled with winter-dirty cars—bearing, beneath their fenders, chunks of blackened snow that melted throughout the day, covering the cement floor with filthy water—led to the Coffman Student Union. There stairs rose to the Terrace Cafeteria (controlled by medical students from the University Hospital across the street), where I stopped to have a cup of coffee before walking into the huge student lounge, where I always breasted my books in a spasm of self-consciousness.

That afternoon everyone I saw looked ridiculously safe and secure to me, immune to the panic and despair I was feeling. The abortion I was scheduled to have at six-thirty that evening consolidated all the fears that had evolved in my first twenty-one years of life. The countdown had started early that morning and accelerated all day long, until now, as I waited for Shay and Eli, my anxiety was pumping like a generator. Something horrendous was going to happen to my body. Something savage was about to happen to the most intimate part of me. I felt a panic similar to the one I'd suffered during my initial sexual encounter that had resulted in this pregnancy.

Combined with my physical anxieties was a brand-new terror about breaking the law. There I was, the nice girl, the dependable girl, the older sister, waiting to get her internal organs scraped out during an illegal operation. Not only did I fear an inadvertent slip of the knife, I also feared the police crashing into the place to arrest the doctor and me. Guilty demons were hurtling through my head and I could not bury the demons, stop the clamor, the vibrations, the anticipation. Wrong, wrong. Wrong. What would be the end result of this wrong? Who would claim me for punishment, for disciplinary action, for revenge?

But I proceeded with our plan because I was willing to die rather than live with this shame, the horror of an illegitimate pregnancy that I couldn't halt in any other way. Certainly Shay tried to comfort me during that long gray ride as Eli drove us to St. Paul, speeding away from the safe familiar campus while my heart scrambled around in my chest. I sat between them in the front seat, feeling the panicky pumping of all the organs locked inside the darkness of my body.

The sudden ring of Marge's telephone so startles me that my elbow jumps and knocks over my wineglass, pouring pink onto Marge's tablecloth. I lift the receiver while watching the blot spread across the cloth. Marge runs into the kitchen for a sponge.

"Nat? Did you get there okay? Is everything all right?"

"Yeah, Shay, everything's *great.*"

"I hope I didn't wake anybody up, but Mickey just telephoned to tell me Jerry was shot and you guys went to Minneapolis. I mean he called before, but I wasn't here. But, really, this is the worst thing that's ever happened to me in my entire life."

"In *your* life," I hiss. "You know, you're a pathological egomaniac, Shay. Somebody else gets shot and you scream you're wounded."

Standing up, I walk the length of the telephone cord into the hallway so Marge can't hear me.

"Oh, Nat, ple-ase. Mickey is just furious at me. Who's this crazy cop who keeps butting his nose into our business? Somebody is really jeopardizing my relationship with Mickey." She begins to cry. "You didn't tell Mother anything about any of this, did you, Nat? I don't want her to know."

"No. I haven't. Yet. But there definitely seems to be some sort of statute of limitations on secrets around here."

Shay suppresses her sobs for a moment as if she's digesting my comment. Then she begins crying even harder.

"Do . . . you . . . still . . . have . . . the . . . interview?"

"Yes."

"Oh, burn it, Nat. Ple-ase. Right away."

"What the hell good would that do? The people who want it won't know I burned it."

"*Natalie!* I'm trying to get us out of a lot of trouble. Do you want to get all of us gunned down in the street by some hoodlums?"

"You should have thought about that before. You didn't mind *me* taking the risk when you were doing it for the Duke."

But I don't know if she can hear anything I say because her sobs are so loud and harsh now.

"You've really outdone yourself this time, Shay. Why don't you call back later, after you get a grip on yourself? I can't hear a word you're saying."

I replace the receiver very quietly and return the telephone to the dining room. Marge is still rubbing at the wine stain on her white linen cloth.

"Gee, I'm sorry, Mom."

But instead of helping her, I walk into the living room and sit down in a turquoise armchair with a matching hassock.

My Abortion
Act II

The three of us had walked up an outside staircase to the second
floor of one of those muted, weathered-gray, two-family duplexes
that stud the Twin Cities. A young man admitted us into a barely
furnished flat. An examination table, complete with stirrups, was
set up in the kitchen. One bare bulb hung from the ceiling on
a long umbilical cord.

The man who admitted us was now joined by another medical
student wearing a not-too-clean white jacket. I heard some hurried first-names-only introductions. Then Shay and Eli went into
the front room to wait and I, burning with shame, removed my
pantyhose and lay down on the table. Following instructions, I
ignominiously spread my legs and hooked my heels into the stirrups.

"Scoot down," one of the students said.

Then they instructed me on how to administer gas to myself
through a mask that I kept over my mouth and nose. I used this
mask to cover my shame as well as my pain.

Again Marge interrupts me.

Having left the tablecloth soaking in the kitchen sink, she
insists on kissing me before she goes to bed. Meanwhile, my own
fatigue has evaporated completely. I am no longer tired. Instead,
I'm wired. I turn on the television set to watch some convention
coverage, scanning the crowd of political hacks and groupies and
junkies and scribes for a glimpse of my husband, whom I do not
see. Then I go hunt through the refrigerator, where I finally find
a bottle of Amstel Light, which had rolled to the rear of the
bottom shelf. This time when the telephone rings my heart
jumps, but at least I don't blow away my beer.

"Natalie?"

"Yes."

"It's Bo Culver. Sorry to be calling you so late. I called information there, in Minneapolis. Only one Karavan listed in the Twin Cities, so I knew it had to be your mother."

"Good detective work," I say wryly, even though I know he's just warming me up. Prepping me. "So? What's happening?"

"Your house got hit again a few hours ago. It was completely ransacked. Looks like Nagasaki. One of your neighbors called it in around ten o'clock tonight. I went right over."

"Oh, no." Dread begins playing kettledrums in my head. "What should I do, Bo? Should I come back? Oh, Bo. We've got to return those papers. I can't go on living like this. If they'd shoot their own lawyer, they'll kill me. Or Shay. Or someone. I want to give the interview back, Bo. Right away. Please. Can you arrange that?"

"Okay. Sure. I'll get in touch with Jerry. Or his wife. Or his doctor or the cops or someone. Don't worry. I'll get word to him first thing in the morning that we're ready to return the stuff. Maybe I'll call Mickey and see if he can go see Jerry and cut the same deal he wanted to make before."

"That's a good idea, Bo. Do that. Mickey can go to the hospital; he can ask Georgia to take him over there. It's the best way to do it, and I'll get the first plane out of here tomorrow morning. Maybe we can give them back to one of Jerry's people in D.C. Whaddaya think, Bo?"

"Sounds sensible. Doable."

"I'll leave Amelia here and be back in D.C. by noon tomorrow. There's a seven o'clock plane in the morning."

"Don't expect to stay at your own house, Nat."

"Oh, God. It's that bad?"

"Yeah. It is. Anyway, call me as soon as you get in tomorrow."

When the line clears, I dial the number of the Atlanta Omni, which I now know by memory. This time Eli picks up his extension.

"Eli! Where have you been? Why haven't you called me?"

"Did you call here? I didn't get any message."

"Oh, Eli, I started calling you Sunday night and I've called you at least a hundred times since then. I just stopped leaving messages. Didn't you even know I'd been trying to reach you?"

"Honey, I've been in and out a lot, but I never got a single message. And the phone never rang once while I was here."

"But, Eli, you were *never* there."

"Nat, this hotel's a zoo. The switchboard looks like a Christmas tree. You know how it gets during a national convention."

Silence, so he can hear his own words.

Of course I know how it gets during a national convention. This is the first one I've missed.

S N A P S H O T

Here's a picture of us on our way to a one-thousand-dollars-minimum Democratic donors' dinner dance at the 1972 Democratic National Convention in Miami. A friend of Eli's gave us some free tickets. That night I looked like someone I had always wanted to look like. Maybe Ali MacGraw, someone who wasn't me. That night I had looked glamorous in the way I know Eli admires. Over the years I'd noticed the kind of women *he* noticed, and since it was the absolutely thinnest moment of my life, I wore a shocking red-and-navy-blue-striped floor-length T-shirt evening dress I borrowed from Shay. You can see Eli standing beside me and looking down at me *very* appreciatively. That night he had the hots for me and I loved it. That night Eli looked like he wanted to get all over me. Is that any reason to remember that night? *You bet your ass it is.*

"Please, don't get all bent out of shape over nothing, Nat."

"I'm not bent out of shape, Eli. I'm just not very happy."

"Nat, believe me . . ."

He's too obsessed with establishing his innocence to hear what I'm saying.

"Listen, Eli. A lot's happened since we've been in touch."

"What do you mean?"

So I tell him about our bedroom windows and my going to the

Hamptons and Jerry Russo being shot and my coming to Minneapolis and our house being vandalized just a few hours ago. I tell him everything, but I also tell him nothing, because I don't factor my feelings into the narrative. There is just enough emotional content for him to realize I am in a very different place from when he last saw me.

I feel some sweet vindication as he slowly begins to react to my recitation of disasters. His shock is authentic. At least, I have the Pyrrhic victory of knowing he's not been with Shay, because everything I tell him extracts cries of surprise and distress. His ignorance is so real that it eliminates Shay as his possible companion down there—which I had never totally discounted. I never count Shay out of anything until it's absolutely over.

In his extreme upset, Eli begins to stutter slightly as he asks questions, trying to clarify the sequence in which things happened. The magnitude of the events I'm recounting dwarfs whatever he's been experiencing in his personal life down there in Atlanta.

There are some calamities even more compelling than adultery.

"Eli, I'm leaving Amelia here with Marge and flying back to D.C. first thing in the morning. I want to see the house and then I'm going to return those goddam papers to Jerry Russo's clients or whoever wants them. But I really want you to meet me there, Eli. I want you to leave Atlanta first thing in the morning and come home. I need you. I've never asked you to help me ever before in my life, but I want you to come home tomorrow, Eli. I mean it."

"Oh, Nat. What are you saying? How can I? I'll lose my job. They'll go crazy at the paper. I can't do that. This is the biggest story of the year, for chrissake. You know that."

"Come home, Eli. Someone is trying to kill me."

"Do you want to come down here, Nat? Would that help?"

I hang up.

The balance between Eli and me has shifted imperceptibly in my favor. I, at least, am defending what was once our life. He has effectively abandoned any responsibility for it. If our relationship is over, I, at least, pay it some tribute by defending it now. Eli's a double loser for not doing the same.

My Abortion
Act III

I was groggy when it was finally over. They told me I could get dressed and for a moment I didn't know what they meant. One of them pointed toward an apple-green wooden chair, where I had left my underpants and pantyhose. When I tried to sit up, both of them hurried to help me.

Then Shay was there.

"You don't need your pantyhose," she said, balling them up inside my panties and ramming them inside her coat pocket.

I slipped my bare feet inside my boots. The boots felt furry and soft but I knew they would rub against the backs of my ankles when I started to walk.

Eli paid one of the med students, who said to him, "Be more careful next time."

"I'm not . . ." Eli started to say, but then stopped.

Shay walked over to stand beside Eli and reassert her ownership. She didn't like errors about her status. I stood up and felt warm blood slide down my bare legs into my boots. It squished beneath my feet as I started toward the door. I was weak. Maybe I stumbled. Eli and Shay surrounded me. They helped me down the icy wooden staircase, which was vibrating in the wind.

Two years later, after Eli and I had been married awhile, we talked about that gray day in St. Paul. We didn't yet know that the abortion had ruined me so that we would never have any children together. We told each other our very different memories of that event and Eli said, "Isn't it odd that I was there?" What I said was "I think I was already in love with you." Then he put his arms around me and rocked us both back and forth, as if we were the child we didn't yet know we'd never have.

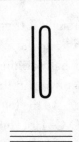

I fly back to D.C. first thing the next morning. Amelia gets hysterical when she understands I'm leaving her behind. Marge and I try to be reassuring, but eventually I simply must go downstairs and get into my taxi while Amelia continues shrieking "No, no, no" inside the apartment. I feel heartsick. Amelia must feel the way I did when Eli left for Atlanta. Not only left *behind,* but left *out.* It's a shitty way to feel.

As soon as I'm strapped into my airplane seat, inhaling the stale, stingy air, I check the Fawn Hall papers for the tenth time. The innermost pages lining my bag are still smooth, the outer ones crinkly and wrinkled from too much contact and handling. Because I've taken so much of the heat generated by these papers, I now feel that they rightfully belong to me, to do with as I want. *That* settles *that.*

During a winding ride home from the airport, in an un–air-conditioned taxi driven by an Iranian who understands English but prefers speaking Farsi, I realize that the leaves of the trees have begun to turn. The drought is triggering a premature change of color in July. *The middle of July.* Recently *The New York Times* predicted that if global warming continued at its present rate, palm trees would be growing in Rock Creek Park instead of pines. By 2050, D.C. could have the temperature profile of Dallas.

It is hot back here in D.C. Hot, humid and hazy.

When the taxi stops in front of my house, my pain revs up like a sports car zooming from 0 to 60 MPH in six seconds flat. I start to decompose. I am afraid to go inside. The damage to my home is an obvious symbol of my disintegrating marriage. Although my key to the front door won't work, it doesn't matter. The lock's been sprung.

Inside I feel as if I'm viewing my own funeral. My home has become a ghost house. Everything that wasn't nailed down has been moved, upended, torn apart, opened, turned, smashed or broken. There are papers strewn about everywhere on the floor: bills, checks, letters, envelopes, newspapers. Like a zombie, I walk slowly from room to room. The kitchen has sustained the most violent damage and, beyond its glass-brick wall, I can see that more of the shrubs and flowers in my garden have dried up and died as if nature were offering a sympathetic protest.

Only a Martian could miss this message.

It's coming in loud and clear.

Someone wants what I have in my purse. Bad.

I touch the papers like a talisman and then telephone Bo.

"I'm glad you're back," he says, magically appearing at my front door ten minutes later.

He surveys my face with affection, making me smile a little.

Then he comes inside, walking with his usual grab-ass pitch and street-smart roll. He looks as if he's lost a little weight; he's trimmer and even lighter on his feet than usual. I'm starting to like this guy so much. I think he can walk on water.

In the kitchen he methodically picks up all the chairs and

replaces them around the table. I start to make us coffee, ignoring the silverware strewn across the counters, the tipped apothecary jar full of flour, the chaos spewed out of junk drawers. Unwilling to confront the damage, I sit down beside Bo as if nothing's the matter.

Maybe I'm crying a bit by now, but I don't know for sure.

"Do you have the papers?" he says softly.

I nod.

"And you want to go through with this?"

"Yes," I say, my voice breaking.

"All right, champ. It's all set, then. Mickey went over to see Russo in the hospital this morning. With Georgia. He said Russo was plenty glad to guarantee your safety in exchange for getting the interview back. He kept saying Mickey was saving his life, that they would've killed him if he didn't recover those papers. So Russo's arranging for us to meet José Ocheros—Mr. George-town—tonight at that after-hours club of his, Ariel. Ocheros launders money for the contras through his club. I know Arturo Cruz's a member."

I don't respond.

Bo turns his chair around so he's facing me. "I'm not going to deny you've been catching it in the neck," he says with a tender smile. "But you've taken it like a real champ, Natalie Karavan Myers. My hat's off to you."

I grimace. "Thanks."

"I even freaked out when I saw this place last night."

I smile through my tears.

"I told Mickey what'd happened to your house when I talked to him last night and he freaked out too. Anyway, he was sup-posed to catch a plane and fly to D.C. right after his visit to the hospital. He's going to stay at the Washington Hilton and he thought you should get a room there too. You should, Natalie. You can't stay here."

"Yeah, I know," I murmur.

Complications . . .

I go to the telephone, get the number of the Hilton from information, call the hotel, make a reservation and leave a message for Mickey saying I'll call him when I check in. I feel ill as I go through this procedure. I can feel disaster stalking me. Flares have been going off and warning alarms ringing, ever since I left Minneapolis. The anxiety that's tracked me since the bullets shattered my bedroom windows is beginning to peak. Panic is in hot pursuit of my composure.

Next I call Marge to brief her on the condition of my house. I let her believe it was a random act of vandalism, but when I say I'll be staying at the Washington Hilton she realizes how much damage was done and she grows quiet. Then Amelia picks up another extension.

"Hi," she says.

"Hi, sweet Amelia. How are you, my love?"

"Good."

My heart is breaking. "Are you going to go swimming with Marge?"

"Yes," she says and then mumbles something.

"What, sweetheart?"

"Am I going home, Auntie Nattie?"

"When are you coming home? Real soon, baby. I'll tell Shaysie to call you up tomorrow, okay? I love you."

"I love you too," she answers.

I stare out through the smooth glass-brick wall and think about my family. My sister has finally ruined my life as completely as if she'd nuked me. She's won.

I'm homeless, unemployed and about to be divorced.

Bo gets up and pours us two cups of coffee. Then he motions me to sit down again, so I do.

"Listen," he says. "This is no time to zonk out on me, to start feeling sorry for yourself, Karavan. This thing isn't quite over yet."

Bo's clearly still hoping that we'll somehow blow the cover off the whole national-security establishment and its underground drug economy.

"You know, I still haven't gotten my car back, Bo. I have to go pick it up this afternoon; I really need it. But if you put me in your paddy wagon, I'll take you out for lunch. We can go over to Herb's."

He's surprised, but pleased. Very pleased.

I wash up in the powder room while Bo works on the front-door lock.

"It's only fixed temporarily," he says when I'm ready. "But it'll keep the drug users out, if not the pushers."

We get in his car and cruise down Columbia Road. The street is churning with people. After Minneapolis, Adams-Morgan looks like a Third World refugee camp. Most of the new residents have fled wars and revolutions in their homelands, so they bring a south-of-the-border battle fervor to the streets. Adams-Morgan has no stores like T. J. Maxx, Trak Auto, Color Tile, Mattress Discounters, K mart or Toys "Я" Us. There aren't any no-tell motels like HoJos or TraveLodges in Adams-Morgan.

Here there are only a few bed-and-breakfast guest houses on Mintwood Place and stores like Little John's Used Furniture, which sells junk to people who prefer it, Fasika's Ethiopian Restaurant, Horizontes Servicios Sociales Para Jóvenes, the Montego Bay Jamaican bakery, Miss Susan's Palm Reading Studio (where Shay once suggested we get "hand jobs"), the Aprendes Ingles School, with its hours posted on the door, and Bick's Books.

"That's where one of the dealers Fawn Hall mentioned operates out of," Bo says, pointing to a building beyond the Safeway. On the next block, he says, "That another one. We know some pushers live in there, but it has a hundred and fifty units and most of the tenants are Hispanics. We can never infiltrate there. Those people don't even mix with the Anglos, so they're really hard for . . . us."

By "us" he means black cops.

He drives up Seventeenth and then parks in front of the precinct station on V Street.

"I've got to pick something up," he says, taking his keys out of the ignition.

I roll down my window.

A white man, clearly a cop, comes out of the building. It's strange how I'm beginning to notice the whiteness of white people before anything else. Back in the Twin Cities they used to say that blackness "doesn't rub off," but it can certainly change your point of view. I've begun to see some things through Bo's eyes.

"Here comes my partner," Bo says uneasily, nodding toward the man approaching our car. "Chuck Connors."

Chuck Connors?

Chuck Connors inserts his head inside the car, invading my airspace. He's a white version of Bo, beefy and out of shape, but not as open or friendly. He's *very* white, in fact, as in: That's really *very white* of you.

"I bet this is the little lady who lost her Ford, am I right?"

I nod. He is busy psyching out the scene. Checking me out. Baiting Bo.

"Pretty lucky to get your car back, you know that? And how 'bout those papers? They looked real important to me. Bet you were glad to recover those, weren'tja? You must be a reporter or something, right?"

"Wrong," I say. "I'm a social worker."

How white of you to ask.

But he is not interested in what I do during the daytime. He's only interested in figuring out what's happening between Bo and me. What we're doing together. What's going on. Indeed, he's clearly enjoying the distress he's caused by discovering us together.

"I know your house got hit real hard," he says sympathetically, looking off into the middle distance. "Sorry 'bout that. We've got a pretty tense situation going on right now. I know Bo's briefed you on what's happening. But we're on the case, so not to worry. You're gonna get first-class police service."

I give him a grimace, a grin, a thumbs-up.

"Well, I won't keep you," he concludes in a hearty-hearty voice. "It's getting near lunchtime."

The mention of lunch is to let us know he suspects some

hanky-panky. Then he drums his hand on the roof of the car—
boom-boom-de-boom—and walks away.

"Nice guy," I say sarcastically.

"He thinks we're making it," Bo responds flatly. "He's gonna give me the business. He's not gonna let me forget it. Anyway . . . hang on a sec."

He gets out of the car and jogs into the red-brick building. Seconds later a cluster of black kids emerge from a neighboring apartment building and congregate in a circle on the sidewalk to stare at me, wondering how a white lady ended up in a squad car. When Bo returns, they scamper away. Downtown, Bo parks illegally at a bus stop right outside the entrance to Herb's.

Why not? It's his town.

It's only at night that he loses control of it.

Herb's is a George Raft kind of restaurant. The decor is late-night-movie 1940s. It's the quintessential cocktail lounge with an overlay of *Key Largo* atmosphere, a mixture of all kinds of romance distilled from corny paperback mysteries. There's even some off-Broadway ambiance created by photographs of local artists, actors, writers and musicians on the walls.

I can hear the buzz of social expectation as soon as we descend the stairs to the outdoor terrace. It's like the sound of a flashbulb or the sizzle of electricity. The hum of anticipation lasts until the new arrival is recognized or dismissed as being an unknown. An authentic celebrity always creates a ripple of motion, a breeze of silence. An anonymous interracial couple like us only qualifies for a quick once-over.

We sit in a booth. It is as safe as a crib, cool as an ice bucket. I feel special, pretty, as if there's a big satin ribbon wrapped around me. Bo is in a teasing mood. He orders us a carafe of wine and toasts Jerry Russo's health. My friend Herb comes over and makes a big fuss about my tan and my haircut, which mellows me. Then he sends over another carafe of wine that mellows me out even more.

Bo and I both order salads.

"When's your sister coming back?" Bo asks me.

"Don't know."

Translation: *Please don't remind me of my hump when I'm so happy.*

"You're foxy, you two."

"Whaddaya mean?"

"She's in Atlanta with your husband and you're checking into the Hilton with her . . . whaddayacallim? It's sorta crazy. Why didn't you go to Atlanta?"

The wine hits my body with a rush right at the same moment I feel a lazy tug on the invisible cord tying Bo and me together.

"My husband didn't invite me to go along this time."

Translation: *You don't have to be a detective to figure that one out.*

Bo lifts an eyebrow and helps himself to my butter.

"You having a little domestic fra-cas over there?" he asks in a droll voice, as if he's heard it all before, as if he can't be bothered.

"Maybe," I answer.

Translation: *I'm not so sure what I'd do if you came on to me, but I think you're really . . . neat.*

Now I'm on a slippery slope, sliding tentatively closer to this man. I am getting drunk. My words are becoming both more deliberate and more slurred around the edges. I have begun to unravel. Bo pretends not to notice, but he does smile and say no when our waitress asks if we need more wine.

Lunch is on Herb; we feel stroked. We walk back outside into the burning sunlight. From here it looks like downtown Washington is melting. The new glass buildings on N Street are shimmering in the sunlight, waves of hot air curling around them, liquefying and setting them in motion. The visual effect of this Greenhouse Summer is a halo that shimmies around objects, haunting them until nothing seems solid any longer.

Bo says Mickey and I should meet him at Ariel at nine. Then he folds himself back into his car and takes off. I get a taxi to the Motor Vehicle Department, which provides transportation to its various metropolitan car-storage lots. When I finally find my Ford, I'm told it can't be released until I cough up payment for three outstanding parking tickets—which have doubled in price. I charge these tickets to Eli's Visa card, knowing our marriage will probably expire before the card does.

Then I drive back home, pick up the luggage I brought back from Minneapolis and go to the Hilton. After I shower and change clothes, I ring Mickey's room and arrange to meet him in the lobby bar. He is waiting for me beside an old-style popcorn popping machine. He looks like a *GQ* model in his lean white linen slacks and a cream-colored crew-neck Polo sweater.

He kisses me lightly before we choose a table and sit down.

"You know we're all supposed to go to a club in Georgetown called Ariel for dinner tonight," I say. "Bo and you and me?"

"Yeah. I was there when Jerry set it up for us. But I didn't know your cop friend was coming along." Mickey speaks wearily. "I know you like him, Nat. I do too. He's a nice guy. But he really fucked up by going to Russo's house on his own that first afternoon. He blew me right out of the water with that one—and it might even be one of the reasons Jerry got shot. Georgia thinks someone saw Bo and Jerry together and got scared they were making a deal. Anyway, what bugs me is why Bo thinks everything that happens is being engineered from higher up by the contras."

"Because they're the ones bringing the drugs into D.C., Mickey. They're the ones responsible for what's happening to the blacks in the city."

"Yeah, yeah, I know, Nat. But I just want to stop the attacks on *us,* understand? You and me and Shay. And Amelia. Us *white* folks. Bo can't stop cocaine from coming into the United States, but he sure as hell could try to stop people from shooting through your windows and tearing your house apart. It's the local pushers who are ruining your life, not the kingpins in Guatemala or the drug lords in Colombia. Bo thinks those little guys are insignificant; that makes me think he's just on some big power trip and not taking care of the real business."

We talk and talk. We drink a lot of drinks. We don't agree on anything. It's almost six-thirty when Mickey signs the tab. We take the elevator, but when I step off on six, he also gets out and follows me to my door.

"What do you want?" I ask.

"You. It's all I've been thinking about. How decent you've been—running around the country, dragging Amelia everywhere, and always being so nice to everybody at the same time."

"Patsies are always nice," I remind him. "It's part of the Patsy Girl's Code of Honor."

I smile and turn to insert the plastic key card inside the door slot.

But he puts his hands on my shoulders and pivots me around so I'm facing him.

"What I really want to say is that I think you need a lover, Natalie. Someone to love you right now. When you need it. *A loaner.* I definitely think you need a loaner."

"Oh, great," I laugh.

A loaner.

At first I thought he was saying *loner.*

But no. That's what *I* am.

He's the *loaner.*

And why shouldn't I borrow him for a while? Who other than my sister's lover could offer me the opportunity to screw him, her and my husband all at the same time? To get behind enemy lines and do some real damage? Talk about a home run with the bases loaded. An emotional grand slam.

"I want to make you feel good about yourself, Natalie. At least better than you do right now. And since Eli's not around, I'm volunteering my services." He puts his arms around me and spreads confident hands across my back. "I want you to know how gorgeous you look. I want you to know how sexy you are. I want you to *feel* sexy."

I insert the key card and hear it click. Mickey follows me inside the room. I put my purse down on the bureau top and look at myself in the mirror.

"I've never done that before," I say. "Cheated on Eli."

"Really? Well, it's no big deal. It's no different than rotating your tires every year. It's good for the car."

He's done with the discussion.

He walks over and folds back the bedspread.

I call room service and order a bottle of white wine.

A minute afterward the telephone rings.

"Nat!" It's Eli. "I just called Minneapolis and Marge told me you were at the Washington Hilton. This is insane."

"I think so too."

"Are you all right? You must be ready to cave in. How bad's the house?"

"Awful, Eli," I say in a flat, uninflected voice that's as accusatory as any scream of outrage. "They knocked over everything. Half the breakable stuff is ruined. It's a mess. Your papers and books are all over the floor in your study. I'm just going to stay here at the Hilton until you get back. When're you coming home?"

"Tomorrow night. I've got the last plane out of here. I think it leaves at ten. I can get a tape of Dukakis's speech from the office."

Mickey walks over to where I'm standing and touches my face. I don't say anything for a few seconds. I feel my body beginning to remember how to respond. Then:

"Did you have to take the very *last* plane, Eli?"

"It was the only one I could get into National."

"Great," I say.

Mickey's hand drifts down the front of my blouse. He touches me with rude, probing fingers until my nipples stiffen. Then he flicks them back and forth with his fingertip.

That doesn't happen to be one of my things.

"What're you going to do about the papers?" Eli asks.

"I'm supposed to give them to some guy who owns a nightclub in Georgetown tonight."

"Who's going to be with you, Nat?"

"Don't worry about it, Eli."

He accepts that insult in silence.

Then he begins to ramble. He says he's been working very hard and that maybe we should take a little vacation together, get away for a while, so we can think things through. Blah, blah, blah.

"Hmmm," I answer.

Eli is audibly pained by my indifference.

"What's the matter? Is someone there?"

"No." I brush Mickey's hand away. "I just don't feel much like talking right now, Eli. Give me a call tomorrow, okay?"

And I hang up just as someone knocks on the door. Mickey admits the waiter, takes his tray, signs the bill and shows him out. Then he opens the wine bottle and fills the two goblets before sitting down on one of the beds.

I join him.

"He knows," Mickey says.

"Who?"

"Eli."

"Knows what?"

"That you're starting to pull back from him. Feel more independent."

"How do you know that?"

Translation: *You're absolutely right.*

"I could tell from what *you* said. I bet he suggested that you two should go away somewhere together. To talk."

"Well, he did," I admit reluctantly. "Actually, I feel sort of bad about everything. About . . . this."

I wave my hand vaguely to encompass the present situation.

"Well, don't. I knew you would. He's just responding now because you've begun distancing yourself. That's the only reason. What's happening here is *his* fault, so he'll just have to eat shit for a while." Mickey hands me a glass of wine and then lies back against the pillows. "Hey! He shouldn't've cut you off the way he did. I saw what he was doing to you last weekend when we stayed at your place. He was cold-cocking you. I don't know why, but he was. Anyway, he should've lightened up when your car got

ripped off and Shay stuck you with all that garbage of hers."
Mickey pauses to evaluate the effect of his words. "Well, *bube-leh?*" he prods. "Am I wrong?"

"*Bubeleh?*" I laugh, leaning back against the pillows.

What am I doing?

S N A P S H O T

There's Eli, dressed in his tuxedo, standing in the doorway of
the Shoreham ballroom with three other reporters who are also
covering Reagan's 1985 inaugural. Whoever took this picture
caught Eli at a perfect moment because he's displaying his secret
weapon—that magnetic smile which effortlessly sucks people
into his orbit. What's exciting about Eli's smile is that it momentarily cracks the abstracted, abstentious expression on his
face so the recipient feels as if he's just been voted into office
with 68 percent of the vote. Eli's smile extends credit and con-
fers value, makes the recipient grateful—as if he's being rushed
by a first-class fraternity on a Greek-dominated campus. It is
that momentary evaporation of Eli's reserve which is as thrilling
to me as the Stones on one of their comeback tours, tearing up
the stage while brandishing their guitars like huge sexual organs—public instruments of love.

Mickey and I start fooling around. I let him undress me in
stages while we're kissing. It's with relief I feel my tummy retract
as I flatten out. Some higher power clearly peeled those pounds
off me just in time for this encounter. But maybe I've been
anticipating this moment; it's hardly a hostile takeover. The fact
is I *want* to be subsumed, absorbed, recapitalized. I want to put
myself in fresh managerial hands. I have to accept that the old
jungle-fucks Eli and I once enjoyed are over and gone. Over and
out. I know there *has* to be a reorganization.

So I put my arms around Mickey, feeling the ripple of muscles
beneath the skin of his back. In these first early moments, I own
this man because his satisfaction resides within me; I own him
because I control the means of production.

Sex always offers possibilities—primarily the chance for some spontaneous combustion. That's the winning number in the lottery. It's possible Mickey could become chemically addicted to me, sexually dependent on my presence, so that he'd be compelled to keep me beside him to ensure his own future pleasure and satisfaction. It's happened before. Lots of times. Lots of women engage in sex like Christians casting their crumbs upon the water. Fucking is kissing the Blarney stone, knocking on wood, making a rice-paper rubbing of some religious relic, clutching a crystal for good health or good luck.

So I shut my eyes and do what I always do. Mickey is doing, I assume, what he always does. Actually he feels me up quite a bit, which is nice, since Eli doesn't bother with that much anymore. Revenge, of course, sweetens everything. The juxtaposition of love and hate always heightens the thrills of sex. Hateful love—like a whiskey priest, criminal lawyer, defensive weapon or peacekeeping missile—is an exotic concept that spices all sorts of different experiences.

"You see? It works just like it's supposed to," Mickey says, holding himself up for inspection.

"Why shouldn't it?"

"You're too sheltered," he complains. "In New York, maybe only one in five works. Or at least that's what I hear. Twenty percent."

So I look at the unfamiliar organ he's holding.

It could belong to a dinosaur.

It is primitive, primeval, prehistoric.

A blunt, unrefined, undefined part of human anatomy. It is large and red and ugly as sin.

Old as Man.

"Your Eli must be some hero," he says.

"I really don't want to talk about *him* right now."

"Sorry about that."

Then, like teenagers with two straws stuck in the same soda, we begin to keep company. Seek a rhythm. Find a beat. Work it out. At first I don't like the way he does it very much. I'm probably too used to Eli. Mickey is totally different. Everything feels somewhat strange and offbeat. It's all right, but not great. Just okay. This must be what methadone feels like after years of heroin. The craving's cut, but the high's not the same.

Then I realize:

This is just recreational sex.

This is like the recreational shopping we did in Southampton. It doesn't *mean* anything. It's like playing tennis or golf or going horseback riding on a dude ranch. You do it just to do it. You do it just to see how good it can make you feel. You do it to kill off a July afternoon when your life's falling apart and you're powerless to impede its collapse.

Mickey's in no hurry. He starts things and then drops them. The minute we get some real major mo going, he stops and sits up on the edge of the bed. He studies my body. I dig my nails into the palms of my hands to stifle an almost overwhelming impulse to cover myself. Next he gets up and refills our wine-glasses. He messes around with the radio until he finds some sixties-style music station. Then we just hang out for a while, sipping our wine.

"I guess I'm as different from Shay in bed as I am out of bed."

I hand him that remark as if it's a box of candy from which he must make his own selection.

"Oh, you know Shay," he answers lightly. "She gets carried away about everything."

"Sex too?"

"Yeah. Sure."

"Oh," I say, deeply wounded.

"Hey," he cajoles. "Now what's the matter?"

"It hurts my heart to hear you say that."

"Why?"

"I don't know. It sounds like she even has better sex than other people."

"Hey, I didn't say *that*. And don't sell yourself short, kiddo. You dig it plenty. You just have to play a little catch-up."

"What does she like?"

"Different things. Have you ever tried amyl nitrate?"

"No."

"Well, what are you waiting for? Your cardiologist to prescribe it?"

I laugh, although I'm not totally certain what he means, what people do with all their sex enhancers. My sister is part of a bevy of worldly women who know tricks to which I'm not privy. I don't even know why bidets are such a big deal. This is a bit embarrassing because I don't like to look primitive.

Anyway, I do what Mickey tells me to do when he tells me to do it, since he seems to be in active pursuit of my pleasure. Indeed, he is exclusively concerned with pleasure. Mine and his at the right time in the right way. Do I like *this* or do I like *that*? Do I like *this* better than *that*? Should he do *this* before he does *that*? After a while I'm so wired I can't tell the difference between doing this or doing that in any particular order.

But then he stops again, totally derailing me.

"I'm crazy about you, Nat. . . . Shay's an acrobat. You're more of a sensualist."

I can live with that.

As a show of appreciation, I get on top the next time.

"I knew you'd be fabulous," he says much later.

There is no sweeter report card than a good sexual one.

At the right moment, Mickey takes an amyl-nitrate inhaler from the pocket of his shirt and presses it beneath my nose. I inhale, and suddenly all erogenous sensations are taken to the max. I exist in a state of suspended excitation, an exquisite, seemingly eternal moment of stasis, before I experience a gorgeous explosion of nerve endings that touches off equally dizzying reverberations. I am dazzled and delighted by my own body, thrilled by Mickey and me. This is the kind of selfish pleasure that makes me feel wealthy. Affluent. Benevolent. Magnanimous.

A regular sexual philanthropist.

Often when a woman doesn't go to bed with a man she desires, she'll impulsively jump into the sack with the next guy who comes down the pike. It's a way of punishing herself for missing the real thing. By substituting a lesser experience, usually in the form of a more "appropriate" man, she expresses her own self-contempt and pays reparations to the gods for lost lust. Or lost love.

Mickey and I have a bedroom fight before he leaves. He starts bad-mouthing Bo again and I get angry. He says Bo's a loose cannon and there's no way to know how he'll perform once we're at Ariel. I object strenuously.

"You know, we don't even know for sure that Jerry got shot because of the Fawn Hall papers," Mickey says, using aggression to shore up his defensiveness. "Jerry Russo was knee-deep in a lot of illegal shit. He's got plenty of enemies who might have shot him. It's also possible he might not have gotten shot if Bo hadn't gone over there. Your house obviously got looted because those hoods were still looking for the fucking interview. We could have avoided both those events if I'd been allowed to proceed with *my* plan, if I had just returned the damn papers. But macho man had to hightail it over there to do his number. Shi-iit."

I reject this analysis. I get stubborn, angry. I tell Mickey he doesn't have to go with us, that I'll go alone with Bo. Then, rolling his eyes as if I'm nuts, Mickey leaves to dress for dinner. What should have been a creamy postcoital scene turned into a political pissing contest.

Of course I still take great pains to glamorize myself when I get dressed. Women are supposed to look good after they make out, as a compliment to their accomplice. So after I shower, I finally open the suitcase containing my loot from Southampton. I put on a white silk suit with a tropical-print blouse that cost almost as much as our monthly mortgage payments. Sexually speaking, having delivered the goods, I now feel entitled to some of the spoils—the bad goods.

I look fine on the outside, but inside my heart is banging around like an unlatched screen door in a thunderstorm. I can hardly look at Mickey when we go to retrieve my car from the garage. He drives and I sit beside him, feeling remorse and regret beginning to seep through my system.

Oooh! Why did I do it?

Why did I go to bed with him? And why am I now on my way to shake hands with the Devil again? Rolled up tight like a miniature poster in my evening bag are the famous Fawn Hall papers, ready to be returned. Suddenly I am acting totally out of character—with reckless speed and self-destructive relish.

Georgetown.

Ariel.

Valet parking. A velvety entrance into a large Art Deco space, elegantly decorated. A Republican aura of power-without-grace. Silky strokes from an elegant maître d', who leads us to our table. The crystal sounds of cultivated voices, mannered laughs, expensive foreign accents. Self-confident Clint Eastwood– and Khashoggi–type men are sitting at white-skirted tables with good-looking younger women in black sliplike dresses. Satin spaghetti straps drip down over their slim, sexy shoulders as they pose and posture, telling little jokes to provoke salty male laughter.

These women interest me. They are not like any of my friends or colleagues. These women are a different country—bunnies and bimbos still living off men, still using sex to survive, afraid or unable to upgrade, reeducate or retrain themselves. Shay should write an article about America's need for rehabilitation centers to retrofit and retrain capitalist geishas.

Bo arrives and joins us at our table. He's looking good, as usual, dressed in his vanilla suit, but there's a subdued air about him tonight. He shakes hands with Mickey. Smiles. Means it. Then he looks at me.

A long moment passes.

He *knows*.

He knows Mickey and I have become lovers.

He knows that after I left Herb's I went to the Hilton and made out like a bandit with my sister's lover.

Bo is hurt bad.

Kicked in the balls.

He sits down, starts to fidget with his cigarette lighter, adjusting the dial that regulates the height of the flame. He is trying to hide his confusion. He cannot look at me. He is shy, as if *he* and I had spent the afternoon making love to each other.

Maybe that's what should have happened.

Mickey eavesdrops on our silent conversation. Although he hasn't got a clue about our feelings, he's aware of a cosmic disturbance in our vicinity. Reverting to form, he summons the waiter and orders champagne. This at least provides us with the distraction of a wine ritual—the silver bucket, the napkin wrapped like a bunting around the waiter's arm, the expensive explosion of cork and the giggle of liquid into our glasses. We cleave to the ceremony, seeking recovery time.

I begin by just sipping my champagne, but soon speed up the tempo. I am heartsick, crushed that Bo knows I slept with

Mickey. Everyone is tense and unhappy, feeling either betrayed or alienated. The waiter refills our glasses. Once. Twice. Another bottle. We look around at the other people, the elegant bone-china men and their crystal women.

Bo is desperate to say something.

"I wonder if Ocheros'll sit down and talk," he says. "This might be the only crack I ever get at him. Excuse the pun."

He gives me a swift sidelong look, demanding I laugh.

So I do. He wants me to laugh, I laugh.

But Mickey is too pissed off at Bo to be accommodating.

"What I can't understand is why the police weren't watching Nat and Eli's house," Mickey says, smearing sarcasm over his words like a thick syrup. "The place just got shot up a few nights ago and yet there wasn't any surveillance or protection last night. No nothing. Seems like there should have been some sorta extra security."

Bo's face becomes an iron curtain.

"Also you guys should have come up with some suspects by now. It's not like you don't know who's involved. In fact, that's what's causing all the trouble, isn't it? The names in Fawn Hall's interview? You must even know their addresses by now. I bet the only thing you don't have is their shirt sizes. Why don't you round them up for questioning? I thought the cops were supposed to chase the robbers. So how come the robbers are chasing us?"

When he stops, silence explodes like a bomb at our table.

The waiter brings menus. I open the heavy leather folder. They have given me a woman's menu, without any prices. Nothing costs anything. Señor Ocheros has never heard of nouvelle cuisine. The menu reads like a takeoff on the Palm restaurant. It's basic roadhouse fare. Ariel may be the last place in North America where a twenty-ounce porterhouse steak and a baked potato with four kinds of topping don't attract any attention. Here good and bad cholesterol wrestle for dominance in public view.

"You're right," Bo says with a sudden squirt of laughter. "We've been a little outta sync up till now, but it looks like we're gonna turn it around tonight. We'll give the bad guys everything they want and then they'll leave you alone. Works out perfect."

"Save me from any sermons," Mickey says coldly.

"I want to tell you something," Bo adds. "I'm going along with this gag because Natalie has the right to call the shots and she's decided to return the interview. But if she gave me the high sign, I would blow this off in a minute. I think anyone who wanted to release that interview to the press could use the subsequent publicity as a shield. No one's blown away a whistle blower yet."

I feel gross. Mickey is treating Bo contemptuously, as if things got fucked up because Bo was somehow limited, incompetent. Bo is hanging tough and I'm in the middle; it is going to be a very long evening. It is nearly ten o'clock and Ocheros is late, but the night is still young here at Ariel. People continue arriving, surveying the scene, drinking champagne and starting to party. We order dinner.

As I get drunk, my discomfort decreases a little and my tension subsides. This kind of triangle is new and spicy for me. Two handsome men, one I just slept with and the other jealous about it, flank me like bookends. This is how my sister lives her life— sitting in silky restaurants with attractive admirers, locked in sexy triangles that produce involuntary body rushes.

Talk about strokes.

Our food arrives, elegantly presented.

Mickey studies his platter. "This looks good," he says. "I propose a truce while we eat."

He must be hungry. He eats everything. Fast. The next thing I know he's back at it again.

"Bo, tell me—why're you so hung up on there being higher powers involved in all this drug shit? Does that make you feel bigger and better or something? It wasn't Noriega who ransacked Nat's house, you know. Some small fry did it and you could round them up in a minute. Shit—even *I* could."

"Don't turn around," Bo orders, without raising his voice, "but our man Ocheros just walked in with another clown I know.

Ocheros is the little guy. The tall one is some Columbia Road *jefe*, a bagman for the contras. He's probably here picking up proceeds, drug money. This is the connection I've been talking about."

I turn slightly and look toward the doorway, where I see the two men. The small skinny guy is wearing a white Armani suit. The tall one, the bagman, is wearing a flashy silk jacket with slacks that probably cost a thousand dollars.

There are big differences between a bagman and a bag lady.

"I couldn't have wished for anything better than seeing those two pricks together," Bo says with sweet surprise. "Right in front of my eyes."

The maître d' approaches our table with his wine steward in tow. He looks back and forth between Bo and Mickey for a moment and then, of course, hands his wine list to the white man.

"Mr. Ocheros would like you to select a wine or champagne with his compliments. He'd like to come over and join you."

Mickey orders an expensive bottle of champagne, which arrives only moments before Ocheros does.

Up close the Nicaraguan looks even smaller and thinner than he did from a distance. He has a sharp copper-colored face, narrow and pinched. His straight black hair sports a wet look.

"Well, I never thought I'd be doing business with you, Mr. Culver," he says to Bo with a laugh as he slips into our fourth, empty chair. He has an accent like Desi Arnaz.

I see Bo flinch as if taking a hit below the belt.

"Howya doin', José?" he asks dryly.

"*Mister* Ocheros," the man responds with a quick smear of a smile. "People call me *Mister* Ocheros until I tell them not to bother." Ocheros smiles at Bo with false indulgence. "And who're your friends here? We should have some introduction."

"This is Natalie Myers. She's a social worker who lives in Adams-Morgan."

"Madam's Organ?" José Ocheros asks with a laugh.

He has clearly made this little joke before.

"This is Michael Teardash. A businessman from New York."

Since both Ocheros and Mickey are seated, their handshake is an awkward one.

"Mr. Ocheros," Mickey says, "I'm a good friend of Natalie here, and also her sister, who's out of town. I'm also an acquaintance of Jerry Russo, whom I saw this morning."

"Yes, how is he?" Ocheros asks, frowning. "It was a terrible thing, someone shooting him like that."

"Would you excuse me for a moment?" I ask, rising unsteadily to my feet. "I'll be right back."

I begin a long trek toward the rest rooms. My legs feel weak. I have drunk much too much. The other guests, who had seemed so distinct when we entered, are now blurred and imprecise. Inside the women's lounge, I finger-comb my hair in front of the mirror until two older women finish smoking their cigarettes and leave. It is good to see my own reflection. It helps me remember who I am.

Then I open my evening bag, remove the papers, reroll them even tighter and carefully insert them, horizontally, inside my bra. After checking my silhouette in the mirror without detecting any disfiguring bulges beneath my blouse, I reclose my evening bag and walk back out into the restaurant.

The papers scratch uncomfortably against my breasts, but I feel a comfortable sense of closure. If Fawn Hall could hide documents in her undies to get them out of the White House, I can hide her testimony in my bra to avoid returning it to the criminals who want it.

Mickey eyes me critically as I sit down again.

"I guess I'll have to recap a little," he says to announce his irritation. "Natalie, you know someone inadvertently removed some papers from Mr. Russo's home and that now we're going to return them. Mr. Ocheros and I have come to a clear understanding that, upon their return, all efforts to recover them by any interested parties will cease. There will be absolutely no more acts of retaliation. In other words, Nat, you'll have nothing more to worry about or fear."

"I was sorry to hear about your experience," Ocheros says to me with mock shock.

I smile.

"So?" Mickey prompts me. "If you can give them to Mr. Ocheros we'll just finish up our coffee and get going."

"I've done something very stupid," I say, feeling myself flush. "I had them in my other purse, my shoulder bag, and I forgot to transfer them into this one."

I place my evening bag on the table.

"I don't know what to say . . . I've been so busy, not at all myself lately. Stupid. Really stupid of me," I repeat. I now inject a little nervous stammer for authenticity's sake. "I mean . . . I mean . . . I knew we were c-coming here just to deliver them." I pause to smile nervously at *Mr.* Ocheros. "But I can b-bring them by first thing tomorrow. Or in the afternoon. Or whenever you want. Whatever . . ."

All three men are looking at me with genuine amazement. I look around the table at them.

"I'm sorry," I say, shaking my head. "I'm . . . uh . . . really, *really* sorry about this."

"Well, we can wait until tomorrow," Ocheros says very precisely as he removes a small silver card holder from inside his jacket. "Here is my card. Please telephone my office before you come and someone will meet you here," he says, nodding toward the doorway.

"Thanks, Mr. Ocheros," I say with a smile. "Thank you."

And then he gets up and walks away, stopping to bend and sway like a palm tree over various tables as he greets special guests.

I drain my champagne glass.

Now Mickey is furious.

"I hope to hell you're telling the truth," he says to me. "Because if you're pulling a fast one, if you're still thinking about releasing that damn interview, you're on your own. You're responsible if anyone gets hurt. And that includes Michael Dukakis. That story could hurt him a lot. I wish you'd get your head out of the sixties, Natalie. It was fun while it lasted, but it's over now."

"You're playing right into the Republicans' hands by letting them get away with all this," I say, suddenly hot and focused. "There's been a big cover-up here, Mickey. A White House secretary admitted using drugs and no one turned her confession over to the Justice Department. No one made any effort to have her prosecuted even though she was holding a sensitive government job. It was a complete cover-up. I don't want to sound like some bleeding-heart liberal, but, jeez, I see old ladies eating cat food and sleeping in the streets while these Republicans are snorting coke in Georgetown and sending millions of dollars to the contras."

"Christ, Natalie," Mickey says. "How retro can you get? This isn't the time for all that shit. If the Democrats want to get their man in the White House they've got to forget about the war in Nicaragua and Salvador. They've got to show they can run this government. Run this country."

This time I don't answer him.

Bo signals the waiter for the bill, but the man comes over to say there isn't any charge. Bo leaves a twenty-dollar bill on the table and then leads the way to the door. The minute we step outside, one of the parking jocks sprints off into darkness and returns within seconds in my Ford. Mickey tips him and gets into the driver's seat.

"Well, I'll be in touch with you folks tomorrow morning," Bo says.

I can hear a smile in his voice.

Then he turns and starts walking up Thirty-first Street toward Wisconsin Avenue.

"You could've asked him if he wanted a ride," I complain, sliding into the passenger seat.

Mickey doesn't answer. He doesn't speak at all during our ride back to the hotel. When the elevator from the garage stops at the sixth floor, he gets off with me.

"Oh, no," I laugh nervously. "I'm done in, Mick. No more for me tonight."

I move quickly. Standing on tiptoe, I give him a sisterly peck on the cheek and then hurry toward my door before he recovers. I let myself into the room, turn the night lock and fling myself down on the other, unused bed.

I wake up before seven the next morning in the weird light of a hotel dawn and dig through my suitcase to find my old jeans, which are daily growing bigger on me, and a shirt. Then I dress, check out at the front desk, put the charges on Eli's Visa, load up my car and drive home.

I want to go home.

No matter how dangerous it is, I want to go home and put some order back into my life. Tonight Eli will return and I want at least to have our bedroom fixed. I want to cleanse and restore our house to make it a home again.

I begin on the first floor by uprighting little end tables, returning drawers to their desks and replacing books on their shelves. Plants have been pushed over and their pots broken. Eli's study is a disaster. I do a little work in each area before I decide to concentrate on one room at a time. Of course I choose to begin in the kitchen, my beautiful kitchen, with its wall-length view of Rock Creek Park.

I become totally absorbed. No—transported. Since everything is out of order and space is up for grabs, I begin to improvise, improving upon my original organization of the pots and pans. I am so into it that I don't even hear the footsteps in our gravel driveway.

"Natalie? Nat?"

It's Mickey.

I open the back door. He comes inside without looking at me. He seems to be suffering from the same reticence I felt last night. I, also, have refused to run the rushes from yesterday.

"My God," he groans, looking around the kitchen. "Whadda disaster. Why'd you come back here all alone, Nat? It's still dangerous. Especially since we didn't complete our mission last night."

I have to smile at his delicacy.

"Well, I can't just abandon it, Mick. It's the only thing we own, Eli and me. And I don't like being homeless. I work with homeless women. I know what it does to people."

"But I thought all the locks were broken—"

"I'm going to get everything fixed. It's my house. My home."

"Well, I wanted to warn you Shay's coming back early. She says she wants to help you. Clean up the place, I guess." He studies the pieces of a broken platter on the floor. Then he looks up and meets my eyes. "I think she was maybe getting suspicious. About us."

"Really?"

Translation: *Infidelity and adultery are surefire topics to grab her interest. That negative attention span of hers can be corrected and converted with the right ammunition.*

"Yeah. Really."

"So's she coming back to restake her claim?"

"Yup. In about an hour and a half. The flight gets in at eleven. She phoned at seven. I called your room right away, but you'd checked out, given me the slip. You didn't go to Georgetown already, did you?"

"No."

"Well, I want to go do that with you, but it'll have to be early, because Shay wants us to go back up to the Hamptons tonight." Mickey smiles sheepishly. "Apparently Long Island is *the place to be* between conventions. Shana told her that. She bumped into Shana. Or else Bianca. Or someone."

"She's still a groupie," I say, starting to scrub one of my countertops with cleanser on a sponge. "A groupie grandma still chasing after the band. A real Democratic party girl. Well, tell her she has to pick up Amelia in Minneapolis because I'm not going back there and I won't let Marge make the trip. I really mean that, Mickey."

"She did say she misses the baby."

"Oh, that's *real* cute," I snicker.

"Don't get bitter," Mickey counsels. "Half your charm is not being bitter when you could be. I just hope she doesn't pick up any vibes about us. You and me."

"Don't worry about it," I say sarcastically. "Shay's never seen me as any kind of threat, let alone a *sexual* one."

"You won't say anything, then?"

"Hey! I'm disappointed you felt it necessary to ask."

"Wait till she sees how you look," Mickey says ominously. "She's not stupid. You look gorgeous. You look like you've been getting it."

Although there's an element of truth in what he says, I know the minute Shay gets here I'll experience the same old anonymity that blankets me whenever she's around. I'll start to feel like a missing person again. Some shadowy figure in a witness-protection program. A *desaparecida*.

"Would it be okay if I borrowed your car to go get Shay?" Mickey asks. "Yours or Eli's?"

"Sure. Take mine. I'll run up to Georgetown when you get back. Don't worry about it."

At 10:00 I give him the keys and he leaves for the airport. At 10:02 I take a bottle of Chablis out of the refrigerator and slowly sip wine from a coffee mug while I sweep broken shards off the floor.

Still, I think, things *could* be worse.

I mean, with my luck, I could have ended up being the sister of Scarlett O'Hara or Zelda Fitzgerald or Daisy Buchanan or Elizabeth Taylor or Cleopatra or Queen Victoria or Holly Golightly or Brett Ashley or Temple Drake or Princess Di. I might have been born the sister of Bette Midler or Angela Davis or Madame Ngo or Jane Fonda or Marie Antoinette or Mrs. Dalloway or Zsa Zsa Gabor or Anastasia or Rosa Luxemburg or Connie Chung or Hannah Arendt or Madame Chiang Kai-shek or Viva or Ultra or Simone de Beauvoir or Dorothy Lamour or Dorothy Parker or Dorothy Day or Georgia O'Keeffe or Frida Kahlo or Tokyo Rose or Joyce Carol Oates or Queen Esther or Golda Meir or Whoopi Goldberg or Cher.

Who needs trouble like that? Shay's bad enough. As far as I'm concerned, *she* takes the prize.

When I've finished sweeping I get out the bucket and mop the kitchen floor.

I'm always surprised how little wine there is in a bottle.

"Hiiiiiii."

They're ba-aaaack.

She's ho-ooome.

Heee-ere's Shaysie!

The back door swings open and Shay rushes into the kitchen.

"Jeez, do I ever need to use the toilet," she squeals. "Ohhh my-yy God. Look what they did to your house!"

Today Shay is dressed in a drumroll of royal-blue spandex bike pants, a neon-green sleeveless T-shirt, black running shoes and double-density yellow socks.

"D'you cut your hair?" she asks, barely looking as she rushes past me to the powder room with her huge red suede shoulder bag slapping against her thigh.

From my bag-lady clients, I have learned that women use a

purse or shopping bag as an extra appendage, an externalized auxiliary organ like the pouch of a kangaroo. Women like to transport essential ego props in detachable containers strapped to their bodies. I have never seen Shay enter a bathroom without her purse. It is not only that she carries and uses coke, but also that she keeps her private agendas and alternative identities inside its zippered compartment, just as Hannah keeps her survival supplies in a torn L&T shopping bag.

The powder-room door slams shut.

I feel mugged.

Robbed.

Whiplashed.

Okay, so I am also a little shitfaced, but *really*!

Did I cut my hair? What did she think happened to it?

Oh, I am pissed. *Really* pissed.

Mickey comes inside carrying Shay's bags. Somehow my sister has already acquired several summery-looking suitcases covered in a hot-Day-Glo-print fabric that I have never seen before.

Big Difference #291: Shay was born to shop. She is the only woman I know who can find time to do some serious shopping while covering a national political convention. I *hate* to shop. I only shop when I'm in Southampton, about to prostitute myself.

Mickey sets down the luggage and comes over to me. He looks numb, like a spectator at the Ice Capades.

"Not to worry," I whisper. "She hardly *looked* at me."

"Nat, something happened on the way home from the airport . . ."

But then the powder-room door swings open and slams against the wall, vibrating loudly until it shivers to a stop.

My sister is seated upon the toilet, her pants down around her knees, peeing in front of both Mickey and me.

"I have *got* to tell someone," she yodels. "I have got to tell my sister. *You*, Natalie. Mickey and I are going to get married. We just decided on the way home from the airport. It's the triumph of hope over experience. We're going to get married!"

"Oh," I say, my voice flat and uninflected. "Great. That's really wonderful."

But I am running on empty. Shitfaced or not, I can't cover my shock at Shay taking a piss in front of us. I glance at Mickey, who looks totally pussy-whipped. Then—half to scare him, half to hide my hurt from Shay—I cross the room and plant a light kiss on his lips.

"Congratulations," I say, flashing the sexual chip on my shoulder. "This is a real surprise."

Dear God, I pray. *Let me get through this. Let me swallow this like everything else. Let me eat the fact that my sister, even in her ignorance, trumped my ace. This is a toughie, but when the going gets tough the tough get going. . . .*

Numbed, I now turn around. Shay has finished wiping herself and is simultaneously flushing the toilet and dragging her pants back up over her body.

"I know you must be happy," I say, giving her a stiff little hug when she reenters the kitchen. "But don't forget you're already married. I don't think you're supposed to double up like that."

"I know. I've *got* to take care of a lot of stuff with Christopher," she agrees. "But he's still down in Atlanta chasing after all *my* Washington friends. *What a loser!* Anyway, I'm going to help you fix up the house and everything, but first I've *got* to have a decent lunch. I'm *starving.* I'd kill for a huge Caesar salad. I've gotta have one."

Our Lady of Gotta. Our Lady of the Blue Gotta.

Shay is a transitive verb. Everything she does takes an object. My sister is a tidal wave, a *tsunami,* an oceanic surge of wants. She can keep busy just satisfying her own appetites. One whim follows fast upon another. Gratifying her own desires and impulses can fill her days. It's amazing she ever had time to work or be promiscuous, so prolific are her wants.

"Why don't you and Mickey go out and have a celebration lunch alone, Shay?" I ask in a saccharine voice. "I've got to go to Georgetown and drop off the papers at Ariel. Did Mickey tell you about last night?"

"Yes, he did. *But we're not going to go out to eat without you,*" she howls, genuinely astonished at such an outrageous idea. "Come on—we really need a field trip. All I have to do is change into something cooler." She bends over to lift one of her suitcases up onto my kitchen table. "Spandex doesn't breathe."

Oh, no no no.

In less than a moment she is down to transparent bikini underpants and a cleavage-creasing bra. Then she begins rummaging through her suitcase, inspecting and rejecting various pieces of clothing, pausing only long enough to toss her cosmetic bags, shoe bags, beach bags and satin jewelry bags out on the table. In a manic monologue, she begins babbling about the Masters and Johnson prediction that AIDS will soon invade the heterosexual world in a serious way. She says the whole theory is tainted by their claim that normal Americans have only three sex partners a year.

She says to her that sounds like a long weekend.

Mickey laughs, which encourages Shay to walk over and rub the back of his neck. He shrugs his shoulders to slough her hand away, glancing at me to acknowledge his show of independence. Then he asks her if she went to Tom Hayden's book party. She nods, so he asks whom she went with.

Shay says she doesn't usually carry sand to the beach.

Then he really laughs.

Jealousy is a crab crawling around inside me, starting to eat my guts out.

Attacking her suitcase again, Shay reports everyone clapped when Tom Hayden said he sometimes likes the old Tom better than the new one. Then she begins naming the various journalists and celebrities Mort Zuckerman entertained at his rented gym in Atlanta. The bratpack from Hollywood seems to fascinate Shay these days. She discusses Rob Lowe, Ally Sheedy, Molly Ringwald and other young actors I don't know.

Finally she pulls a white cotton dress out of her suitcase, puts it on and disappears with Mickey to assess the vandalism in my house. She looks genuinely shaken when they return to the kitchen, although she refers to the damage as if it's been caused by an act of God. I am beginning to feel ill. I am sick and tired of my sister. I am sick and tired of her silly chatter, her fucked-up values, her demagogic behavior.

"I promise that after lunch I'll spend the rest of the day helping you, Nat," Shay says. "We'll call repair people and contact your insurance company and everything. I just have to get up to East Hampton sometime tonight so I can begin working on my article. It's due Monday and I'm going to have to work around the clock for a couple days."

"What about Amelia?" I ask her bluntly.

Shay looks startled. "Well, what about her?"

"You can't just leave her in Minneapolis. Marge is exhausted. You've got to fly out there and pick her up."

"I can't go to Minneapolis before I write my article."

"You can write it on the airplane en route. You love to write on airplanes. Remember?"

"Oh, shit. I can't write a whole article in three hours," Shay squeals. "And I certainly can't work with both Amelia *and* Mother around."

Something in this moment finally ignites the flammable mass of my grievances—forty years of tinder-dry resentments. The slow burn I've borne all my life now begins racing toward a fiery climax.

"You are going to go get her," I say shrilly. "I have taken enough shit from you in this past week to last me for the rest of my life. Can't you get it through your head that someone shot bullets through my bedroom windows? That I had to take Amelia and run away from my own house? Go to the Hamptons? That from there I had to go to Minneapolis? Do you understand that Jerry Russo got shot? That my home's been destroyed? Do you understand we're being *hunted,* Shay? Can you even guess how sick I am of cleaning up your messes for you?"

"Eat shit and die," says my forty-year-old sister.

"Sha-ay!" Mickey moans.

"Well, what am I supposed to say?" she yells defiantly. "Do you think I wanted all this to happen? Do you think I would put my own little granddaughter in jeopardy if I'd *known*? Give me a break, wouldja? I mean *gimme a fuckin' break!*"

"Well, I'm really glad Mickey was around to hear you say that, Shay. We don't often have witnesses to see or hear the *real you*. And that was such a *you* thing you said: 'Eat shit and die.' You've got a lovely bride here," I say, turning toward Mickey with a vicious smile.

And that's when the doorbell rings.

Loud and long.

Standing in a little huddle in the middle of the kitchen floor, we look at each other helplessly. Finally Mickey walks down the hallway. Shay opens her purse and takes out her hairbrush. I get a glass of water, although I'd really prefer wine. Mickey returns with Bo and Chuck Connors. Shay is still brushing her hair; she doesn't stop. I have watched my sister brush her hair while speaking to a Supreme Court justice at a cocktail party, sitting in a synagogue, and eating in a four-star restaurant.

Mickey introduces everyone.

Shay becomes busy as a bartender carding the men. She gives Chuck Connors a once-over-lightly, then turns her attention to Bo. *So this is the detective,* I can see her thinking. *Hmmmm. Interesting. So this is the big black hunk Natalie's been running around the country with. Not bad. Maybe Miss Goody Two-Shoes isn't as gooney as she looks.* She begins back-brushing her curls.

I watch my sister brushing her hair.

Mickey watches my sister brushing her hair.

Chuck Connors watches my sister brushing her hair.

But Bo is watching me.

He has a complicated smile on his face that I can't immediately decipher.

"So this is the famous Shay Karavan," Chuck Connors croons. "It's a real pleasure to meet you. We were just cruising past and decided we would offer you folks some free delivery service. We can run those papers over to Señor Ocheros for you, Ms. Myers. Looks like you've got enough to do around here."

"Oh, that'd be very convenient," Shay says with one of her more glamorous smiles.

Instinctively, Shay takes anything that's offered to anyone in her presence.

No flies on *my* sister!

I look at Bo, who dons another demismile and shrugs.

"As a matter of fact, I was just leaving to do it myself," I say in a chilly voice. "I really don't need any help."

The three men all back off, alarmed by my show of anger. Shay's eyes narrow suspiciously as she watches me prepare to leave. Both Chuck Connors and Bo are eager to leave now and they let themselves out through the front. I pick up my purse and walk toward the back door.

"This won't take me but half an hour," I say.

"Should I go with you?" Mickey asks.

"No. But I'd appreciate it if you'd bring in my luggage from the trunk."

"Sure." He follows me outside. "Everything happened so fast, Nat," he says as soon as we hit the gravel driveway and he knows the crunch will cotton his words. "She came at me . . ."

"You sure know how to hurt a girl," I say in a teasing, old-fashioned tone of voice. But then the lightness I'd wanted to project evaporates. An enormous, raw, ragged-edged hurt rises up within me. "Why'd you do me like that, Mickey?"

"Whaddaya mean?" he mumbles, flushing.

"Was there some reason you wanted to make me feel lower than whaleshit? I mean, did you have to fuck me over like that? Fuck with my head? I mean, how did you think I'd feel, hearing you got engaged just one day after . . . yesterday?"

"Hey! You're giving me more credit than I deserve, babe. I didn't know it was going to happen. How 'bout that? It happened all of a sudden. I didn't orchestrate it."

"You orchestrated yesterday afternoon."

"That wasn't so hard; you wanted it too."

I flinch.

He leans up against the door of my car so I can't escape. After a few seconds the metallic heat must have penetrated his clothing because he suddenly jerks away.

"Hey, we didn't *meet* in that bar at the Hilton. We *knew* we had some unfinished business from out at the beach. You're a very attractive woman, Nat. More attractive than Shay in lots of ways. So at least we got it over with. At least it didn't happen *after* the wedding, right? That's good. We wanted it and we did it and now it's over, finished. I wasn't trying to fuck you over. Believe me."

"But how do you think I feel now? Tell me that. Or don't you care at all?"

"I'm sorry," he says miserably. "I'm sorry. It must feel shitty. I even feel shitty about it. But didn't Shay sleep with Eli before you married him? All you did was even up the score. Try to look at it that way. We were both a little lonely."

"I was fine."

"Fine? You were *terrific*. You were *fabulous*."

"Oh, God." I begin to laugh. "You really are something. You're really full of shit."

"Now why'd you want to go ahead and say something like that?"

"Doesn't matter." I shrug. "You'll get yours."

A look of uncertainty wings across his face. He knows I'm referring to Shay but he hasn't got the nerve to ask specifically what I mean. A moment later he takes a deep breath, straightens his shoulders and accepts the challenge of a future life with Shay Karavan.

I get into my car, flip open the trunk and watch him collect my luggage. When he starts carrying it toward the house, I back out of the driveway and pull onto Adams Mill Road.

Shay and I are up in my bedroom folding clothes to put back into the drawers. By the time she and Mickey returned from their celebratory lunch, the bride-to-be was inebriated and ebullient once again. She insisted upon helping me clean my bedroom even though she was "exhausted."

"Oh, I'm so happy, Nat," she says in her breathy baby voice, carefully creasing Eli's boxer shorts. "And I'm so glad you had a chance to get to know Mickey a little this week. Don't you think he's great?"

"Really," I murmur. "He's really great."

"And he's *so* rich, Nat! I'm going to be the wife of a multimultimultimillionaire! He might even be a demibillionaire for all I know. I'll be the new Ivana Trump. Of course I'll have to sign some sort of prenuptial agreement. He says his lawyer will insist on that, but anyway, even if it doesn't last forever it will be fabulous while it does. I'll be able to buy Mom and you and Steven a lot of stuff. And I'll take Amelia to F.A.O. Schwarz and let her go crazy."

I can almost guess which picture Shay will send to *The New York Times*—a close-up Dad took of her a few years ago. In it her hair is pulled back very tight, showing off her razor-sharp cheekbones. Her eyes look light and provocative because her face is, as usual, tan, and she is wearing a shirt with the first three buttons open so that a slight swell of bosom is visible in the V below the mandatory premarital pearls.

I could write the story:

SHAY KARAVAN WEDS

Stephanie Ann (Shay) Karavan, 40, free-lance journalist, was married yesterday to Michael A. Teardash, 38, in a private ceremony in East Hampton, L.I. Ms. Karavan, the daughter of Marjorie Karavan and the late Morton Karavan of Minneapolis, married Mr. Teardash, Chairman and Chief Financial Executive Officer of Communications USA Corporation and a Manhattan real estate developer. Ms. Karavan will keep her own name. It was the third marriage for each.

Mr. Teardash is the son of Nathan Teardash, partner in the firm of Paul, Weiss, Rifkind, Wharton & Garrison, and an overseer of the Harvard Corporation. His mother is Cynthia Paisley, children's book illustrator of Greenwich, Connecticut, and Kennebunk, Maine. The groom's stepfather, Dr. Reynolds Paisley, retired as the Chief of Pediatrics at Yale University Hospital last year.

Mr. Teardash is a grandson of the late Edgar Teardash, a member of the New York Stock Exchange and senior partner in the New York brokerage firm of Baker, Weeks & Company, and Amanda Teardash Twomey of Manhattan and Southampton. His maternal grandparents were former Massachusetts Senator William O'Reilly of Boston and Wellfleet and the late Louise O'Reilly Goldman of New York and Hollywood, Florida.

Mr. Teardash graduated from Swarthmore College, where he was a member of Phi Beta Kappa, Fordham University School of Law and Harvard Business School, where he received an M.B.A. His marriage to Anita Louise Barker, who was presented at the Assembly Ball in Greenville, South Carolina, and is a member of the Junior Leagues of Memphis and Manhattan, ended in divorce, as did his marriage to *New York Times* Living Section editor Demi Martin, former Editor and Chief of Correspondents at *Newsweek* magazine.

Ms. Karavan attended the University of Minnesota and did graduate work at the University of California at Berkeley. At the request of the Vietnamese government, she brought back to the United States the ashes of MIA American pilot Warren Carmino. Her marriages to Barney Yellen, 1960s political activist and Washington D.C. attorney, and Christopher Edmonds, former Legal Counsel to the U.S. Senate Foreign Relations Committee and currently a fellow at the Woodrow Wilson Institute of the Smithsonian Institution and a 1988 winner of a MacArthur Fellowship, both ended in divorce.

A reception for 1,000 people is scheduled to be held at the Plaza Hotel early in October. Honored guests will be the son of Ms. Karavan, Steven Yellen, 19, a premedical student at McGill University, his daughter, Amelia Yellen, 3, and the three children of Mr. Teardash: Emily Teardash, 15, by his first wife; Maggie Teardash, 12, and Zachary Teardash, 5, by his second wife. Until then the couple will reside in the seafront home of Mr. Teardash in East Hampton, Long Island.

More wretched excess.

Will *Entertainment Tonight* have to cover Shay's reception because of its glitzy guest list? Will news helicopters have to hover overhead taking aerial shots à la Madonna's wedding? Will *People*

magazine have to use a telephoto lens to get a cover shot of the
new fun couple at the East Hampton Writers and Artists' Labor
Day baseball game, which Shay hasn't missed in six years? Will
Baba Wawa have to do a duo interview with the new lovebirds
in their fabulous house with its wraparound porch full of white
wicker furniture?

Will Mr. and Mrs. Teardash take a honeymoon at some fashionable spa where everything costs 40 percent more than it does
ten miles away because getting rooked makes Shay feel rich? Or
will my sister, the surf Nazi, the sun-and-fun fanatic, visit some
foreign country she views as a duty-free specialty shop: Mex-
ico=silver and turquoise, Spain=leather goods, Morocco=djel-
labas for loungewear. To Shay, Ireland is a cable-knit fisherman's
sweater outlet, France a huge perfumery. Now the world will
really become my sister's boutique.

"Do you still have the key to Christopher's place, Shay?" I ask.
"I wouldn't mind having it in case I decide not to sleep here. And
it'd be nice to be able to take a swim."

"Oh, of course, honey," she purrs.

Shay darts for her purse. She is genuinely thrilled to provide me
with a little luxury. Although she's greedy, she's not selfish.

"Nat, I'm so glad you returned the papers and everything is
going back to normal now. This was a *terrible* week and I really
mean it when I say thank you for doing everything you did. I'm
terribly sorry about what happened to the house." She pauses
briefly to look around regretfully. "Anyway, here's the plan we
worked out at lunch. Mickey and I are flying out to Minneapolis
tonight, spending a little time with Mom and then bringing
Amelia back to New York. I'm sure I can find someplace to leave
her while I work on my article."

The sleaze factor has just kicked in. My sister is probably going
to spend *one night* with our mother. My sister the scuzz ball is
looking to unload Amelia even *before* she picks her up. My sister
the scum bag has absolutely *no* shame at all.

"Maybe Yvonne's folks up in Vermont would enjoy having Amelia during the summertime for once, instead of always at Christmas," she says. "I think I'll give them a call."

"They live in New Hampshire, Shay."

"Oh, right. Anyway," she sighs, closing Eli's top drawer and ignoring the rest of the clothing still on the floor, "I've got a shitload of stuff to take care of so I think I'll just sit in the kitchen and make my phone calls. Is that okay?"

"Shay, why did you tell Mom about my abortion?"

She flinches, pales, begins talking too fast:

"Because she couldn't understand why you never had any kids."

"There's lots of reasons women can't get pregnant. She didn't even *ask* you. You just *volunteered* it. You just wanted to tell Mom the worst thing you knew about me. Why are you so destructive? You know how rough it's been for her since Daddy died."

"Listen, Nat." Shay is rushing to find a cigarette, a match, a prop. "I know you hold me responsible for what happened at your damn abortion, but that's just because you're such a *blamer.* First you thank me a million times for arranging everything and then, when you find out they've botched it, you blame *me.* Is that fair, Natalie? First I'm the good guy and then I'm the fall guy?"

"I don't blame you for what happened, Shay. All I want to know is why you had to tell Mom about it. *Two decades later.*"

"I told you—because she couldn't figure out why you never had any kids."

"Shay, you told her because you're jealous of how close we are. That's the real reason. You wanted to turn her against me."

"Okay, I'll tell you how it happened," Shay says. "I was talking to Mother on the phone a couple weeks ago about the abortion issue. Not *your* abortion issue, Nat. *The* abortion issue. And I just happened to mention some of the medical consequences of illegal abortions. And I guess that's when the cat slipped out of the bag."

"You're sick, Shay. You're a bad seed." Bitterness hardens my words like heat caramelizing sugar. Raw rage pumps through my system. "You were always competing with Mom for Dad's attention. All you ever wanted was to have Dad to yourself. That's why you kept getting into trouble, so he had to deal with you all the time. And you're still doing the same damn thing. Making trouble so people will notice you."

"Oh, stuff it, Natalie."

"And that's probably why you can't maintain any real relationships now, either. Not with your son or your daughter-in-law or me or Mom. Or anyone. Except men. You'd ball *anybody* just to get them to pay attention to you."

For one dizzying moment I think of screaming out that I'd slept with Mickey to finally repay her for every wrong she's done me. But then I realize that she is close to hysteria. I can sense her upset percolating dark and strong and pungent within her.

Turning, she runs toward the stairs.

I lie down on my bed and stare up at the bullet holes in my ceiling.

Although the sheer membrane separating us often clouds my reason, I think some of what I said to Shay sank in this time. In real life it's often hard to identify watersheds or Waterloos. They come and go too quickly, and most relationships are as absorbent as cat litter when it comes to ruptures. But my sister and I are fast approaching a turning point. This time Shay has gone too far. I cannot let her get away with her current destructiveness much longer. Hopefully, this fight will finally lance our abscessed relationship. Hopefully it will cauterize the source of our sickness and let some of the infectious poison drain away.

I fall asleep and don't wake up until Shay walks back into my bedroom.

"So listen," she says, shaking my shoulder until I open my eyes. "We're leaving."

"Oh."

It's as if the abortion issue had never come up.

"I've called almost everybody in the Western world, so just save your phone bill and I'll pay you for all my calls. I made our plane reservations and spoke to Mother. She's going to bring Amelia to the airport to meet us since it's an hour earlier out there and it won't be too late. Then I called Steven and we talked for a long time. I mean, I told him I was going to marry Mickey and move to New York and we discussed whether he wanted Amelia to live in Manhattan. Actually, I've been thinking I might go visit Yvonne at Hazelden when I'm in Minneapolis. Steven thought that'd be a good idea."

For a moment I wonder if Amelia could live with me for a while in some nice clean apartment near Columbia Road. That should please Steven more than having Shay drag her up to New York, where she'd quickly be turned over to hired help. Quietly I deposit this thought in my mental hope chest.

"Anyway, we're ready to leave," Shay says.

I walk downstairs with her. I see the yellow cab in front of the house. Mickey embraces me with a tenderness that almost makes me cry. My sister kisses me with a chilliness that makes me want to die. The cab driver comes inside to carry some of their luggage. After they're gone I walk around my house, feeling more alone than I've ever felt before. Eventually I end up in Eli's study, where I use his telephone to call the Omni. Eli answers his extension on the first ring.

"Hi," I say. "I just called to get your flight number so I can pick you up at the airport tonight."

"Honey, I was just about to call you. It's weird—I had my hand on the phone. They want me to stay down here one more day to do a big wrap-up. An Atlanta-after-the-convention takeout. You know? Delegate feelings . . . all that kind of shit."

I am too tired to manufacture any light response.

"Now don't start thinking the worst, Nat. This doesn't *mean* a thing. It's just that I'm the only one down here who can do it."

"Eli, call them back. Tell them there's a huge story waiting for you in Washington. A great big scoop with your name on it."

"Whaddya mean?"

"It's the Fawn Hall interview, Eli. Shay doesn't want to do it anymore. She's just going to chuck it. But since I've taken all the heat for it, I decided it belongs to *us* now. I mean, to *you.* I've also learned a lot about the drug scene in D.C. and there's a huge crack-cocaine-contra connection. It's a big story, Eli. I *mean* it. It could win you another Pulitzer."

"Natalie, we're right smack in the middle of a presidential election campaign. Nobody's interested in drug stories right now. Besides, didn't you return it last night? Over at that nightclub?"

"Eli, listen. There's all sorts of stuff breaking loose up here. This cop, this black detective who heads the D.C. drug squad—"

"Nat, I know you want me to come home. I know you've had a rough week. But I can't tell Benson I won't take this assignment. There's no one else to do it. He's my boss, Nat."

"Well, I guess you have to do what you have to do," I say quietly. Then: "Shay and Mickey are getting married."

"I know. I bumped into Christopher. He told me. He asked if he could fly back to D.C. with me so I said I'd try to arrange it."

"When will you come home?"

"Sunday at the very latest."

"Sunday?"

It is painfully clear that Eli does not want to come home.

Now I know he's shacked up with someone.

In truth, I do not think Eli necessarily wants a different woman. I think Eli is just tired of being married. Or maybe he's just tired of being married to *me.* I know he's weary of putting out, of reassuring me about things, of sharing his privacy and diverting his energy into sustaining and maintaining our marriage. I think he's grown tired of talking, bored with listening, weary of acting interested when he's not—or affectionate when he isn't. It's almost biological. It's almost as if he can't get it up to care about us as a couple anymore.

Again I hang up without saying good-bye.

That's getting to be par for the course.

I sit at Eli's desk until the telephone rings around seven o'clock. It's Bo: "What time does your husband get in?"

"He's not coming back tonight after all," I say in a flat voice.

"No?"

"No. Change of plans. Not till Sunday."

"When's your sister leaving?"

"They're gone."

"I'll come past at nine. We'll go get some supper."

He hangs up.

A moment later he calls back.

"Is that okay with you?"

I have to laugh.

"Absolutely. But listen. Pick me up at nineteen twenty-four Reservoir Road. That's my brother-in-law Christopher's house. I have something I want to do over there."

There's one more bimbo on my shit list.

"Sure. But do me a favor, willya?"

"What?"

"Take your car keys into the house with you this time."

13

I let myself into Christopher's house and hunt around until I locate Shay's black Rolodex on the coffee table in her former study, right off her former bedroom. Flipping through the cards, I find exactly what I'd hoped for—a directory of Washington's media stars fingerprint-coded as to frequency of usage. Suddenly a glorious giddiness overcomes me. I feel empowered and anointed. Running back downstairs, I start my telephone crusade from inside the citadel of the kitchen.

Beginning with the *A*'s, I work my way through the entire deck of Rolodex cards, dialing each D.C.-based print or broadcast journalist whose name I recognize. The reporters' reputations are reflected in their addresses. Upper Northwest streets are laid out alphabetically, starting with the letters and then continuing through one-, two- and three-syllable words. Big brand-name journalists live either on the lettered streets of Georgetown or high up in the third alphabet. It's a primitive process for determining status, but it works.

Most of the journalists I reach know me through either Eli or Shay. None of them question the legitimacy of my announcing a press conference. Of course I'm too insecure to call it that. I simply say I've come into possession of some interesting documents about Fawn Hall that I am duplicating for distribution at six o'clock tomorrow in a storefront shelter called A Home Away from Home at 2121 Eighteenth Street, off Kalorama Road.

I feel flushed with great confidence about the future. I know I can do what has to be done because I have long harbored my own grudges against the Reagan administration. Like any administrator deprived of operating funds, I know where the social-services monies I needed were diverted. Everyone knows those dollars went for military expenditures. Money for the homeless was wasted on violence and destruction.

When Bo arrives I lead him through the house and outside into the garden. Darkness is shifting down upon the grounds, rubbing the surfaces of Christopher's patio furniture. I flick on the pool light and Bo slices off a low whistle through his teeth.

"Nice spread," he says.

Bo always comments on "nice" houses, "nice" gardens, "nice" neighborhoods. Sometimes I feel he views me as that kind of "nice," too.

"Wanna take a swim?" I ask, moving toward the tiled margin of the pool.

He looks at me questioningly.

"There're lots of suits in the house. I'll get you one of Christopher's."

Bo squats down and touches the water.

"Come on," I say, reaching out for his hand to pull him to his feet. "I'll find you some trunks. It'll feel great. It'll cool you off."

"I don't know how to swim," he says.

I look at him.

He doesn't know how to swim?

But why should he?

He was a poor black kid who grew up in D.C.

Where the hell would he learn how to swim?

In the private pools of friends or relatives living out in the suburbs?

In the fountain in front of Union Station?

In the Tidal Basin, where Fanne Foxe took her dive?

In the polluted Potomac River?

S N A P S H O T

This is Dad and me all dressed up to go someplace together on a Sunday afternoon. I'm about six. Now I can't remember where we were going. I know we drove downtown on the Floyd B. Olson Memorial Highway, past a public housing project, where most of Minneapolis's small population of blacks lived. That day I began to ask questions. Why do only Negroes live in the Project and no white people? Dad explained that the city built special housing for poor people unable to pay regular rents. Why are only Negroes poor? I asked. Dad explained that there were also poor white people. Why didn't some of those poor white people live in the Project with those poor Negro people? I asked. I don't know, Dad answered. Maybe he didn't. Anyway, that was the day I became the Emma Goldman of our family.

"Well, we could sit on the stairs, Bo. In the shallow part. Just to cool off," I offer.

He shakes his head.

He's afraid of the water.

Jesus.

Suddenly a soft panic, sired by regret and born out of sorrow, begins to stir me. I look into Bo's face, which has now become completely legible to me. Immediately I read that he is painfully embarrassed about not knowing how to swim. Humiliated.

A succulent sadness, ripe as a fruit, passes between us.

This man is complicated. Now there is a jeering look on his handsome face, plus a souvenir of anger. His expression reminds me of a joke:

What does New Jersey look like?

The back side of an old radio.

I can almost see the mess of wires, bulbs, conduits and connectors in his head—the whole complex system by which he operates. As easy as it was to get it on with Mickey, that's how tough it is to connect with Bo, to dig through all the debris and to avoid the celestial stadium of invisible spectators watching us.

"Are you worried Christopher will show up and do a Carl Rowan in reverse?"

For a moment Bo looks blank, but then he expels a short, reluctant laugh.

"Listen, I wanted to say something to you," he says. "I'm sorry you slept with your sister's boyfriend. He was just using you to get back at her and you should've known that. It was a piss-poor performance on your part and I can assure you that it didn't rock my boat."

Of course that's what's eating him. He's still pissed about Mickey, and I don't blame him.

"Let's go," Bo says in a tired voice.

There's a heaviness about him now as he drives up Wisconsin Avenue to a Brazilian restaurant near the Dancing Crab. The place is crowded; the air-conditioning is quaking from the magnitude of its mission. We order Brazilian beers, but after I taste mine I start to feel queasy. Bo orders *feijoada*.

I tell Bo that Shay and Mickey are going to get married. He asks if that's a problem for me and I assure him it's the perfect solution, the right resolution. But I flush as I speak, sorry that Bo knows about Mickey and me. Sorry that there was a Mickey and me. Feeling raw and injured, I lower my head so I can revise my face a little before I speak again. Erasing the hurt from my expression, I pencil in some pride and apply a light dusting of dignity to my image.

"Bo, I didn't return the interview yesterday. I thought about everything—all the risks and everything—and I decided that I wanted to release it. I mean, until late this afternoon, I thought maybe Eli would do it when he came home. But when I talked to him today, I realized he really isn't interested in working on *any* story at the moment." My voice falters. "I think he's with . . . someone, a woman, down there in Atlanta. Probably some journalist covering the convention. Seems he's taking a little sabbatical from our marriage. Actually, he might be getting ready to throw in the towel altogether."

Bo looks solemn. "You've definitely got a doubleheader going here today," he finally says. "Both your hubby and your sister's beau—that's B-E-A-U, right?—you're really stacking 'em up."

"Anyway, that's why I went over to Christopher's house. I used Shay's Rolodex and called up all the bigwig journalists in town. I'm going to release the interview tomorrow at a press conference in my shelter at six o'clock. It'll either fly or it won't, but I really think Contragate is ten times worse than Watergate so I just had to do something about it."

"Well." He smiles. "I'm proud of you."

I grow warm beneath his praise.

"I always thought the best defense on something like this was an offensive move," Bo continues. "The publicity will shield you better than anything else. Once it's out there, you'll be too visible to hit." He looks at his watch. "But we better think about Ocheros for a minute. It's ten-thirty. By now he knows you're not going to show. This is your most vulnerable time, Nat—from now until the press conference. You can't be alone. I'll just stay with you tonight, wherever you go."

"I've had worse offers."

Surprise freezes his face.

Then pleasure chases the surprise away.

Sitting in this brightly lit, overcrowded restaurant, it is difficult for me to look directly at Bo. In Christopher's garden, the darkness had smudged some of our disparities. The night had softened the differences between us. Now everything has become hard-edged again, and I feel shy.

Once more I've become the White European Woman, laden with all the burdensome baggage assigned me by history. Bo and

I both have a lot of baggage. Each of us is dragging around a lot of memories in the little red wagons of our pasts.

"Look," he says, "this is tough."

"What?"

"This."

I decide to take a chance.

"Why is it tough?" I ask, accepting the assumption of our feelings for each other and meeting his eyes for the first time since we sat down.

"Because I'm having trouble forgetting about you being with Teardash," he says simply. "Why'd you do that?"

I shrug, miserable.

"I'm sorry you did it. It makes things real tough for me. I'm a . . . finicky man. Were you . . . doing your sister?"

I shrug even more speculatively.

"Did you enjoy it?"

"I guess it was better than being alone."

He shakes his head regretfully.

"But you *weren't* alone, Natalie," he reprimands me. "And you *knew* that."

He's right.

Shay was right, too. I *should* eat shit and die.

"I was scared, Bo. Everything felt so scary."

"And sleeping with Teardash made you feel safe or something? That was safe sex?"

"Well, yes. I suppose. In a way."

"Look," Bo sighs as if to launder his voice so he can launch a fresh explanation. "I go around to D.C. high schools and give lectures on safe sex. It's not part of my job, but I volunteered to do it because I think safe sex is important."

He looks around the room at all the overwarm but still enthusiastic people enjoying their ethnic dinners, super-conscious of their surroundings and their titillating certainties.

"You know, sex is real risky," Bo continues.

He's talking more than condoms. I nod.

"But then it's always been risky," he continues. "Even before AIDS. It'll still be risky after they beat AIDS. Sex in the modern age is a dangerous thing."

I look at Bo. He's talking feelings now. He's talking about the chances people take. He's also talking racial risks. The racial perils:

1. Doing it to show there are no racial reasons for *not* doing it, or

2. Not doing it to show there are no racial reasons for *having* to do it.

Although I don't know any of the people in this restaurant, they are, for the most part, people like me—white liberal professionals living amidst walloping contradictions without any power to resolve them. Even if offered the opportunity to make some social repairs, these people would probably fuck up, since that's what most people—including myself—do despite their best intentions. Anyway, at the moment they are eating and happily guzzling Chardonnay, having discovered—just as I did—that wine can get them drunker faster for fewer calories and less money than booze while letting them feel virtuous about not drinking hard liquor anymore.

"Is that good, Bo?" I ask, pointing at his almost-empty plate.

"Yeah. It's their national dish," he answers. "Want a taste? Before it's too late?"

"Okay." I nod. "I'll taste it."

Bo spears a piece of sausage plus a couple of beans, and extends his fork across the table.

I M A G I N A R Y
I L L U S T R A T I O N

This is my mental picture of a scene from *Under the Volcano*. The always-drunk British Consul in Mexico and his estranged wife are standing on a balcony; her hand is resting on the balustrade. The

Consul thinks that if he can reach out, right at that moment, and place his hand atop his wife's, their estrangement will be eased, perhaps ended. Just as he steels himself to do it—to reach out and touch her—a sudden breeze stirs and his wife slowly lifts her hand to repair her hair. With that motion, the moment is lost. The Consul suffers a fatal loss of will, thereby ensuring the loss of his wife and, a short time later, his life—in a dramatic, violent death.

I do not reach out for Bo's fork.

Instead I lean forward and open my mouth. He places the food between my lips, steadying the fork until I've wiped it clean.

My face is hot.

I feel a million eyes on me.

I settle back in my chair and look around.

Okay, not a million, but a few people are watching.

An older, obviously indignant couple seated nearby are discussing me, bothered by a White European Woman tasting food from the fork of a black man. And though I sense them watching me, I don't really mind. I just chew my mouthful and smile at Bo. He smiles back at me as if he understands the test I just administered to myself.

And passed.

A short while later, he pays the check and we leave. Outside, Wisconsin Avenue is humming with heat as we walk toward Count Western's jeans store, where the car is parked. Suddenly, with a reggae rotation of his shoulders that makes him totally appealing, Bo starts to sing "Don't Worry, Be Happy" in a dark husky voice that has an island heat to it.

I suffer a meltdown.

"We can't go back to your place," he says in his cop voice as soon as we get into the car.

"I have to get my suitcase, Bo. It's right in the kitchen. And I have to get a book too. Something I need for the press conference."

So he drives back to my house and parks in the side driveway.

When he comes around to open my door, I start to get out but miss my footing and suddenly his arms are around me.

Bo is holding me. He is holding me, but also holding *on to* me, with a kind of a democratic neediness that corresponds to my own. Being near him is like being next to a big shade tree that offers shelter on a hot summer night when there hasn't been any rain for seven weeks.

"No sex tonight," he says, smoothing my hair away from my temples, where it's pasted down with perspiration. "No condoms, no sex. I can't tell those kids not to do something if I do it, right? You don't want me to be like our mayor, do you?"

But we *are* having sex.

Our bodies are like relief maps—hardened protuberances and absorbent valleys. We are having sex and it is safe, the safest sex I've ever had. No demands, no danger. No requests, no risks. I am in the hands of the law, and although they are not soft, they seem gentle.

He has taken me into protective custody.

Maybe that's the definition of love.

After a long while, Bo cuffs my chin gently.

"Let's go in. I have to call my office."

Once inside, I leave Bo in the kitchen and run upstairs, turning on lights as I go. I walk into Eli's study and suddenly remember the millions of times Eli looked up from his desk to smile at me when I appeared in his doorway. Now my heart turns into a fist and I experience a moment of pristine longing for the past. I would have liked my life to stay the way it was, but it was silly to think that what was good for one person would necessarily please the other forever.

I kneel down and begin sifting through the piles of books that have been dumped on the floor around Eli's desk. I'm lucky to find the paperback anthology, edited by our friend Scott Armstrong, titled *The Chronology: The Documented Day-by-Day Account of the Secret Military Assistance to Iran and the Contras.* When the fat little paperback finally surfaces, I shove it into my purse. Then I pick up Eli's answering machine, which is lying upside down on the floor, and reset and return it to his desk before I hear Bo calling me.

"What's wrong?" I ask, trotting toward the stairs.

"Something's the matter with your telephone," he says from the first-floor hallway. His voice sounds different. Emphatic, insistent. "I think we should get out of here."

I hurry down the stairs and follow him back into the kitchen. Flicking off the overhead light, he walks over to the glass-brick wall and stands there looking outside. When he finally turns around I realize something terrible is happening. Unconsciously, I back up against the refrigerator.

"Jesus," he hisses. "There're men out there. Maybe two or three."

Panic begins playing loud kettledrums in my head.

"What should we do, Bo? Who is it?"

"I don't know. I can just see shadows moving around outside. There's too many fucking trees for me to see."

"So we'll just wait," I say loudly enough to make myself heard over my internal rock band. "We'll just stay right where we are until they go away. They can't get in."

The next time I hear Bo's voice it's only a hoarse whisper.

"Get down on the floor, Natalie. Lie down."

I do.

I know Bo is nearby but I can't see him.

Now there is the sound of glass breaking.

My kettledrums are thundering.

"Where'd that come from?" Bo demands. He is across the room, flattened up against the wall near the stove.

"Upstairs," I say. "Maybe the bathroom. There's a big bay window in there."

Next comes another cascade of falling glass that seems to be from a more distant place. Maybe the window in the cellar door. Could someone reach inside and open the door that way? But there's mesh wire over that window and the basement door into the kitchen is always locked.

Now I hear a car engine revving up. The sound comes from the side driveway, where our cars are parked. For some reason the sound of the engine seems to get louder.

"Oh, God." I begin panting. "Someone's driving around the side of the house, Bo. On the grass. They're driving through my garden."

"Which side?" he howls.

Suddenly headlights pour into the kitchen, splashing up against the walls.

"Go!" Bo shouts. "Get out of here. Run down the hill. Go toward the zoo. Keep your head down. Go, Natalie! *Now!*"

I crouch over and start to run.

The back door sticks.

I feel the key begin to bend from the force of my turning it. I lighten the pressure a little and finally hear it catch.

Turn. Click. Open.

I edge outside onto the patio. I am waiting for something to slam into me, but I keep moving, hunching along the hedge, running away from the headlights. And that's when the car, racing its engine, smashes into the glass wall of my kitchen like a plane into the side of a mountain.

I half roll over the waist-high brick wall that reinforces our patio. When I hear a rally of gunshots I stop for one second to look back. With the headlights illuminating the kitchen, I can see Bo explode through the wall of shattered glass and head toward the retaining wall I just hurdled.

"Get him," a man yells.

And then light comes stuttering out of the darkness and Bo leaps up into the air like a deer and flings himself toward the wall.

I stand up and start to run. The din of death and destruction fills my head as I lunge through the thick underbrush down the hill toward the parkway. I am crashing through roots and vines, swinging around trees as I skid down the steep incline.

The animals in the zoo are shrieking and screaming and roaring. I feel hunted. Like an animal. I feel the killers coming after me. Quietly trying to find and finish me.

My ankles are burning as if I'd been ice-skating. Someone is making sliding, scraping sounds behind me, crashing through the undergrowth like I did, but I don't know who it is. It might or might not be Bo. I'm afraid to call out. I don't think it's him. Or it might be him with someone else in pursuit. I don't want to reveal where I am. I can't see anything. I am afraid of everything that touches my arms or legs. I flatten out on the hillside and wait while three cars speed past. When it's dark again I cross the hard flat road of Rock Creek Parkway.

Now I'm inside the zoo, running along the pathway down a hill toward the bears, toward the safety of the animals, where I can hide until daylight. But I am out of shape and unable to run anymore. I sink down on my knees behind an enormous tree. Now that my fear of the human terrorists subsides a little, I begin to panic about the animals—possible refugees from the zoo as well as the wide assortment native to this heavily wooded area. Snakes, skunks, rodents and opossum come out of these woods at night to invade adjoining properties, scavenging for garbage and causing panic in those who come upon them. I am hard-pressed to keep hysteria at bay.

But not very long afterward, I hear a police car come screaming along the main service road of the zoo, its red light spinning crazily atop its roof. Then I hear Bo calling out over some kind of bullhorn.

Calling me.

"Natalie. Natalie. It's Bo. Come on out. Don't be afraid. Are you hurt?"

For a moment, I don't believe it's Bo. If Bo is in that car, who was running behind me? Maybe Bo was hit by the bullets. How many people were up there at my house? Who smashed into my wall? I didn't give them what they wanted so now they want me. Maybe there are still some of those men wandering through the zoo, hunting me, waiting for me to disclose my hiding place behind this tree.

"Nat?"

This time I know that it's Bo's voice. So, dazed and slow, I stand up and walk back toward the service road. That's when I see Bo coming toward me, skewered by the headlights of the squad car. And then there's a crazy circle of people forming and reforming around me, big in their blue uniforms.

Bo clasps my shoulders.

"Answer. Are you all right?"

The heat hugs the darkness like a satin lining. It is difficult to breathe. I am hyperventilating, unable to speak. Each breath is uncomfortably shallow, unsatisfactory.

I can hear traffic on the parkway, the distant rumble of people on Columbia Road. From deep within the zoo, I hear a hyena. Once. Twice. Three times. Everything is getting crazier. Everything seems upside down.

Bo guides me toward a squad car. Someone else is in the driver's seat. Bo opens the back door for me and I get in. He rides shotgun in the front. The overhead light is on. Bo turns around to look at me.

I am out of it.

There are no handles on the inside of the back doors. This is something I'd never heard about. No back-door handles. If we have an accident, I won't be able to get out of the car. I lean back and close my eyes. I seem to have had a date with death tonight, but he stood me up. Through a fluke, I escaped dying. I avoided being murdered. I have to think about that. I have to study and memorize it, maybe even do a translation.

"I'm pretty sure I know who it was," Bo says soberly.

I don't respond.

"Do you want to know what happened?"

I can't answer.

"Your neighbors saw that car in your driveway and called the precinct even before they smashed into your wall. The squad car they dispatched was on your corner. Pretty lucky, huh? I saw it pull into your driveway before I started down the hill. I knew they were there; I had that edge over you."

He smiles at me; I don't smile back.

"But since they'd never gotten out of their car, they got away. They smashed down half the back wall of your house and then just drove away. I'll keep security there until we can get it fixed. Listen, Nat, where would you like to go? What about your brother-in-law's place in Georgetown? Brian here will stay with you."

I nod. "My purse?" I ask.

Bo bends over and lifts it off the floor.

"Got it—I grabbed it when I went back." He grins. "I even threw your suitcase in the trunk. How 'bout that?"

I look at him, but don't answer.

No one speaks again until we are on Reservoir Road.

The driver keeps the engine running while Bo walks me to the front door. He has to unlock it because my hands are shaking too much. He comes inside.

"I've got to get back to the station," he says. "You go upstairs and find a bed. My man will stay downstairs here all night. Okay?"

I do as I'm told. I run up the stairs and into the master bedroom. From there I stagger into the bathroom. A wild woman looks back at me from the huge mirror over the sink. It's not the raw red scratches on my neck and shoulders and along one side of my face. No—my entire expression has changed. The attempt on my life, my crazed run through the zoo—this steamy Graham Greene night of crazy dangers has written a new message across my face. It has made me someone different, though I don't know who.

After I hear the front door slam shut, I take a long shower and then crawl into Christopher's king-sized bed.

I sleep until noon. When I get up, I put on a bathrobe from the closet and go downstairs to make coffee. Brian, the cop, is walking around outside near the pool. He waves to me; I hold a coffee mug up in the air, but he shakes his head. I do not let myself rerun the rushes from last night. I do not let myself think about my house.

Midafternoon I begin to get nervous, so I dig the Scott Armstrong book out of my purse. I've read hunks of it before, but now
I flip through it with a greater sense of purpose. Oh, yes. It's all
so clearly documented. Oliver North was a traitor and Fawn Hall
was his accomplice. There's no way around it.

Oliver North usurped authority from the president, from Congress, from America's citizens. He traded arms for the release of
our hostages in Iran but failed to secure their freedom. He took
funds from Iran and other countries and secretly sent it to the
contras. Presumably higher authorities were unaware of those
activities; anyway, there is no accounting for what happened to
all the money.

Oliver North, Fawn Hall and Arturo Cruz, Jr., were their own
government. They conducted their own foreign policy. After
rereading several sections of the book, I replace it in my purse.

Around three o'clock I shower, fix my hair and put on a khaki-
colored sundress that makes me feel as if I'm going off on a safari.
At four o'clock Brian drives me up to Eighteenth Street, where
I enter the Pronto Press and wait while the clerk makes sixty
copies of Fawn's interview and sixty copies of a medley of quotes
I compiled from *The Chronology*. Walking up the block to A
Home Away from Home, I read through my handouts:

- Reginald Bartholomew, the American Ambassador in Leba-
  non, reported on September 4 [1985] that "North was handling an operation that would lead to the release of all seven
  hostages. [A U.S.] team had been deployed to Beirut, we were
  told. Ambassador Bartholomew had been alerted directly by
  the NSC and would assist." (Shultz, 12/86)
- [May 1986:] The NSC suggests that Reagan ask Saudi Arabia
  to contribute money to the contras. During the summer,
  McFarlane calls Shultz to inform him the Saudis have donated
  $31 million to a contra group. It is not clear whether this
  includes an earlier $20 million donation received before
  McFarlane left office late last year. (*NYT* 1/13/87)
- [April 14, 1986:] It is reported that the CIA spent several

million dollars refurbishing the image of the United Nicaraguan Opposition (UNO), the contra umbrella organization,
despite a congressional ban on aid to the rebels. (AP 4/14/86;
CRS "U.S. Intelligence: Issues for Congress, 1986" 1/5/87)
- [May 2, 1986:] Lt. Col. North informed VADM Poindexter
that he believed the Contras were readying to launch a major
offensive to capture a "principal coastal population center" in
Nicaragua and proclaim independence. North warned that if
this occurred "the rest of the world will wait to see what we
do—recognize the new territory—and UNO as the govt.—or
evacuate them as in a Bay of Pigs." He suggested that the U.S.
should be prepared to come to the Contras' aid.

I concluded these quotes with an excerpt from Seymour
Hersh's introduction:

The Iran-contra affair has correctly been viewed by most Americans as a serious foreign policy gaffe, but it is more than that—it
is a symptom of a government gone amok. We do a disservice to
that truth by dealing with Iran-contra merely as a scandal to be
resolved. . . . One of the major issues that emerged . . . was whether
the President would be willing to admit he had "made a mistake"
in authorizing his subordinates on the National Security Council
staff to attempt to trade arms for hostages through Iran. . . .

Unlocking the padlock and untangling the chain, I push open
the door and go inside the shelter. A month without any ventilation has turned the small front room into an oven. The heat is
impacted like a sick tooth, but I am afraid to even leave the door
ajar because some drunk could enter and trap me inside. Dust has
settled on the floor, atop the piles of thin, narrow mattresses and
inside the two huge shipping boxes containing all our linens and
pillows.

There is a foul smell in the room. I open the bathroom door.
In the sink is a backed-up pool of yellow water. Holding my
breath, I stick my hand down inside the mess, but when I finally
get the drain unstopped, I can't find anything on which to wipe

my hand so I end up drying it on my dress. Then I walk into the little back annex that is lined with clothes racks. There I see a streak of black race along the rear wall toward the alley door.

A rat.

I suppress a scream and run outside, where I wait until the first few male journalists arrive. Then, mistakenly viewing them as protection, I lead them inside. These well-dressed, well-seasoned journalists are clearly unnerved by the sight of the miserly camp mattresses stacked in the corner. But I don't feel apologetic about having summoned them here, because this is my office. I am using my office for a press conference just as any other professional might. The fact that my office smells and is about 120 degrees, with no windows, no ventilation, no chairs and no semblance of civility, is not my fault.

It has to do with the political values of our whacked-out local and federal governments.

Not mine.

As more reporters arrive, I notice them watching me with equal amounts of eagerness and suspicion. They are curious about what contribution I might make to the presidential circus snaking through Washington. But they are also silently praying I won't embarrass them with any more facts or statistics about homelessness or the shortage of shelters in D.C. They want information, not a lecture.

By six o'clock there are some twenty-five reporters standing in the claustrophobic heat, waiting for me to begin. I am impressed by their commitment. A camera crew from CBS, which I'd never even contacted, has also arrived and started setting up.

But I am waiting for Bo. He finally appears about six-ten. He's all business today. But he's looking so good my hormones start to jangle. His beard and hair have been trimmed, highlighting their silvery slivers. He's wearing tan cotton slacks and a white cotton shirt with epaulets, which, like my dress, has a safari flavor. Then brown loafers without socks, as usual.

Although I've never addressed such a large or sophisticated audience before, I sound fairly cool when I begin.

"Thank you for coming. I'm Natalie Karavan Myers. Yes, I'm Shay Karavan's sister, but I'm not a mover or shaker like her." Gracious smile. "I'm a social worker and I run this shelter for homeless women, which is temporarily closed because we've run out of operating funds. You can probably tell that our most pressing need is for an AC or at least some large floor fans." I look at the impatient faces watching me. "I know newspaper policies about never paying for stories, but if you *can* make a contribution before you leave, a lot of women would be very grateful. You can just leave it up front on that windowsill there."

Embarrassment twists through the crowd like a small tornado.

"Anyway"—I smile to let them off the hook a little—"today I'm going to distribute an interview that Fawn Hall gave to some DEA agents last summer in which she admitted to being a weekend cocaine user."

A delicious hum stirs the room. Breathing rhythms change like the tempo of a band shifting from a waltz to a fox-trot.

"I guess I don't have to explain why it was never released, why the DEA suppressed it. Nobody wanted Fawn Hall discredited before she appeared in front of the joint congressional committee. The Republicans didn't want her testimony in support of Oliver North tainted by any confession of drug usage. They didn't want her to become a symbol of the corruption in the Reagan administration. They didn't want the issue of a possible breach in national security raised by Fawn's being a cokehead."

The journalists start asking questions, but I cut them off.

"Please, wait. Let me finish first. What Contragate shows is that government officials made private deals without congressional or presidential knowledge. We know Oliver North's gang sold arms to Khomeini and independently negotiated for the release of our hostages. We know he solicited funds from other countries, which he then sent down to the contras in Nicaragua. In other words, Reagan's National Security Council staff did whatever they wanted to do whenever they wanted to do it. They altered, shredded and stole official documents. Ollie North's secretary, Fawn Hall, dated Arturo Cruz, Jr., the contra leaders' son, and did coke in Georgetown during the time she was working for North.

"I'm no foreign-policy expert but, having lived in D.C. as long as I have, I do have a certain sense of the contradictions and inconsistencies that exist here. However, just to refresh your memories, I've also photocopied for you some excerpts from Scott Armstrong's chronology of Contragate. So please pick up one set from each of the two piles."

There is a long quivering silence during which only the TV cameras whir and the print photographers click their shutters. Everyone is sweating profusely by now. Everyone is eager to pick up a handout and get out of here.

"Okay," I say, pointing to the two stacks of papers set atop two mattress piles. "Help yourselves."

There is a wild flurry as they begin grabbing copies. Then there is a silent pause while they read Fawn Hall's statement. After that the questions come skidding at me like baseball grounders:

"Where did you get this information, Ms. Myers?"

"Why didn't your husband want this story?"

"Is Shay Karavan involved in any way?"

"Does the DEA know you are in possession of this document?"

"What do you hope to accomplish, Ms. Myers, by releasing this?"

"Do you work with the Dukakis campaign? Are you supporting Dukakis for president?"

"Have you ever been to Nicaragua?"

"How did you come into possession of this interview?"

"No comment," I say.

"No comment," I say each time they ask how I came into possession of the document, and each time they ask about Shay or Eli. Some of the other questions I try to answer; Bo fields different ones. But when he stands up, clearly prepared to make a statement, I listen like all the reporters in the room.

"Some of you might have seen a small Metro article in the *Post* this morning about an attack on a Northwest home last night. A car carrying three narcoterrorists smashed through a glass wall of Ms. Myers's house. They were attempting to find the original copy of the interview that Ms. Myers just distributed to you. She's behaved both coolly and bravely. Because of Ms. Myers, and her neighbors, who came outside in time to get the license-plate number of the car, we were able to find the registered owner. Two of the men in the attack car are well-known dealers linked to José Ocheros, the owner of the Ariel club in Georgetown. They were inside the house of the registered owner, just sitting in the goddam kitchen—making microwave popcorn," Bo chuckles. "They were arrested, taken to the Second District lockup and, by morning, had agreed to testify against Ocheros. So he was picked up and brought in for questioning around eight-thirty this morning. Our drug operatives have always suspected Ocheros laundered drug money for Nicaraguan contras by buying Georgetown commercial real estate in his own name. We've got plenty of evidence ready for presentation to the grand jury that's currently sitting."

Surprisingly, this information seems to interest the reporters, most of whom cover only national news and usually consider local stories beneath their dignity. They question Bo and he provides a number of details about the arrests and the detainment of Ocheros at the D.C. lockup. He also provides detailed background material about the contras' involvement in the D.C. drug trade. People listen to Bo because he speaks with an air of urgency that sounds both dramatic and authentic.

It is toward the end of this question session that Hannah suddenly appears in the doorway, sporting a brand-new costume, pushing her Safeway shopping cart and swinging her Lord & Taylor shopping bag from one wrist. Today she is wearing a woolen serape over a large pink beach towel she has tied around her waist.

Pausing, she surveys the well-kempt, dressed-for-success-in-the-tropics crowd.

"Whazzall this?" she asks me in a loud raucous voice. "They're making it too crowded in here."

An uncomfortable chuckle passes through the crowd. Here is a street person turning up her nose at an elite congregation of top-flight correspondents who are slumming only long enough to score a story.

"It's too hot in here," Hannah repeats in the silence that follows in her wake. She wipes her face with the clawed fingers of one hand. "Better in the park. Better in the zoo."

"I can borrow a fan somewhere so you can stay here tonight, Hannah," I offer.

But she has turned around and begun pulling her shopping cart back toward the doorway.

"The park's better," she says, nodding cordially to the people making way for her. "It's not so hot."

Now none of the journalists know where to look, how to avoid meeting each other's eyes and acknowledging the implicit meaning of Hannah's impromptu, but perfectly timed, visit.

"Why didn't the Justice Department do anything about Hall's confession?" a young woman asks me.

"I personally don't think they knew about it," I answer, still watching the impact of Hannah's departure. "I think DEA just sat on it and never turned it over to Justice. I guess you folks are going to have to investigate that whole scenario because I can't. I'm not a journalist. I work, you know."

They appreciate my little joke.

By now I too am unbearably hot. My clothes are sticking to my body, my hair to the sides of my face.

At last the reporters begin to drift off in twos and threes. Most of them pause to leave some money on the front windowsill as they pass through the doorway. Some of them are still reading my handouts; others are talking excitedly among themselves like students leaving a college classroom after the return of their blue books, rereading their own answers while comparing grades with each other.

When everyone is gone, Bo walks over to me.

"What do you have to do now?" he asks in a new, very private and personal way.

"Nothing. I did it, I think."

"I'd say so." He grins down at me proudly.

My heart goes crazy.

"So c'mon then," he says, jerking his head. "Let's go over to my place. We'll break a few eggs and make a coupla omelets."

Ahhhh. A rich image.

"Okay. Just let me lock up, Bo. And count the loot."

"Looks to me like you did pretty good," he chuckles.

"I think so too," I agree.

In fact, I think I did great.

14

Eli is standing outside the doorway, squinting in the still-harsh sunlight.

I am so shocked to see him that I don't say anything. I just stand there, perfectly still, staring up at him. In one hand I'm holding the ninety-eight dollars contributed by the reporters and, in the other, my keys to the storefront. Bo is at my side.

"You were great, Natalie. Real professional," Eli says with quiet approval.

His forehead is blistered with beads of sweat. His shirt, wet with perspiration, sticks to his chest, drawing a damp map of some unknown continent.

"I did it because you said—"

"You did it because you *had* to," he voices over me. "And you did it *very* well."

Interior commotion. Then:

"Eli, this is Bo Culver, the detective I told you about? Bo, this is my husband, Eli Myers."

They shake hands.

"Been past your place yet?" Bo asks.

"Just long enough to shove my suitcase inside. Looked pretty bad. I hear you had quite an experience last night."

I don't ask how he heard; I only nod.

"I guess I owe you some thanks," Eli says formally to Bo.

Bo shrugs. "Not really. Well, I'm outta here. Back to the precinct. Lots of paperwork to do."

He shakes hands with Eli again, nods at me and then walks back toward Kalorama Road.

I feel like I've just lost my best friend. After a moment, I look at Eli inquiringly. No—apprehensively. He looks back at me with deadly resignation.

S N A P S H O T

This is the photo taken by the wife of the justice of the peace who married Eli and me in Green Bay, Wisconsin, at eight-thirty in the morning after our night drive from Minneapolis. Although still early, it had already begun getting hot, and when we stepped outside onto the porch for our wedding picture, we were looking directly into the sun. Eli had frowned; I had squinted. But as years passed, and I studied that photo more carefully, I realized there was more than sunlight in Eli's eyes. I think he was crying, not from joy or excitement, but with sadness. I think he loved Shay so much he married me, on the rebound, so as to stay faithful to her in his own strange way. Or maybe he just wanted to stay in her life.

Although my heart still hurries when I remember the "us" from long ago, it is clearly too late to think about any of that now. From this moment on, our relationship is totally different. We are like formal friends now, polite and careful.

"Want to get something over at Millie and Al's?" Eli asks.

"Sure."

"Your hair looks real good like that, Nat. And you've lost some weight."

I decide not to respond.

We cross the street and walk up the block to the tired old restaurant that doesn't even try to compete with its upscale neighbors. The heat and humidity slap up against us. Eli's hair is curdling atop his scalp. We walk close beside each other, like we always do, but I can feel his determination to say what is necessary to end our marriage. He is going to take care of this last piece of business with the same thoroughness and dispatch as he does everything.

I feel myself filling up with dread now that it's about to happen. I am suddenly afraid to attend my own sentencing. I want to postpone it in hopes of some sudden clemency.

Inside Millie & Al's, we sit down in the same scarred old booth where we've always sat. Eli orders us beers and smiles nostalgically at the waitress.

"What made you change your mind about returning the interview?" he asks me.

"Oh, different things. You were one of them. Listen, I've got to wash my face," I say. "I'll be right back."

What I really want is to see how I look. I want to take a mental snapshot of myself in the mirror so when I remember this encounter I'll be able to know how Eli saw me. The light in the ladies' room is dim and the mirror cloudy, but I can see how I've begun to resemble one of those female models in a black-and-white Calvin Klein ad. Despite the cuts and scratches on my face, I've begun to look like one of those existential-eyed women, leaning up against a thick, sun-bleached wall, on the hillside of some Greek island that is eternally erupting and tumbling back into the sea in an orgasm of beauty. Drama has begun to adhere to me.

I *like* how I look because now I look the way I feel.

I try to calm down as I walk back to rejoin Eli in our booth, but a symphony of contradictory emotions is roaring through my head.

Seated, I pour beer from a bottle into my glass.

"This is hard to say," Eli begins. "I really don't know exactly how to say it. Except, well . . . it really isn't working out, is it, Nat?"

"What?"

"Our marriage—it isn't working out."

Though I've been waiting for this pronouncement, the passive construction of his sentence sends rage whipping through me. A hard stubbornness establishes a beachhead in my breast.

"You know what I regret?" he asks.

"What?"

"That we didn't adopt any kids."

That's an easy charge to rebut.

"It never really seemed like you wanted to, Eli. I mean, whenever I tried to talk about it, you mostly just grunted."

"Grunted?" he repeats, insulted by the word. "That's not true."

"And when we *were* ready to do it, you accepted the San Francisco assignment, and the waiting time ran out on us."

He shrugs.

"Well, you're only forty-five, Eli. You can still get married and have ten kids of your own."

He looks away, silenced by this truth.

"Is that what you're going to do, Eli? Remarry and start a family? That seems sort of unfair. My turn is over, huh? I'm like one of those Middle Eastern queens who gets deposed for failing to produce a male heir."

"That's not why. If it was about kids, I wouldn't have stayed this long."

"Well, what *is* it about?"

He doesn't answer. He is looking off toward the front window.

"Eli, were you still in love with Shay when we got married?"

He sighs with ancient disapproval at my question.

"Please, tell me."

"Of course I wasn't."

"Did you ever really love me?"

"Of course."

"But now you've just stopped?"

Silence.

"You know, in a weird way I'd feel better if I knew you never loved me, Eli. It would make *this* a little easier."

He grimaces with impatience. "I'm not going to say that, Nat. All I can say is that it just isn't working out anymore."

"What's 'it'?"

His face clouds over with anger.

"Well, maybe this is just as well," I say, shrugging. "You always made me feel pretty shitty about myself, Eli."

Since he doesn't ask what I mean, or deny it, I say it again: "You always made me feel second-class."

"I didn't mean to, Natalie. I'm sorry if I did. And you really look astonishingly beautiful right now. Do those cuts on your face hurt?"

S N A P S H O T

Here's me and Eli and the Nelsons in Moscow last year, shivering in our bulky, shapeless overcoats and boots. We're standing in knee-deep snow with the crest of the Kremlin behind us. Something had happened that morning which hurt me a lot. We'd been eating breakfast in the Nelsons' big chilly apartment and talking about the cold war and Russia's current posture in the world, especially in Eastern Europe. I had disagreed with what Eli and the Nelsons were saying. I even made a short but impassioned speech about Gorby and the movement toward a U.S.-Soviet political thaw. Then Eli had turned to me, put his hand atop mine on the table, and said, "You don't understand, Nat." "I *do* understand, I just see it differently." But then he'd patted my hand so patronizingly that I'd flushed and fallen silent with embarrassment.

"Not as much as some other things."

For a while he doesn't speak, can't speak. Then:

"You took off like a bat out of hell at that news conference, Nat. You really did a great job. You're going to get a lot of exposure from that. You'll see. You'll be playing in the majors from now on."

"What about our house?" I ask.

"I'm sure the insurance will cover it, but it will take a long time to get it repaired. We'll have to put everything into storage for a while because there's no way to secure it with that back wall smashed the way it is. And since we can't stay there, we might as well use this opportunity to try living apart for a while. Each of us can try out some new things, on our own."

I can't tell how far Eli's progressed in his thinking about divorce. If we do split, we'll have to sell our house. Eli will probably try to be fair about dividing our assets, and I am self-sufficient anyway. But I know I will never again have a beautiful home or the security and fun that Eli once provided for me.

"I'll never live in another house," I say.

He dons his Columbo confused expression and slumps over in his Matthau manner. What he's trying to establish is that, while what I've said is probably true, he can't help it. It's not his fault I'll never live in a house again and, anyway, that's hardly an earth-shaking tragedy.

"Were you with a woman down in Atlanta, Eli? Someone else?"

"Yes. Yes I was."

I have to recoup for a few minutes before I can speak again.

"Well, does that sound reasonable to you?" Eli prompts me. "About the house and all that?"

Rage erupts inside me.

"Would you please tell me why you want to do this, Eli? I mean, where do you get off unilaterally deciding you're going to turn my life upside down?"

"It's not an easy thing, Nat, but I'm burned out. I've got nothing left inside. For me or for you."

"Well, you've got *something* left for her."

Carefully I pour the remainder of my beer into the glass, which I tilt so as not to raise any foam.

"Do you like that cop?" he asks me in a gentle voice.

I ignore the question and ask where he's going to stay.

"I'm not sure. I'll find someplace to camp. I wanna see if I can get a sabbatical from work. Spring myself loose for a while."

"I was almost killed last night, Eli. Some men came to kill me."

"I know, Nat."

"How'd you hear about it?"

"Someone from my office called to tell me. So I just went out to the airport and I got on the first flight outta there. It sounded like a god-awful experience."

"And how'd you hear about my press conference?"

"Same way."

We've finished. We both smile vaguely at each other.

I feel forlorn. Bereft. Like one of Jean Rhys's abandoned female characters anguishing over the advisability of ordering a second Pernod on the shadowy terrace of some stingy, street-front café, where she wants to linger, watching the gaiety pass by, and thus delay returning to her morose hotel room, where memories wait to riot during the darkness of her barren nights. But she cannot order another drink because she fears the opprobrium of the proprietor . . . the cashier . . . the waiter . . . the other patrons . . . the passersby. . . .

Eli pays our bill and we walk outside.

"What are you going to do now, Eli?"

"Go back to the house."

"It's such a mess." I grimace. "But, then, so's life."

Now he seems somewhat reluctant to leave.

"How 'bout you? Where're you going?"

"I don't know. Maybe Christopher's. I can stay there until he gets back."

"Well."

Eli sighs, but he can't think of anything else to say. After a while he hooks his arm around my neck and awkwardly draws me close enough to kiss the crown of my head.

Then he turns and walks away.

I go half a block in the other direction.

From an outdoor telephone booth on the corner, I call Bo, who exudes excitement when he hears my voice. He says he was waiting by the phone, that he'll be over in five minutes to pick me up, that he's going to take me home to his place—if I'm still free for dinner.

But when I get in his car, I suddenly feel enormously shy. I don't want to talk about Eli or what happened. I don't even want to think about it. He, of course, asks immediately.

BO: So? What happened?
ME: (Silence.)
BO: What'd he say?
ME: We're going to close up the house for a while. We're going to have a trial separation.
BO: How do you feel about that?
ME: Pissed.
BO: Just pissed?
ME: (Silence.)
BO: One of my sisters just got divorced. Last year, actually. She's forty-five and she said if she'd known how it felt to start dating again, she'd never have left her old man. She says now she spends her Saturdays getting ready for dates with men who don't like the same movies she likes and who don't want to buy her any popcorn.
ME (looking out the window): Nobody ever said it's a barrel of fun trying to find someone to be with after you've hit the big four-oh. But I don't think I want to talk about it right now.
BO: Okay.

He turns on the radio; NPR gives us a heavy dose of Dukakis. Ugh.

Bo lives off Sixteenth Street in a large apartment complex. After parking in a subterranean garage, we take an elevator up to the twelfth floor. The lights in the elevator glare like theatrical spots. I feel tired, awkward, out of it. Bo is also quiet. He seems to have difficulty opening the lock on his front door. Finally I realize his hands are shaking.

This must be as hard for him as it is for me.

His apartment is a basic L-shaped job, not that different from Marge's. It is furnished with a begrudging nod toward fashion. A leather couch and matching easy chair with a large footstool. A couple of glass tables. Beige carpeting. He means for it to look okay, not great. That touches me for some reason.

"If you want to wash up . . ." he says, gesturing down a narrow hallway.

This is going to be too painful to bear.

I shake my head and follow him into the kitchen. It is narrow and suddenly I feel claustrophobic. We keep bumping into each other and apologizing as we start to make drinks. People often pretend that they stumbled into sex because they drank too much, sat too close, did some drugs, lost control. But we can't pretend it's that way. My presence here has an air of intentionality that makes it seem low-budget, garish, obvious.

I feel brazen. Brassy. Ballsy. Bad. Like Shay when she would decide to make it with some guy and simply set about doing it. Crude. Gross. Like Gary Hart finding the *Monkey Business* on which to sink himself. Definitely low-budget. On the other hand, this prelude also seems embarrassingly profound. Significant. Momentous. Big-screen. Either way, it's too much for me to handle. I am rendered speechless. I begin losing it. Falling apart.

Bo opens the refrigerator and instantly encounters a strong sour smell that completely distracts him.

"Jesus, something went bad," he groans, and then he begins to hunt frantically through various tin-foil-wrapped packages.

White European Woman notices for first time that black men blush.

"Maybe it's some cheese," I say, meaning to be helpful.

But instantly I see my remark upsets him even more. It's as if whatever spoiled has spoiled everything between us. Now he is banging around on the metal shelves. Miserable. Unhappy. Finally he finds some package that he deems the culprit and runs out into the hallway to throw it down the incinerator.

Actually his kitchen is clean, tidy and nicely outfitted. He has blue French cookware and everything looks well scrubbed, even the burners on the stove. When he returns from the incinerator, he sets me to work chopping vegetables on a thick wooden cutting board. I dice everything very small. This helps kill time but doesn't appease my uneasiness. I feel miserable. Pitiful. Hopelessly teenaged.

Conversation is becoming more and more difficult. Bo has already related most of the anecdotes stemming from the arrests of the drug dealers in Mount Pleasant. He has already told me what a fuss Ocheros made at the precinct after he was brought in. I have already analyzed the reporters' reactions to Bo's announcement and to Hannah's visit. We have already discussed where to buy floor fans with the journalists' donations.

Neither of us mentions Eli.

While the omelets are cooking, Bo sets the dining-room table: place mats, large-sized dishes, silverware, wineglasses. There is an unattractive furniture-outlet-type bar set up against one wall in the dining area, out of which he takes a bottle of red wine. Then he looks over toward the sink, where I'm rinsing off the cutting board.

"Or do you prefer white?" he asks formally.

"Yes, I do. Thank you."

Oh, God. I can't go through with this, I think, rushing cool water over my wrists. What happened to the safe sex of married life? What happened to those big easy encounters that were as predictable as Monday-night football? I'm not up for major surprises anymore.

Damage control is where it's at now.

When the omelets are ready, Bo places them on a serving platter and brings them to the table. Then he makes a great deal of noise sliding each piece off the dish with a spatula, like some waiter in an expensive French restaurant ritualistically scraping pastries off a silver serving tray. I sit at the table and chugalug my first glass of wine like a teeny-bopper. I had wanted to charm and disarm Bo, but instead I am making him enormously uncomfortable.

"Would you like some catsup or A-One sauce?"

"No. This is fine, Bo. Thanks. It's really good."

Our silverware keeps scratching against our dishes. Every time I break off a piece of omelet, my fork screeches across my plate. So does Bo's. The noise is outrageous. Having consumed a year's worth of cholesterol and all the cacophonous scratching I can endure, I quit eating. So does Bo. After a while we carry our dishes and wineglasses back into the kitchen. Bo washes our two plates and two goblets before starting to scour the black iron griddle. I wipe the silverware with a somewhat tired dish towel.

S N A P S H O T

Dad took this picture of Shay and me about fifteen years ago—a few days after our Bubbie died. Shay and I had both flown home to attend the burial at a suburban cemetery owned by the Twin Cities Workmen's Circle. This fierce fraternity of socialists had bought a piece of foreign soil on which to regroup after death. My family created a small island of life in that deserted landscape. The first generation of middle-aged affluent assimilationists, swaddled in mink and cashmere overcoats, sat on folding chairs set upon the frozen soil. I stood among the crowd of our cousins, all in their mid-twenties and thirties—intellectuals of varying persuasions— and surrounded by their own waist-high children. It was this second generation that formed the ambivalent, neurotic wing of our family. Our clan of cousins, all pampered children of prosperous professionals, had been subverted by the smoldering socialism of our grandparents, eternally caught between a seductive style and an alien analysis.

Finally I say: "I'm pretty tired, Bo. Maybe we should call it a day."

His relief is palpable, visible, audible.

"You *should* be tired," he says sympathetically. "I'll drive you wherever you wanna go. You wanna go back to your brother-in-law's place?"

Abandoning the griddle, Bo takes the dish towel away from me to wipe his hands. Suddenly we are caught up in a great rush of preparations. In his eagerness to get me out of there, Bo loses his car keys and has to hunt around his apartment to find them. This gives me a little additional time to edit my departure.

"You know, I don't think I've had time to process everything that's happened," I say by way of apology, while staring out of the big bay window at the blackboard night outside. "I mean, in one week I had my sister on my hands and my car stolen. I've been out to Long Island and Minneapolis. My house has been shot into, vandalized and rammed by a car. I've messed around with my future brother-in-law and met a wonderful guy—a police-man. . . ."

"Your sequencing's all screwed up," Bo says in a flat, dead voice. "Anyway, don't kid yourself, kiddo. It's just because I'm the wrong color for you."

"Oh God, Bo," I gasp. "I thought we were such good friends you wouldn't think that. It's only because it doesn't matter that I can say I'm not up for it tonight."

"Well, I'm not *up for it* tonight, either."

So I deliver my headline:

"Eli's in love with another woman," I say with a sob, sinking into the leather armchair.

"Oh yeah, that's a pisser. I'm sure you're hurting," he concedes coldly. "But I've been there too. My wife, the woman I'm sepa-rated from, she doesn't love me anymore. It'll do ya every time. Now Bernice, my first wife, whose son got killed, she's begun to phone me up. Wants to start dating again. . . . Nothing ever really ends anymore. . . ."

"You must be tired too, Bo," I say. "I mean look at all *you've* been through. I mean, people get tired, right? We're not kids anymore."

"Right."

But there's a look of closure on his face that frightens me.

S N A P S H O T

This is another photo from that funeral weekend—Shay and me and some of our cousins. Estranged from our country-club parents by the radicalism our immigrant grandparents had bequeathed to us, we kept our distance from them at that cemetery. The old socialists, lying beneath their tombstones, had won our hearts and minds through years of bedtime stories that fixed our political vision, forever estranging us from easy assimilation or conformity. We cousins, who straddled both worlds, felt drawn toward the small group of old Jews standing haughtily apart from the immediate family of mourners. These were the last survivors of the Twin Cities Workmen's Circle, three old men wearing black fedora hats and hand-me-down overcoats, one withered old woman in an ancient chocolate-brown fur jacket. Like pilgrims from some Yiddish short story, they had come to bury their dead, routinely attending the funeral of each member or mate of their original group. When the service was over they limped back to the rented limousine that had been retained twenty years before—prepaid to transport the dwindling tribe of survivors to each of the burials until the last of the eternal exiles arrived in a hearse.

"Well, maybe we could just stay here and get some rest," I say, loud enough so he can hear me above the hard-rock beat of my blood.

"I don't think tonight's a very good night to try that," he says conclusively.

Already I feel lonely. Already I have begun to long and ache for him, yearn for his attention. I scramble to get up and out of the slippery concave chair; Bo bends over to help me and then I'm in his arms again, leaning against the proud stubborn wall of his body. I lift my face upward and he kisses me. I can taste my own salty tears on our lips, but the kiss is still sweet. Soft. Simple.

And then there is no stopping or retreating, no more equivocating or procrastinating. This is inevitable. This is a passion so sudden and deliberate that it has become my destiny. I walk down the long hallway to his bedroom with his arm around my shoulders. The bed is beautifully made, covered with an old-fashioned chenille spread. I touch the Braille-like pattern of big flowers.

"My grandmother's," Bo says proudly.

For one moment, I think of Eli. I know I have come to a point of no return, that I have embarked upon a solitary voyage without any map. But the thought disappears and I surrender to sensation, reaching for Bo with a thirst born of loneliness.

This is what I want.

This is the best way to talk about love.

In its silent language.

The wordless dialect.

The dazzling vocabulary of sex astonishes me all over again, the primitive but perfect grammar of internal dialogue, the eloquence of its syntax.

It is sweet to be near this man. Like a big shade tree, he offers me solace and shelter. My body nurses on him; I inhale and heave around him, hold him tight, absorbing his silent and silencing movements.

Is this for real?

Has any man ever felt so good, so nourishing, during a drought? We are in some alien dimension where time has been tamed and defanged. We loll about in perpetuity until we reach a place that proves unendurable, and then we crash, smash and splash into a million pieces, multicolored shards in all the hues of a rainbow. We don't sleep until dawn. I lose count of our couplings. All physical and temporal perimeters are lost in the darkness.

Right before dawn I hear myself begin to cry in my sleep.

Bo rolls me back into his arms and holds me until I grow quiet again.

The next morning I am half-asleep when he comes back into the bedroom. He has showered and put on fresh Lagerfeld and is holding *The Washington Post* open in front of himself like a shield. There is my picture in the left-hand bottom corner of the front page under the headline

D.C. SOCIAL WORKER LEAKS DEA DOCUMENT
I look like Sigourney Weaver in *Gorillas in the Mist.* I look like an absolutely ballsy, self-composed, self-edited, purposeful, com-

mitted, independent and unafraid woman. I look unflappable. I love the way I look. It's the way I've always wanted to look. Sweat has put a glow on my skin despite the scratches and cuts. The humidity has ruffled my straight limp hair into confusion. My eyes are fiery; I have a purpose. Although America has no stereotypical female intellectuals, no prototype like Simone de Beauvoir, I guess I look like the progressive political activist I've always wanted to be. Jesus, I look great!

"What do you think of that?" Bo asks.

I watch the center of the newspaper stir and bulge of its own volition.

"Looks great," I say.

"Wait till you read the story."

He hands me the newspaper. I don't mention his aroused condition, although I experience a rush of proprietary pleasure.

The transcript of a Drug Enforcement Administration interview with Fawn Hall, secretary to Lt. Colonel Oliver North when he served as Assistant Deputy Director for Political-Military Affairs on the National Security Council, was released late yesterday afternoon by Natalie Karavan Myers, director of A Home Away from Home shelter for homeless women at 2121 18th Street N.W.

Ms. Hall, who, during testimony before a Congressional Investigative Committee, admitted altering and shredding official government documents and concealing other papers on her person to pass through security at the Executive Office Building, admitted to DEA investigators that she used cocaine on a number of weekends during the period she worked for Colonel North. Ms. Hall's attorney later denied she'd admitted to extensive drug use.

Ms. Myers, who refused to divulge her sources or tell how she came into possession of the interview, said she was operating as a private citizen in making charges against a person imperiling U.S. national security.

Allllll riiiiiight!

When he's dressed, Bo kisses me good-bye and leaves for work. But ten minutes later he's back.

"It's me. Don't get scared," he yells from the hallway. Then he rushes back into the bedroom. His arms are full of newspapers—*The New York Times, The Washington Times, USA Today* and more copies of *The Washington Post.*

"You've just replaced Fawn Hall as the woman of the hour. The week. The month. The year. You're a star, Natalie."

He is smiling. He is happy. He hands me the newspapers, kisses me again and then jogs back to the front door.

I am also on the front page of *The New York Times,* below the fold, with a jump to page A24:

TRANSCRIPT OF DEA INTERVIEW WITH FAWN HALL REVEALS COCAINE USAGE

There is a sidebar to the story describing who I am, and another attractive, but totally different, photograph of me. Alongside my picture is one of Fawn Hall. We look like we're from different planets.

This is really a photo finish.

I go into the kitchen to put up some coffee.

Suddenly I wonder if Eli has seen the papers. I pick up the telephone and dial our number. After four rings, I hear my own voice on the answering machine. I hang up and dial the code that lets me hear the messages:

- "Well, you really take the cake, Natalie, you bitch. Call me the minute you get this message."
- "Good morning. This is Caitlin Gregorson at ABC News. Mr. Peter Jennings would like to speak with you to get some background information since you have been proposed as a possible choice as 'Person of the Week.'" (She laughs.) "Which isn't bad for the same week as the Democratic National Convention. Please call us collect at 212–555–6937. Thank you and congratulations."
- "This is Carl Badeiner at *The New York Times.* I've been

assigned to do an in-depth person-in-the-news–type interview with you this afternoon, if possible. I am here in the Washington bureau and will wait to hear from you. I've known Eli for years and look forward to meeting you. My direct number is 555–4399. Thanks for returning my call."

- "Hi, Natalie. I'm Cynthia Credenzia from *People* magazine. You are the talk of the office today. What a ballsy thing you did. I bet Ms. Fawn Hall would like to get her hands on you this morning. Of course we want to do a photo/interview story—you know, follow you through one of your days, catch you at the shelter where you work, that sort of stuff. If your sister's in Washington, maybe we can get some shots of you two together. Well, again, it's Cynthia Credenzia, at 212–555–2341. Please call back ASAP."

- "Brava, lady. You're a tiger. Don't worry. Be happy. I'll defend you pro bono. Call me at home. I want to talk to you about Amelia, too. Boy, you really struck a blow for freedom."

- "Hello. This is Mr. Fitzgerald from the Whistle Blowers' Association. Your name has been placed in nomination for induction into our organization. My number is 555–8976. I'm eager to speak with you. Frank Fitzgerald."

- "Natalie! Oh, this is really so great. It's Marcia Prouty from the Statehood party office. I've been trying to reach you for days. Thursday afternoon we had a citywide Coalition for the Homeless meeting over at Saint Mark's Cathedral. There were reps from about ten different groups and we finally hammered out a charter and an agreement to band together for all our fund-raising activities and campaigns. Oh, it's too complicated to tell you everything, but please call me up. Call me at home at 555–4657. Anyway, I think we can use all this publicity you're generating to make a real strong fund-raising pitch, so call me as soon as you can. Everyone's real proud of you, Nat. You did a really brave thing there, lady."

- "Good morning, Ms. Myers. Dean Carlos from *Newsweek*'s Washington bureau. Would you kindly give me a call at 555–9788?"

David Hummings, from Disney's Touchstone studios, tells me where to call him collect at any time. There are also calls from *Good Morning America* and the *Today* show. I scribble down the names and numbers as fast as I can, but the first call I return is Marcia Prouty's.

"Marcia, it's Nat Karavan Myers. I just got your message."

"Oh, boy. You did *good*, Nat." She gives a war whoop and a laugh. "You really stuck it to 'em. Listen. I know you're probably crazy busy right now, but we're finally getting our shit together. Mitch brought over four groups besides his own to the meeting Thursday and we formed a steering committee and laid out some plans for putting pressure on Human Resources. I think we're finally in business. And we voted you in as co-chair in absentia. Will you take it? We really need you."

"Will I ever! Oh, that's great, Marcia. I'm so excited. Now we'll have enough muscle to make some waves. Look, I'll probably have to go to New York to do the talk shows—there's a million messages—but I should be back in a week. Then we'll really dig in and show our stuff. Okay?"

"You got it."

Next I call Barney.

"Jesus, Natalie," he laughs. "You're spread all over every newspaper in the country."

"I know. Isn't it wild? You should hear the messages on my machine. *The New York Times, Newsweek, People,* Peter Jennings . . ."

"You did a great job, babe. Really great. This story isn't going to go away. We can really stick it to them now."

"They want me on the *Today* show Monday."

"Go."

"But then I can't do *Good Morning America;* I'll have to choose."

"Check it out. You want the largest exposure possible on a story like this."

"I can probably get enough New York appearances to stay there for a week."

"Don't miss a beat, babe. But, listen, the jury went out yesterday afternoon and came back in at midnight with an acquittal, so I'm high as a kite. I also had a long talk with Steven late last night. He's real uncomfortable about Shay moving Amelia to New York. He isn't too comfortable with me keeping her either, since Vicky works full-time and I work double time. So he wondered what you might think about—"

"Oh, Barney, you think he'll let her stay with me for a while?"

"Could happen. She'd still spend holidays and weekends with me."

My heart is unfurling with joy. I can't even respond.

"Okay, champ, I'll phone you later," Barney says softly before disconnecting.

Champ, I think.

Actually I feel a little bit like Rocky. Like all the push-ups, all the miles jogged and logged, all the workouts, have finally paid off. I will probably have to start a scrapbook. I will probably have to start cutting and pasting and gluing my own news clips and photos and outstanding quotes. Or maybe I'll just send the stuff to Marge and let her catalog my clippings along with Shay's.

Maybe I'll even become an answer in a crossword puzzle.

#1 Down: "Nickname of citizen who leaked Fawn Hall story":

N
A
T

#50 Across: "Big sister of formerly famous New York housewife known as Shay":

N A T

When I finally dial my mother's 612 number, Shay answers the telephone.

"Hold the line," she says. "I want to take this in the study."

Picking up the extension, she yells for someone to replace the receiver in the dining room. Then I can hear her lips making their familiar initial dry-air kiss as she lights a fresh cigarette.

"Well, you must be pretty pleased with yourself this morning," she says fiercely. "You made NBC and CBS news. Not bad for a little sneak. You really have a lot of balls, Natalie, stealing my story like that."

"I didn't *steal* your story, Shay. You *dumped* it on me. I only stole your thunder. And that's fair, since you've been raining on my parade—"

"Oh, please, don't get weird on me now. I just can't believe you didn't return the papers like you said. What a liar you are. And do you realize the kind of danger you've just put us in?"

"Wrong. No one's in danger anymore. Bo's men picked up Ocheros and his two main guys yesterday; he booked them on B and E."

"B and E?"

"Breaking and entering. They broke into my house again, Shay. No—they didn't *break* in; they *drove* in. They drove right through the glass-brick wall in my kitchen. Then they chased me, on foot, down to the zoo, Shay. This hasn't been a lot of fun for me."

"Well, it *seems* to have come out all right. In fact, you've done pretty well for yourself. They definitely made you out to be a heroine on CBS." She falters on the word "heroine," suddenly uncertain whether it is pronounced like the drug or not. "I mean you're getting a *lot* of mileage off of it."

"That's true, and I'm going to use it for a good purpose. I'm gonna—"

"Well, I'll tell you something. This whole thing is making Mickey crazy. I honestly thought he was going to break off our engagement because of this. I mean, he *really* went berserk this morning." She pauses and adopts a more speculative tone of voice. "But maybe that's what you've been trying to accomplish."

"Whaddaya talking about, Shay?"

"You know, Mickey lives in a different world than we do. He can't afford to—"

"There's *nothing* he can't afford."

"Nat, you *told* Mickey you were returning the papers and then you just *decided* not to. You gambled with the only chip we had to guarantee our safety. You've really compromised us now, and Mickey's furious. I mean, he almost got kidnapped once, and he doesn't need *this.*"

"You know what? I'd like to know the real reason Mickey wanted to keep all this stuff out of the newspapers. I mean, he's right up there with Michael Milken, jerking the market around and—"

"Oh, Natalie. Please don't talk about things you don't understand. Just tell me *why. Why* did you do it?"

"I thought it was important, Shay. You didn't."

"Of course I did. Otherwise I wouldn't have stolen it in the first place. Risked my neck—"

"No. You risked *my* neck and then you dropped it the minute it didn't fit into *the Duke*'s campaign plans. You're just a Democratic party girl, Shay. Whoever blows in your ear—or up your nose—last, gets you. For whatever that's worth."

"Up yours, Natalie. You're really something. One minute you're all sweet and nice and the next minute you stab me in the back like we're not even related. You're a vindictive little slut, that's what you are."

"You don't have any principles, Shay. You don't have any politics. You pretend you're politically committed but you're—"

"You're jealous of me, Natalie. You've always been jealous of me. All your life you've wanted to *be* me."

"Which you?"

Long silence. Maybe she's trying to decide.

"Now I suppose you'll want to become a free-lance journalist and—"

"No. I've *got* a job, Shay. I'm a social worker. I know that's not glamorous enough for you, but that's what I do. It's a real thing that I do. And for years the money that should have come to our programs got wasted by the government. So I just blew the whistle. That's all. It wasn't any of your phony photo-ops or Dukakis *shticks*. This might actually make a difference. It might actually stop some other Colonel North from doing whatever the hell he wants to do with *our* hostages and *our* money and *our* foreign policy . . ."

"Save me," Shay groans. "Oh, please, save me. Listen, where's Eli?"

"You know, I really wasn't going to say anything about this, Shay, but Amelia is suffering because of you. You come and you go, you leave her with other people's housekeepers and nannies and maids and—"

"God, you are *such* a jealous person; it's sickening."

"Maybe I am jealous about Amelia—I really love her. But you should have told Steven you were going to Atlanta and—"

"Say, would you get off my back? Maybe I wasn't a perfect mother according to your standards. And maybe I don't meet all your specifications for a doting grandmother, but right now you're hardly a paragon of virtue yourself, you know."

"Is that why you told Mom about my abortion? Because you were afraid she maybe thought I was a model daughter?"

"Oh, this is too sick for me, Natalie. Really, I don't think I can deal with it anymore. Look, let's just forget about seeing each other for a while. How 'bout that? Just get out of my life. Forget my wedding. Forget about being my matron of honor. . . ."

"I've already been your matron of honor *twice*, Shay. I'm not going to be your handmaiden ever again. It's getting boring."

"Look." Her voice thins out, becomes weaker. "Every morning I have to make myself up. I don't mean put on makeup. I have to . . . invent myself."

"Oh, you've got so much style, Shay, that can't be too hard for you."

"That's not style. That's panic. Plus a little imagination."

I have to laugh. She's witty, my sister.

For a few seconds, she laughs along with me before she continues.

"At least you had Eli. You had stability, financial security. That nice house. . . . I always had to play it by ear. Every day. I've never even owned my own sofa; I never got to pick out one *I* really liked. I was always out there on a limb, all alone."

"You were *never* alone, Shay."

"I was so alone I couldn't bear to be by myself for a minute. I was too scared."

Scared?

"You think it was fun being a single parent and having to run around the world just to keep my name out there so I could get my next assignment? That was white-knuckle living. . . ."

"Shay, you've been married to Christopher for the last eight years. That's hardly roughing it."

"Aren't you ever going to *hear* me, Nat? Listen, you don't even know what it *means* to look for a job. For years I never knew where our next meal was coming from. Eli was always there for you."

"Shay, you never—"

"But how could you *not* know?" she wails. "You're my *sister.*"

Jesus. My hump, my burden . . . appealing for sympathy.

"I mean, I *am* marrying Mickey and he *is* rich, but he's making me sign a prenuptial agreement. How's that for romantic?"

"You had Steven, Shay. And now you've got Amelia."

"Well, Steven is talking about Amelia maybe staying with you."

"Yeah!" I say bitterly. "Now, when I don't even have a house anymore, thanks to you."

"I apologize about your house. And don't worry. I'll be able to help you out financially with whatever you need. But if you had stuck by our plan, so that Mickey could've returned the papers to Jerry up in Southampton like we planned, nothing would have happened to your house. But no, you had to futz around with that black cop and let him call all the shots."

"Is it Bo that's bugging you, Shay? Are you threatened by people like Bo who still care about *real* things? That must really shake you up. You're a cokehead, Shay. I think all the coke you've done has fried your brains."

"You're still angry about your abortion, Natalie, something bad that happened *twenty-one years ago.* Anyway, you could have adopted some kids, you know. There're plenty of children who need homes. For a big liberal, you really dragged your ass about adopting. . . ."

"I just can't believe you told Mom. I mean, did you tell Daddy too, before he died?"

An unnervingly long silence.

"Oh, God," I wail.

"Maybe she feels better . . . knowing . . ." Shay sniffles. "So is that why you stole my story? To get even with me for telling Mother?"

"No, that's not *quite* the reason. Anyway, Shay, I gotta go. I've got a million calls to return. *Good Morning America* and the *Today* show and . . . *The New York Times* and the *L.A. Times* . . ."

"Oh, fuck off, Natalie! Listen, does Eli know what you did? Is he still in Atlanta?"

"No. No, he's back in Washington."

"Is he there? I really want to talk to him. And so does Mickey."

Then I begin to cry.

Sitting in Bo's tidy little kitchen, at his little butcher-block table with its two ice cream–parlor chairs, I begin to sob. And then wail. Like a banshee. I start to lose it. I'm out of control. Completely out of control. There is a long silence on Shay's end of the line, a thick, cottony silence.

"What's the matter?" she finally asks.

But I can't speak. Wet gasps keep rising to the surface like waves upon the shore.

"What's wrong?" she asks again, more gently now, reading my sobs as real.

"It's . . . Eli, Shay. He . . . wants us to separate. . . ."

"Oh, Natalie. Oh, honey." There is both shock and fear in her voice. "Was it because of the house, because of everything that happened?"

"No, no. He just said it wasn't working out."

"I can't believe this. What a bastard. You should be mad as hell at him. Well, I'm just going to tell Mickey to go on back to New York alone."

"Oh no. Don't do *that,* Shay."

"Why not? Amelia and I will fly back to Washington this afternoon and then we can all be together. Maybe she'll sleep on the plane and I'll be able to work on my article."

"You don't have to come back, Shay. I'm all right."

"I know I don't *have* to, I *want* to. We can all stay at Christopher's. I have a few things I'd like to discuss with Eli. What the hell bit his ass, anyway?"

"I don't know."

"Well, I'm going to find out, that's for sure."

"Really, Shaysie, it's not necessary. Don't worry. I'll be fine. Don't bother—"

"*Bother?* Hey! Nat! *What's a sister for?*"